3/6/19

Cat Got Your Crown

Also available by Julie Chase

Kitty Couture Mysteries

Cat Got Your Secrets

Cat Got Your Cash

Cat Got Your Diamonds

Cat Got Your Crown

A Kitty Couture Mystery

Julie Chase

CROOKED
LANE

NEW YORK

Copyright © 2019 by Julie Anne Lindsey

Published in the United States by Crooked Lane Books, an imprint of The Quick Brown Fox & Company LLC.

Crooked Lane Books and its logo are trademarks of The Quick Brown Fox & Company LLC.

Library of Congress Catalog-in-Publication data available upon request.

ISBN (hardcover): 978-1-68331-956-6
ISBN (ePub): 978-1-68331-957-3
ISBN (ePDF): 978-1-68331-958-0

Cover illustration by [needs name]
Book design by Jennifer Canzone

Printed in the United States.

www.crookedlanebooks.com

Crooked Lane Books
34 West 27th St., 10th Floor
New York, NY 10001

First Edition: March 2019

10 9 8 7 6 5 4 3 2 1

Chapter One

Furry Godmother's words of warning:
Beware of showboats; sometimes they splash.

Excitement charged the air inside the historic Saenger Theatre on Canal Street. The atmospheric interior had been designed to replicate a fifteenth-century Italian courtyard, complete with inky domed ceiling and "starry sky." I wasn't sure about Italy in the 1600s, but in modern-day New Orleans, the venue was packed to the pylons with one hundred highly trained pets and their anxious handlers. Judges, staff, and volunteers for the National Pet Pageant scampered through the crowded hallways finalizing details for Tuesday's big show. I was doing my best to answer questions, adjust and repair the performers' costumes, and stay out of the way.

"Lacy!" An austere woman wearing a tweed skirt and a deep frown headed my way. "Miss Crocker, a moment please."

I moved carefully in her direction, keeping a vigilant eye on a pair of stubborn cockatoos flying overhead. The intricately detailed ceiling was widely considered a point of interest, but at the moment, it was unwise to look directly up. "Coming."

The woman met me several feet from her assigned table and led me back to a growling cat in a bedazzled carrier. She pinched a battered bonnet between her fingers. The frilly eyelet material had come loose at the seams and one row of ruffles had nearly been chewed off. "Can you fix it?"

"Of course." As the unofficial costume department, I was determined to fix everything. "It's no problem."

"I don't know what's gotten into her," the woman said. "Maybe it's the weather? Or the full moon? This city is strange. Have you seen the cemeteries? Everyone's buried above ground. Is that even natural? And have you taken the ghost tour?" She stroked one long finger against a narrow eyebrow and grimaced. "Jackie and I will be glad to return home to Dallas, where everything is normal."

I opened my jumbo-sized pink tackle box and selected the best tool for the job. "I'm sure it's just nerves."

"There are too many tourists in this town and people in costumes for no apparent reason. A man was playing bagpipes outside my hotel this morning."

I threaded a needle and smiled. Personally, I loved my city, but I could see how someone wearing a bun tight enough to cause a migraine might be put off. I gave her cat a warm smile. "Rehearsal for an event this big would rattle anyone. Right, Jackie?"

The National Pet Pageant was a traveling talent competition for four-legged friends and winged companions. The event was hosted by a different city around the country each year, and thanks to the dedicated petitioning of my mother, this year the producers had chosen New Orleans. The NPP, as my mom called it, was the rough equivalent of Miss Universe, or maybe the Olympics for pets. A lot of money and media attention awaited the winners and their owners on the other side.

I set the final stitch and snapped the thread with my hands. A quick snip of the hanging ends and voila! "There you go. The strings and lace are back in place. You'll want to rinse the bonnet tonight and let it dry on a bed knob to help with its shape." I opened the sparkly carrier and lifted Jaqueline Tabby Onassis into my arms. "Hello, gorgeous." I stoked her fur and rubbed her ears before securing the little chin strap and fluffing the material. "What do you think?" I turned the gray-and-white kitty to face her owner. She blinked big green eyes and yawned.

The woman heaved a sigh. "Bless you." She stuffed Jackie back into her carrier, sans bonnet, and fixed me with a pointed stare. "This is exactly why everyone says Furry Godmother is the best. You absolutely are."

"I appreciate that. Thank you." Furry Godmother was the name of my pet boutique and organic treat bakery on Magazine Street. I'd opened my doors a year ago at the heart of New Orleans's famed Garden District. In the time since, I'd made a name for myself with locals and pet enthusiasts alike. The latter enjoyed spoiling their fur babies with my treats and designs. The former recognized my name from its repeated appearance in newspaper articles on various crimes. I was prouder of one of those facts than the other. Which one depended on the day.

I tossed the needle and remaining thread back into my tackle box. "Let me know if there's anything else I can do." I swept a mass of sticky hair into a loose ponytail and checked my watch. Ten minutes until lunch, and I was already dreaming of fresh air and cold water.

The interior theater doors swept open, revealing the dreamlike courtyard inside. A troop of Dalmatians in top hats and bow ties pranced out. By the look of relief on their owner's face, their final dress rehearsal had gone well.

"Next!" A pale man with a clipboard and newsboy hat pressed the button on his megaphone and aimed it at the crowd. "Number fifty-four!"

A woman in a toga and goddess sandals rushed forward, towing a cat dressed as Cleopatra in a wagon poorly disguised as a chariot. The faux courtyard doors closed behind her with a whoosh and a clang.

Only forty-six acts to go.

"Lacy!" A familiar voice turned my head.

The crowd parted as Mom made her way toward me on three-inch designer heels. Her floral wrap dress was new and her hair was magnificent, either supernaturally immune to the oppressive humidity or simply wiser than to cross her. She was trailed by a gaggle of clipboard-wielding women in coordinating attire. The well-dressed posse was also known as the NPP Welcoming Committee. Mom had started the group months before the show's arrival and arranged every detail that would make the pageant's producers, staff, and crew more comfortable during their stays. I'd been assigned to the committee when another member dropped out. In the last few months, the fashionable group of ladies had become my sisters.

"There you are." She stopped moving and her entourage circled me. Around town, Mom was known as Violet Conti-Crocker, last living heir to the Conti family fortune and virtual force of nature. Mom claimed Conti money had helped build our city, and she worked diligently to see her ancestors weren't disappointed. Everyone knew better than to get in her way. "I'd like you to meet Angelina Smart."

A compact woman with a cloud of puffy white hair and thick cat-eye glasses stepped into view. Her rosy round cheeks and magnified blue eyes made me smile. Her sturdy frame, snub nose, and wrinkles reminded me of a French bulldog, and I immediately liked her. I also liked the vintage pink tweed suit and matching pillbox hat, though I doubted they were vintage to her, probably just another ensemble she'd purchased personally in 1964.

"How do you do?"

"Very well, thank you. I'm Lacy." I extended a hand and squeezed her soft fingers gently. "It's nice to meet you."

Mom clasped her hands at her middle. "Mrs. Smart is the widow of Marvin Smart, creator of the National Pet Pageant. She's here to make sure everything goes according to her late husband's vision."

"I never miss a show," Mrs. Smart said, setting a palm over her chest. "The pageant was his heart. Of all Marvin's accomplishments, this pageant was his pride and joy." She tapped the rubber tip of her silver duck-head cane against the floor beside her white orthopedic sneakers and smiled. "I can't believe I finally made it to the Big Easy. It's on my bucket list."

"We're very excited to have you and your husband's pageant here," I said.

Mom looked me over. "How are you doing with the list I gave you? Have you taken care of your portion?"

My portion of NPP Welcoming Committee responsibilities included obeying her every command and doing it with a smile, but more specifically, I was to oversee the hanging of opening ceremony banners on every light post from here to the Mason-Dixon, or until I ran out. "Yes, ma'am."

Mom nodded. "Good. What are you wearing?"

Mom had been insisting for months that the committee members wear dresses or skirt-and-blouse ensembles in pastels or floral patterns, preferably ones that covered our knees, as a show of unity and proper southern etiquette.

"Jeans," I said, both stating the obvious and continuing to be a disappointment in the coordinating-ensembles department.

"I see that." Mom bristled. "I'm just trying to understand why."

I looked to my committee sisters for support, but they were all dressed appropriately and collectively leaning away. "Honestly," I sighed, "repairing pet costumes is rough on couture. I spend a lot of time animal hugging and crawling on the floor. Dressing up seems almost irresponsible." Plus, I was a sticky, sweaty mess and covered in hair, most of which wasn't my own.

"It's not dressing up," Mom said. "It's called being part of a team."

"My T-shirt's pink." I wiped a bead of sweat off my brow and wished I could do the same for a droplet cruising the valley between my shoulder blades. "There's even a flower on the pocket."

"T-shirts are for men and little children," Mom said. "Then again, so is sitting on the floor." She scrutinized my top. "Did you draw the flower on there?" She rolled wide blue eyes, nearly identical to mine. "Lacy, really."

I looked like my mother. Same blonde hair and ski-slope nose. Same awkward height, too tall for petite clothing, too short for everything else. Unfortunately, for every similarity Mom and I had in appearance, we shared ten differences of opinions.

"Miss Crocker?" A portly woman in high-waisted capri pants and tinted spectacles waved to me. "Do you have a minute? I'm afraid we're experiencing a crisis."

"Of course." I rolled my shoulders and stretched my neck. "Come on, Mom. You can yell at me while I work." I inched between two of my committee sisters and sidestepped a poodle on two legs. The halls and corridors of the historic Louisiana theater looked the way I imagined the backstage at a Las Vegas show might, if that show was *America's Got Talent* meets Barnum and Bailey.

I stopped at the woman and her white Himalayan cat in tuxedo tails. The cat batted a toy piano and meowed.

The woman held a small beret in each hand. "I can't decide. Sequins or suede?" She lifted one to the kitty's face—"Sequins—then the other—"or suede?"

I chewed my lip. The purposely cropped jacket made the

cat look doubly fluffy and squeezable. Sequins seemed a bit much, but suede wasn't doing it for me either. I opened my supply box and fished out a packet of appliques and charms. "Can I see that one?" I took the suede cap and sewed a white band of rickrack into place, then pinned a silver fleur-de-lis front and center. "There. How about that?"

A man's voice boomed in the distance, drawing my attention. Viktor Petrov, the pageant's master of ceremonies, barked orders at a pair of personal assistants until his face turned red and the coeds recoiled. He was easily as aggressive as any reality television chef and, in my opinion, only half as entertaining, but the public loved him.

The woman beside me covered her kitty's ears. "I wish he'd stop that. Negativity is such poison."

Mom scoffed. "He's a showboat, mildly offensive but completely harmless."

Eva Little, the shiest of my Welcoming Committee sisters, turned her wide brown eyes toward the floor. "He can get a little handsy, too," she mumbled.

"Really?" I scoffed.

The entire committee nodded.

Mrs. Smart stiffened. She glared at the self-important man on stage. "Reprehensible."

I frowned. Luckily, I hadn't experienced that side of Viktor, but I hated that most of them obviously had. I swung my gaze back to Mom. He'd be wise to keep his hands to himself with her unless he wanted to lose one.

"I will never understand how that man has fans," Mrs. Smart continued. "Publicity and Marketing have taken advantage of his popularity and used it to increase general interest, but I suppose that only makes them slightly more intelligent than the buffoons tuning in to watch Viktor." She rolled her eyes. "I doubt any of his fans know the difference between a cockatoo and a cocker spaniel."

"Well," Mom interjected, "my committee has worked tirelessly to ensure this year's event will be the epitome of dignity and grace. These beautiful, intelligent, and dedicated animals, along with their trainers, will be treated as world-class performers as long as they are in my city. No buffoons welcome." She swung her gaze in my direction. "Isn't that right, Lacy."

"Yes," I assured her. "Everything's coming together nicely. Elegantly," I added.

Mrs. Smart nodded. "Thank you. Your efforts are greatly appreciated." She produced a handkerchief and drove it under her nose. "If you'll excuse me. I just need a minute and some air."

"Certainly," Mom said, stepping aside to let her pass.

I waited until Mrs. Smart reached the exit, then turned back to catch Mom's narrowed stare and stood a little straighter. "The rehearsal and peripheral details are going off as planned. Yes?"

"I don't know." She made a notation on her clipboard. "Are you still wearing jeans and a T-shirt?"

I closed my eyes and counted to ten. It was my only defense. "Tomorrow I'll wear a dress and bring several changes in case of excessive slobber or a nervous bladder." I frowned. "I'm talking about the pets, not myself."

Mom puffed air into her thick, side-swept bangs and marched away. The committee ladies followed.

I handed the revised beret to the woman and smiled. "Good luck."

"Thank you," she enthused. "It's perfect!"

I scanned the scene for anyone else in need of my assistance.

Chase Hawthorne caught my attention, standing in a cluster of women and pets across the lobby. He winked at me, and a senseless but predictable blush heated my cheeks.

I smiled, and he headed my way with a trademark wicked grin and that ever-present gleam of mischief in his eye.

Chase was an attorney at his family's high-powered law practice, and he understood me in a multitude of complicated ways I didn't like to think about. If the Garden District had had royal families, mine and Chase's would have been at the top, and it was no secret that our parents would die of happiness if he and I agreed to marry and produce heirs immediately, but neither of us were ready for that. In fact, we'd both only recently returned to the district after years of bucking parental expectations and chasing our own dreams. I'd traded the schmancy premed program at my mom's prestigious alma mater for a degree in fashion design from an art institute in Virginia, and Chase had entered the world of professional volleyball instead of joining the family law practice after passing the bar. I'd yet to see him in any suit that hid the hard work volleyball had done for him.

"Miss Crocker," he said, arriving with a dog the size of a woolly mammoth. "You look positively good enough to eat this morning, and you know I'm always hungry."

"Get a bagel," I suggested, dropping to my knees before

the big fluffy baby at the end of Chase's leash. "Well, hello," I said, cupping his honey-hued face in my palms. "I think you're the most handsome man I've ever met." I kissed his nose, then nuzzled my face into his thick fur. "I'm so glad you're here," I said slipping deeper into baby talk. "Yes, I am."

"I don't understand why I never get this kind of greeting," Chase said, looking delighted by the thought.

"You're next," I promised, then giggled when his eyebrows rose.

My relationship with Chase was both intensely beautiful and endlessly complicated. For starters, we were great together, and our families were close, but if we dated and things didn't work out, a lot of people would be hurt, or at least put out. It was a lot of pressure, so we settled for shameless flirting and an appreciation of what could be. Chase had even promised to marry me one day, if that was ever what I wanted, and I had no doubt that we could make a fantastic, fun-filled life together, but there were two big problems with that.

First, I'd been engaged before, and it had ended in betrayal instead of marriage. Some parts of me were still raw from that experience, and I wasn't in a hurry to poke the wound.

The second problem was someone else entirely.

"Hello." A woman only slightly taller than the dog smiled down at me from Chase's side. "Here I am," she said, taking the lead from Chase. "Thanks for watching him."

The giant fluffy beast sat immediately under her control.

"Mrs. Li," Chase said, "this is Lacy Marie Crocker. Lacy, this is Sue Li."

I extended a hand to her. "Nice to meet you."

Sue Li was the definition of petite, with straight black hair and the most beautifully tanned skin I'd ever seen. I envied both instantly. My mother would have appreciated her peach-and-cream blouse and pencil skirt. Not only did both pieces qualify as pastel, but they were clearly couture, and the navy patent-leather belt and shoes alone had cost more than I'd spent on my entire wardrobe in a year.

"Pleasure's all mine," Sue Li said. "Any friend of Mr. Hawthorne's is a gem in my book."

My smile widened at the sound of her addressing Chase as *Mr. Hawthorne.* Chase had grown up and filled out very nicely, but some part of me would always see him as my best friend's boyfriend's younger brother. The district playboy and formerly reckless teen who'd once driven a Segway under the influence and hit a parked sports car.

"This is Big Splash," she said, patting the top of the dog's broad head. "He's my baby, and I love him so much. I will never allow him to go back to that horrific purgatory again," she vowed, eyes misting with tears. "Big Splash belongs with me. Don't you?" She sniffled, wiping wide brown eyes with one trembling hand. "Excuse us." She turned quickly away and led her lumbering giant toward the ladies' room.

I raised my brows at Chase. "Purgatory? Is Big Splash from an animal shelter?"

"No." He checked the crowd before handing his phone to me. "We removed him from her soon-to-be-ex-husband's place back in China."

I gave the phone screen a long look. "Whoa." A ridiculous mansion made of glass and steel clung to the side of a rocky mountain face. "This is the place she was referring to as purgatory?" I asked.

"Yes." He took the phone back and tucked it into his pocket. "I think it has more to do with the man living inside."

"Hence the divorce. Gotcha," I said. "Can I have the wiki version of what you're doing here with Mrs. Li and her dog?" I asked. "I'd love all the details, but my mom is on a rampage, so time is short."

"You didn't wear a dress again," he said.

I gave him a warning look.

He grinned. "I'm representing Mrs. Li in her divorce. She and her husband are both international businesspeople. They both travel regularly between America and China, but after the divorce, Sue wants to stay in Los Angeles, and Daniel wants to remain in China. Those decisions made splitting ownership of their properties easy but custody of Big Splash much more complicated."

"You're handling a dog custody battle?" I asked.

He shrugged. "Big Splash isn't just any dog. He's a golden-haired Tibetan mastiff. The Lis bought him at a luxury pet fair in China three years ago for two million dollars. He was a birthday gift from Daniel to Sue."

My jaw dropped. "Two million dollars for a hundred-pound dog?"

"He was a pup then," Chase said, "and I think he weighs one-eighty now."

"Isn't that what you weigh?" I asked. I might or might not have read all his volleyball statistics online after running into him for the first time in ten years last summer.

13

Chase grinned but didn't ask how I knew. "I wear it better," he said, "and with far less hair."

"Well, I love Big Splash," I said. "He looks like a short-nosed Snuffleupagus. I hope you get his family situation sorted fairly." I wished I could have a big Tibetan moose dog just like him, but my tabby, Penelope, would have killed me, and I didn't have that kind of money to throw around. Or at all. "Two million dollars?" I whispered. "Really?"

"The Lis say he has lion's blood, and they consider a dog like him to be as treasured as China's pandas."

I could have opened a dozen cat shelters across the state with that kind of cash.

Chase swung his gaze to the balcony stairs, where Viktor was still complaining as he made his way back to the seat where he'd been overseeing the rehearsal before his most recent outburst. His clutch of personal assistants was nowhere to be seen. "That guy's something else."

"Handsy too, I hear," I said.

Chase narrowed his eyes.

The lobby doors parted, and my favorite homicide detective strode into view. Nearly a head taller and significantly more handsome than the surrounding humans, Jack Oliver made a straight line in my direction. "Morning, Miss Crocker," he said, his serious blue gaze pinning me in place. The deep tenor of his voice pulled a smile over my lips. His shiny detective badge swung from a beaded silver chain around his neck.

"Morning," I said, a little more breathlessly than intended.

Chase made a puffing sound beside me.

"Hawthorne," he said.

Jack was the NOPD liaison, coordinating efforts between pageant security and local law enforcement. He'd dropped in twice a day since rehearsals began, usually at lunch and dinner, and I looked forward to every meal.

Chase shook Jack's hand, then planted a kiss on my cheek. "I'm going to go see a woman about a Snuffleupagus," he whispered.

I gave his hand a squeeze as he walked away.

"What was he doing here?" Jack asked.

"Custody battle over a two-million-dollar dog."

Jack bobbed his head in mock understanding.

"So, how's your day going, Detective?"

He shifted his weight and smiled. "Better now."

"Me, too. Are you staying for lunch?" I glanced away as a mass of nonsensical butterflies took flight in my stomach.

Lately, it had seemed Jack and I were working on something nice together, though I wasn't completely sure what that was. Thanks to the high rates of homicides and pet-costume crises in New Orleans, Jack and I didn't always have free time at the same time, but we found ways to stay in touch. Sometimes that meant trading texts between errands; other times it meant eating a catered lunch inside an historic theater with one hundred sweaty animal trainers.

The catering staff appeared as if on cue, swinging open the theater doors and delivering long narrow tables to the area below the balcony. The crew whipped white linens into the air and settled them over the buffets, then covered those in silver platters and chafing dishes.

Humans snapped into action, kenneling their pets in the lobby and hallway at warp speed.

I set my pink bedazzled tackle box aside and nudged Jack with an elbow. "Acme Oyster House is catering today. We should hurry." I led him to the front of the line and grabbed a plate.

Viktor grimaced down at us from his position in the balcony. Clearly disgusted with everyone and everything, he stood, arms crossed, before the short ledge, glaring at the lunch line below.

Jack pressed warm fingers against the small of my back and dipped his mouth to my ear. "I was thinking we could get out of here today. Have a quiet lunch. Alone."

Alone? I spun to face him. "Let's do that." I dropped my plate back onto the stack and smiled.

Jack's usual serious expression slid into something unburdened and enticing. "Come on." He clutched my hand in his, and a thrill zipped through my system.

Lunch with Jack. Alone!

A terror-filled cry wiped the smile from my face. My chin jerked upward in search of the sound as Viktor Petrov, the pageant's cranky, handsy MC, fell from the balcony in a blur of tweed and trousers. He collided with the newly set buffet before me, splattering pasta and white sauce over my pretty pink T-shirt, face, and hands. His head and legs were turned at awkward angles and a trickle of red slid from the corner of his mouth. I stumbled back, colliding with Jack's rigid core as

16

the ghastly calamity registered through the thick haze of my confusion.

A bloodcurdling scream burst through me as I whipped my gaze upward in search of a broken ledge or other tragic but logical reason for his deadly fall.

Instead, I found Eva Little, my sweet committee sister, staring down at me.

Chapter Two

*Furry Godmother's words of wisdom: Use care with
unattended livestock, especially a cash cow.*

Jack released me with a curse and broke into cop mode. "Call
an ambulance! Get back!" he yelled, waving his arms at those
closest to the ruined buffet. "Stand down. Security!"

"I'm a doctor!" a man screamed in my ear as he flew past
me with a miniature poodle tucked under one arm. "I'm a
doctor!" He dashed to Jack's side and fell onto his knees beside
Viktor and the broken table.

Jack crouched with him.

I watched in a helpless stupor. What was the man doing?
Could Viktor possibly be okay?

A long moment later, Jack stretched to his feet and sought
my eyes with his. Slowly, he moved his heartbroken face left
and right.

I watched in horror as the doctor rolled back on his
haunches, defeated.

There was nothing anyone could do now. Viktor Petrov wouldn't see another opening ceremony.

The theater's security team arrived seconds later. They stood sentinel around the body, looking to Jack for instructions.

"Lock the doors," Jack ordered. "No one in or out." He twisted at the waist for a look at the balcony. "This auditorium is an active crime scene until cause of death can be determined."

His words echoed in my head. *Crime scene.* My frantic heart hammered harder and ached deeper. My chest constricted with the makings of a panic attack, something I'd become intimately familiar with since moving home last year. "What can I do, Jack?" I choked the jagged words through gritted teeth, determined to redirect the adrenaline into something useful. I caught his wrist in my fingers. "Tell me what to do."

Jack leveled me with a stare. "Are you okay?"

Not at all. I nodded woodenly. "What can I do?"

His chest rose and fell in two full breaths before he whipped an arm forward, pointing a finger at the front of the building. "Help maintain the entrance. No one goes in or out. If they try, take their picture; do *not* attempt to stop them. Watch for police and emergency personnel. Get them inside as soon as they arrive."

I burst into a jog, shamefully thankful to get away from the gruesome scene. I scanned the balcony as I moved, certain Eva had seen the whole thing and praying that this was an overreaction on Jack's part. Maybe Viktor's fall had been accidental. Maybe he'd leaned too far over the edge and lost his footing.

I escaped the faux Italian courtyard and took my assigned position at the now locked front doors beside a man I recognized from the security team. I clenched my trembling fists, desperate to hold myself together in the face of yet another disaster. Adrenaline beat through my veins and whooshed in my ears. Was there this much tragedy everywhere, or did I simply attract it? Jack had once told me that this was the world I'd always lived in, I just hadn't noticed before; but he was wrong, death was his world. Pets and fashion were supposed to be mine.

Restless, I flipped the deadbolt. "I'm going to wait outside," I told the man beside me. I didn't wait for his approval. I needed fresh air.

A rusted white work truck pulled into traffic as I moved onto the sidewalk and paced. Thick Louisiana air curled over my skin like a giant tongue, lapping the air from my lungs and sticking the clothes to my skin. Hot southern sun blinded me as I stared into the distance, willing the emergency crews to hurry.

The low cry of an ambulance and steady din of a bleating firetruck broke my waning composure. Emotion balled in my throat and stung my eyes.

I swiped renegade tears from my cheeks with shaky fingertips and released a steadying breath. I wasn't new to those sounds or to trauma, but the experiences never got any easier. I'd been mugged at gunpoint while walking home from work one night when I lived in Virginia. Sometimes I could still smell the stale beer on the man's breath and feel his grimy fingers on my skin. It was the worst thing that had happened to me until that point. In contrast, I'd been back in New Orleans for a year and had already been accused of murder, stalked by a man in a giant papier-mâché cat head, abducted thrice, threatened by a copycat Robin Hood, and most recently, witnessed a man fall to his death upon my lunch. My therapist was in Tahiti at the moment, or I'd have already called for an appointment. She probably could have funded multiple trips to the moon on my sessions alone.

I waved the arriving vehicles into place and held the theater door as men and women in various emergency responders' uniforms passed through.

"Woof!" A massive brown-and-gold blur rushed past me, knocking me off my feet and bouncing me against the glass.

"Big Splash!" Chase's voice echoed through the controlled chaos behind me. "Lacy!" He crouched before me a moment later and gripped my arms. "I'm so sorry. Are you okay?"

I arranged my feet back on the floor beneath me using Chase for balance and thankful I hadn't obeyed my mother and worn a dress. "I think I was just involved in a hit-and-run."

Chase pressed me against his chest and squeezed before letting me go. "That was Big Splash. Sue was trying to put him in his kennel for lunch when that man fell and everyone screamed. A parrot took off from its perch and Big Splash went after it. Did you see a bird fly out too, by chance?"

A bird? "Are you kidding? I barely got the license plate on the truck that ran me over."

Chase pushed on the door, and a member of Jack's security team stepped into view.

"No one in or out," the man said, dusting his uniform

pants, probably from having also been flattened by one stampeding Tibetan mastiff.

"A dog ran out," Chase said.

"I called it in. Was he wearing a collar with identification and owner contact information?"

"He had a collar," Chase said. "I'm not sure about the rest." He looked at me.

"He had ID," I told the security guy. I'd felt it in the deep tufts of his fur when I'd kissed his big wet nose.

Chase shut the door once more, and I moved into place at his side.

"Do you think he'll be okay?"

"I think so," I said, unsure what people would do when they saw an animal that size running loose in the streets. "Traffic's bad, so the cars are moving slow. At least if he goes into the street, drivers will have plenty of time to see him and stop."

We stared through the glass, our views partially obstructed by emergency vehicles and a growing crowd of lookie lous. Heat hovered over the pavement like an apparition on yet another stifling New Orleans day.

"Any sign of him?" I asked hopefully, as if I could somehow *not* see him if he was out there.

"No, and with the speed he was moving, he could be halfway to the river by now," Chase said. "Sue's going to freak. Hopefully she had him microchipped like those cats you fostered last fall."

I stifled a shiver. Those cats had nearly gotten me killed. "For two million dollars, he should've come with a GoPro and private security detail."

Chase rested his forehead on the window for a long moment, then turned his back to the door. I spun with him, and we stared at the interior theater doors with matching frowns. "At least no one can pick him up, put him in her purse, and steal him," he said.

"No joke."

The security team opened a door and let a pair of EMTs and a gurney inside.

Chase and I inched out of the way.

"Maybe people will think twice before even approaching him," Chase suggested.

"Definitely," I said. I loved animals, but I wouldn't have approached an animal Big Splash's size without his owner present on my wildest day. He looked a little too much like a lion, and I was certain my head would have fit in his mouth.

Sue Li rounded a corner in our direction, moving as quickly as could be expected in five-inch heels and panting. "Did you get him?"

Chase's shoulders sunk.

"Good luck," I said, moving back toward the theater as Jack opened a set of double doors to usher the EMTs inside.

"Is Hawthorne okay?" he asked, steering me down the aisle toward the front of the room.

"He lost a brontosaurus," I said.

Pet owners, staff, and volunteers filled several rows of theater chairs while members of the security team patrolled the aisles.

"You should have a seat," Jack said. "Breathe."

I pulled in a few shallow breaths, and my head spun.

"Can I get you anything? Maybe some water or a change of shirt?"

I cringed at the realization I was still splattered with food a man had died on. My stomach clenched, and I lifted my chin higher, searching for dignity and resisting the urge to be sick.

Jack's jaw locked and popped as he scanned the theater. He was usually on high alert in these situations, but something was off this time. It was almost as if he was taking Viktor's death personally.

"This isn't your fault," I whispered.

Jack slid his gaze briefly in my direction. "I know."

"Do you?" I asked, moving closer. "You seem more on edge than usual. Is it because you're the security liaison?"

Jack didn't answer. He clearly didn't want to talk about it. I couldn't help wondering *why?*

"You met with Viktor a lot this summer," I said, drawing Jack's ghost-blue eyes to mine. "Was he worried about pageant security, or was he worried about personal security?" Given the current state of events, it seemed like a reasonable question.

Jack relaxed his shoulders a bit. "Both," he admitted. "Viktor had questions about the city. This was going to be his last gig with the pageant, and he'd planned to stay in New Orleans afterward. I advised on the best neighborhoods, crime rates, taxi services, and airport routes, among other things. Why?"

I wrinkled my nose. "He needed a detective's advice for all that? Those sound more like Realtor-related questions to me."

Jack crossed his arms and dipped his chin, moving in a bit

closer, ensuring our exchange remained between us. "He was also a little concerned about his security this week. He asked me to take the lead on this and be the police force liaison."

My jaw dropped. "What? Why?"

"He'd received a few anonymous requests for his resignation. He thought the sender might show up at the pageant and make some grand statement. He wanted me to make sure whoever it was wouldn't get any recognition, and that they would be arrested."

"Someone threatened him," I interpreted. "Someone wanted him to quit."

Jack rubbed a heavy hand over his head and gripped the back of his neck. "I told him I'd see to it that he was safe, but things have been quiet. We both thought it might be over."

I ran a hand down the length of his arm. "You couldn't have known this would happen, and you can't be everywhere at once." I scanned the room, fully absorbing the sheer volume of suspects for the first time. "Do you think the person who sent the requests for Viktor's resignation could have done this? Would the person have taken matters into his or her own hands when he didn't comply?"

"Maybe," Jack said. "It's too soon to know anything for sure right now. I have one hundred witnesses, but no one saw anything more than we did."

My heart skipped as I realized he didn't know about Eva. "Eva Little was in the balcony. She must've seen who did this." A shiver rocked through my frame. *Eva could've walked right past the killer.*

Jack jerked his chin upward. He scanned the room before

sweeping his gaze higher into the balcony. "Eva?" he called through the white noise around us. "Eva Little."

She appeared in the balcony, moving slowly to the edge with a grimace. "Here."

"Don't move," he warned.

She nodded, then took a seat, nearly vanishing from sight once more.

"I'll be right back," Jack said. "I've got to talk to her. Wait here." Jack jogged back up the aisle.

I ran after him.

The peal of feedback from a microphone stopped us short. "Attention, pageant participants," a male voice announced. "This is Miles Mackey, your new MC, speaking. Please report to the lobby for an important update."

The suspects rose to their feet.

Jack swiped a megaphone off the floor and clicked it on. "Everyone is to remain seated until you've been dismissed by a member of the New Orleans Police Department."

A unified groan rolled through the auditorium.

Jack hefted the megaphone again. "We'll do all we can to get through this as quickly as possible. Until then, we need your full cooperation. Thank you."

Jack handed me the megaphone and headed for the over-zealous man with the mic.

I jogged along beside him.

He stopped inches from Miles Mackey. "What exactly do you think you're doing?"

Mackey switched the mic off and stroked his beard. "I'm stepping up," he said. "According to pageant bylaws, the head judge moves up in the event of the MC's absence. I'm head judge. Viktor's absent. I stepped up."

I made a face and suppressed the urge to take his mic. "Jeez."

Mom motored into view several feet away. Mrs. Smart and the committee ladies trailed behind her like ducklings. She stopped at my side. "This is terrible."

Jack braced broad hands over narrow hips and fixed her with his steely gaze. "Where were you and your committee members when Viktor fell, Mrs. Crocker?" he asked. "Did you see anything that can help me find out what happened up there?"

"The committee and I were in the lobby," she said, "helping owners secure pets so they could line up for lunch."

"Were all the ladies with you? Minus Lacy and Eva?"

"Yes. I think so." She frowned. "Where's Eva?"

"She wasn't feeling well," Reece Ann answered. "She went to get a bottle of water and a pair of aspirin. I told her it might help her to put her feet up and cool off a bit too."

Mom raised then dropped her palms. "I had no idea."

Jack didn't look impressed. He tipped his head at Mackey and his microphone. "I'll let you take care of this one, Mrs. Crocker."

"Indeed," Mom said, moving closer to Mackey, who slowly backed away.

Jack dashed toward the staircase where I'd watched Viktor disappear an hour before.

I stayed on his heels.

We stalled at the sight of a member of theater security on the landing with Eva.

"What's happening?" Mom asked.

I jumped.

Mom and her entire crew were only a few steps behind us. Mom had Mackey's microphone in her hand.

"Eva was in the balcony when Viktor fell," I whispered.

"Oh dear."

I drew back a step to join her. "It doesn't mean anything," I said, "except that she might be our only lead to what really happened up there."

Jack stopped at Eva's side and spoke quietly to the security member who was holding her.

Mom and I crowded onto the landing with them. The rest of the committee edged in around us.

"Eva didn't do this," Mom said. "Surely you don't think otherwise, Detective Oliver."

Jack pointed down the steps.

We all moved back a few inches.

"I hate to interrupt you all watching your friend get arrested," Mackey called from the bottom of the steps, "but if this place is a crime scene, we're going to need a new venue for the show to go on." He tapped an overpolished dress shoe on the historic marble floor. His voice ricocheted off the high walls and arched ceiling.

"Good heavens," Mom gasped. "He's right, and opening ceremonies begin in forty-eight hours!" She flipped through the pages on her clipboard. "We can't possibly move an event this size to a new venue in that amount of time."

"Have to," Miles stated.

"Shh!" we all yelled back.

Mom closed her eyes and bowed her head. She looked up a moment later with fire in her eyes. "We won't be far, Eva," she said, turning slowly back toward the lobby and gesturing for the rest of the committee and me to follow. She fixed her hot stare on Miles Mackey. "It's not right. There should be a mourning period or a memorial," she suggested. "Viktor was the face of this event. It's callous to go on as if nothing monumental has happened. That's not how we do things here. We celebrate life after a loss."

Miles shrugged. "So we'll add a memorial to the opening ceremonies, but the show can't be canceled, and it can't go on without a new venue. Do you know how many people spent all the money they had to participate in this thing? How many tickets we've sold? How many hotels are at maximum capacity with tourists arriving specifically for this event? The show *must* go on."

Emotion bubbled hotly in my chest. Mom was right, but so was Miles. "I'll run to Viktor's dressing room," I said. "I'll see if I can find that folder he carried with him every morning and look for his schedules and itineraries, anything we can use to stay on track." I grabbed Mom's hand. "Who owes you a favor? Where can we get a venue this size by Tuesday evening?"

"I'm not sure," she said. "I have to think."

"While you're at it, think of where we can get about a million fresh flyers with the new address." Wherever that would be. "The ladies can make calls to relocate staff and redirect traffic. Local media will make the announcement on air and in the paper when they cover the story, because you know they'll be here the second they hear about this."

Mom nodded slowly, color returning to her cheeks. "You're right." She locked her emotion-filled gaze to mine. "We can do this. Go get the playbook from Viktor's dressing room. We'll start there. I'll tell Eva not to say another word until her lawyer arrives; then I'll start calling in favors."

I chewed my lip, attention back on Miles. Was he truly invested in keeping the event on schedule, or did he have another motive for taking over Viktor's role so quickly? Perhaps right after he'd pushed him off the balcony?

"What's wrong?" Mom asked.

"I'm not sure."

"Then move it."

I hurried down the narrow hall to Viktor's dressing room and slipped inside. The space was neat as a pin and smelled distinctly of ginger and turmeric. I shuffled a stack of papers on his desk and opened a few drawers, trying not to be any more invasive than absolutely necessary. Where was that playbook? *Hopefully not in the balcony.* The police would surely confiscate it as evidence if he'd had it with him at his time of death. I struggled to recall whether or not he'd had it with him when I'd watched him climb the stairs.

I tugged the bottom desk drawer halfway open and it stuck. "What on earth?" I slid my hand inside to dislodge the errant flap of an envelope. A three-ring binder lay inside. National Pet Pageant, New Orleans was typed across the cover. "Bingo."

I liberated the playbook and froze when the problematic envelope came into full view. A horde of one-hundred-dollar bills poked out of the open flap. I grabbed the wad of cash and thumbed through it, baffled. "This is thirty-eight thousand dollars," I whispered. I'd never seen so many one hundreds anyplace without a teller.

Why did a pet pageant MC have that kind of money lying around at work?

Sickness coiled through my middle. Maybe Viktor's death was more complicated than someone looking for his resignation. Maybe someone had thirty-eight thousand reasons to want him dead.

Chapter Three

Furry Godmother's fun fact: New Orleans is home to Voodoo. She lives with Dr. & Mrs. Crocker.

My phone buzzed to life in my pocket. I liberated the device and flipped it over. The face of my former nanny and current shopkeep graced the screen. "Hi, Imogene," I said. "Everything okay?"

"Lacy?" She sighed long and loud. "I had a bad feeling down in my socks, so I called to warn you."

Imogene was from a long line of mystics, shamans, and other things I didn't believe in or understand. I tried not to ask too many questions.

"I'm fine," I told her. "It's been a bad morning, but Mom and I are okay. Do you need anything?"

"Yes, please. Your store is swamped, and I'm just one fabulous person. I can't possibly keep up on my own."

"Okay." I looked at my watch. With rehearsal canceled, I had no reason to stay, as long as Jack approved my dismissal.

I had a sneaking feeling he'd be glad to see me away from the crime scene. "I'll be there as soon as I can."

I returned the envelope to Viktor's desk and closed the drawer. "I won't be long."

"You betcha," she answered, whether to me or in answer to an unheard question at the store I couldn't say.

I disconnected and locked the dressing room door behind me on my way out. The next person to wander inside might be tempted to take that envelope of cash. I was certainly tempted, but not because I wanted to keep it. I wanted to show Jack in case the money was relevant to the case, but Jack hated when I disturbed evidence, and I was already worried I might be the reason he'd started buying aspirin and antacids in bulk.

I came face-to-face with an arguing couple in the hallway. They stared wide-eyed. I recognized the young woman as one of Viktor's assistants and the man as a cat owner.

I turned on my heels and headed in the opposite direction, taking the long route back to the lobby.

Mom's voice cut through the white noise of a hundred hushed whispers. She and Mrs. Smart stood on the stairway landing with Eva and Jack. Their expressions were grim at best.

"Eva," I called, climbing the steps as quickly as possible. "Did you see what happened?"

Tears pooled in her large brown eyes, but she didn't speak.

Jack lifted a palm to stop me from getting closer. "Eva was seen fighting with Viktor this morning. She was in the balcony when he fell, and what appears to be one of her hairs was found on his jacket. She's going to the station for a few more questions."

Eva nodded. She pressed a crisp white handkerchief to her nose.

Mom huffed. "I told her not to speak again until her lawyer arrived."

"Hey." I pinned Eva with a meaningful stare. "I know you didn't do this, and everything's going to be all right. I promise."

Mrs. Smart looked at Mom. "What? How?"

Mom rolled her head against one shoulder. "My daughter has an uncanny way of bringing out the truth in these kinds of situations, often at her own peril."

I made a face, but couldn't argue.

A pair of uniformed officers arrived on the steps beside me. "Detective Oliver?" one officer asked.

Jack stepped forward, one hand on Eva's arm. "Take Miss Little in for questioning. I'll be there as soon as I can."

Eva tried to hand her handkerchief to Jack.

"Keep it," he said.

I raised an eyebrow.

He turned his back to the officers as they led Eva away. "What? A gentleman always carries a handkerchief."

"Do you always loan it to women you think are murderers?"

He pressed his mouth shut and edged me forward until we were several paces from my mother and Mrs. Smart. "I never said she was a murderer. I said we have more questions for her. What exactly are you doing?"

"What do you mean?" I blinked.

A vein bulged in his forehead. "You can't go around announcing your intent to obstruct a murder investigation."

I feigned shock. As if I hadn't heard that line before. "I was offering comfort, not obstruction. That poor woman thinks she could be arrested for murder."

He widened his stance. "I'll handle this."

"Okay, but Eva didn't do it, and that's the truth."

Jack dipped his chin. "How about this? I'm going to follow the evidence and every tangible lead I come across until I find a truth that can be proven beyond a reasonable doubt. And you're going to let me."

"Fine."

"Fine."

I spun away from him and headed back to Mom. "I'm going over to Furry Godmother now. I'll be home all night if you need anything." I kissed her cheek and handed her Viktor's playbook. I didn't need it where I was going.

She huffed again, but didn't protest.

I climbed into my car two blocks away and piped the air-conditioning. Thirty years old or not, I felt like a helpless child, and I hated it. The splattered sauce stains on my shirt didn't help. I forced images of the toppled lunch buffet and Viktor's slack face from my mind with a shiver.

Stuck in a line of traffic at the next red light, I sent Jack a text to let him know I'd left the theater and to ask him to call me. I'd forgotten to tell him about the envelope of cash in Viktor's desk drawer.

I pointed a vent at my face and eased along with traffic as the light changed. The temperature gauge on my dashboard read ninety-two. The real feel was probably much higher, and the humidity was at Amazonian levels.

Tourists moved in slow knots and clusters along the sidewalks of my district, snapping photos of themselves with store windows and local artists. Tension fell away in buckets as my shop drew near. Magazine Street was a feast for the senses and a hot spot of activities for anyone in the district. Six miles of eclectic, artsy, and inviting shops selling handcrafted items, clothing, jewelry, and everything in between. Cafés and restaurants peppered the strip, keeping shoppers refreshed and satiated.

NPP opening ceremonies banners hung from gas lampposts on both sides of the street as far as the eye could see. Our family cat, Voodoo, graced the centers in various costumes made by me. Voodoo was the official Garden District pet ambassador for the pageant. Mom had invented the position for promotional purposes, but it was the community who'd crowned Voodoo queen. Mom hadn't even entered her in the contest.

Voodoo was the perfect choice for pet ambassador. She was the latest in a long line of sleek black cats to call the Crocker homestead her home. My great-grandpa had started the tradition when my grandpa was young and their black cat became ill. Instead of talking to Grandpa about things like sickness and death, he replaced the dying cat with an identical, albeit younger, match. Eventually, neighbors began to speculate about the local vet's cat that never aged. Voodoo came up once or twice as a possible reason, and the name stuck. Three generations later, Voodoo was a family institution.

I parked my Volkswagen on the curb outside Furry Godmother and hustled along the sidewalk toward my shop. The
door was held open by a mass of eager shoppers trying to get
inside for one of my custom designs or fresh-baked goods.
Not bad for a reformed runaway socialite.

I made a quick stop at the clothing boutique next door
before going to work. I hated to stay away any longer than
necessary when I knew Imogene needed my help, but my
food-splattered T-shirt had to go.

Imogene was behind the bakery counter at Furry Godmother when I arrived a few minutes later in the newly purchased ensemble I hoped smelled less like white sauce and
murder. She was detailing the list of organic ingredients used
in my peanut butter–and–bacon pawlines. Pawlines were an
all-natural, canine-friendly answer to the famous New Orleans
praline and came in a growing number of flavors. Purrlines
were the kitty-preferred version.

My tabby, Penelope, met me at the counter.

"Hello, honey." I rubbed her head and grabbed an apron.
"Thank you for covering all these extra hours," I called to
Imogene. "I know you hate to work on Sundays."

Imogene loved to claim the Lord's day, but she never went
to church. Normally, she spent the day with her best friend,
Veda, who lived in the French Quarter and ran a magical
cookie shop. Imogene had yet to tell me which was magical,
the cookies or the shop. I didn't push.

She smiled brighter without losing a beat on the ingredients list.

I welcomed guests and rang up sales until my cheeks ached

from smiling. I'd opened Furry Godmother one year ago, and business had grown every month. It was hard to believe with the crowd at hand, but there had been a time last summer that I'd wondered if I could sell enough designs to keep the doors open. These days I worried more about how to keep up with demand, and this week in particular was my busiest so far. The entire world seemed to be in town for the pet pageant, and everyone wanted a piece of Furry Godmother now that my first few pet-friendly food items had gone into mass production with the famous Grandpa Smacker label on them.

Grandpa Smacker was a national condiment and sweets company with local offices and manufacturing. It was just one portion of the enormous inheritance Jack had received when his grandpa, "Grandpa Smacker," died. Jack had asked me to advise on and contribute to a trial line of companion products for pets within the brand last fall, and so far, the trial had been a smashing success.

* * *

By closing time, happy hour and hungry tummies had thinned the herd. I'd sold more than thirty stuffed black kittens wearing tiny National Pet Pageant T-shirts and nearly worn out my new colored pencils designing personalized accessories for folks hoping to take something custom home to their furry loved ones.

I leaned over my full sketch pad on the counter. "There's no human way I can make all these items by the weekend."

Imogene hiked her purse over one shoulder and tossed

her apron onto its hook. "You need to hire some help around here."

I rolled my forehead against the cool laminate. "Writing a help-wanted ad takes time, reading applications takes time, interviewing . . ."

"So make time," Imogene interrupted.

"Pfft." I raised my head to make a face at her. "Now, that's the one thing I definitely can't make."

"Your pecan pie could also use some work."

"Hey!" I straightened. I'd brought a pecan pie to my parents' house for dinner Friday night, and Imogene had been the first to dive in. I suddenly couldn't remember if she'd finished her slice. "That pie was organic."

Imogene rolled her eyes. "Sugar is organic," she said, "and that pie could've used some." She pointed to the far wall, where I kept the turtle tank and shop mascots. "I fed Brad and Angelina at lunchtime. They had their vitamin pellets, sliced heirloom strawberries, and mustard greens."

"Thanks." I deflated into a posture-ruining slouch.

She cocked her head and stepped closer. "You want to talk about what happened at the theater? Your mama said someone died."

I released a long shaky breath, my traitorous eyes sliding for another peek in the trash where I'd tossed my food-splattered shirt at first opportunity. That was the thing about hiring my former nanny and mother's current best friend. Very little in my life went under the radar. What Imogene couldn't tell just by looking at me after eighteen years of making my life her business, my mom told her and vice versa. "Viktor Petrov, the pageant's MC, fell from the balcony at lunch." I fussed with the hem of my new cream camisole top, hastily purchased from the snooty clothing shop on my block, and blinked away the urge to cry. Crying never helped anything. "Jack's looking at Eva as a suspect."

"No." Her eyes bulged. "The little brunette from your mother's Welcoming Committee?"

"Yep."

"She wouldn't hurt anyone."

I lifted and dropped a heavy hand on the counter. "Try telling Jack that. He had her hauled to the station in a cop cruiser for questioning."

"Surely you can help him see reason. That man is sweet on you, and anyone with eyes can see it." She paused. "Except maybe you." Her frown deepened. "And him."

I opened the mini-fridge behind my counter and cracked open a bottle of water. "He told me to stay out of it. Refused to listen to me." I sipped the water. "But I found thirty-eight thousand dollars in Viktor's dressing room. Maybe he'll listen to that."

Imogene's jaw went slack. "Where did the unfortunate soul get that kind of cash? Hit it big at Harrah's?"

Harrah's was the local casino, and more than a few people had made a bundle there. Plenty more went home broke.

"Maybe." I'd have to think about the possibility that Viktor was a gambler later. If I thought about him too long, I'd be in tears all over again. "Looks like the bakery's cleaned out."

"Yes, indeed." Imogene allowed my clunky subject change without protest. "Those Grandpa Smacker labels have everyone clamoring to get a pupcake. Signing that contract was the smartest business move you've ever made."

I agreed, but I hadn't signed the contract as a business strategy. I'd signed it to gain access to the company and help Jack with a personal investigation, but regardless of the reason, Imogene was right. Grandpa Smacker's name was all I'd needed to get people into my store. Once they were in, they were thrilled to make purchases, and I loved to let them.

I shuffled around the counter on aching feet and flipped my OPEN sign to CLOSED. My white floor-to-ceiling shelves were nearly barren. Toppled and damaged boxes of make-it-at-home pupcake mixes were scattered on every flat surface. Brad and Angelina's enchanted lagoon was painted with fingerprints. My delightful pink-and-green decor had lost its charm and whimsy. The only thing untouched by the crush of shoppers was the row of white chandeliers hanging overhead. "I'm going to be here all night," I complained. "I need to get home and work on those design orders."

"And bake," Imogene said.

I dropped my head back and groaned at the ceiling. "And bake." I straightened up and put on a smile. "Go see Veda. Tell her I'm sorry to have ruined your Sunday plans." I dusted an empty shelf and reloaded it with supplies from behind my counter. "How's she doing these days?" I liked to compare Veda and Imogene to my best friend, Scarlet, and me, except we weren't remotely magical or planning to live to one hundred like Veda.

"Veda's fine. We didn't have plans this week. She went to Ohio to meet her granddaughter. She sent a letter first, but the girl never responded, so Veda thought meeting in person would help. Some people just don't trust the things they get in the mail these days. For example, I was told that I'd inherited a small country once, but that turned out to be a scam."

"You don't say."

"Mm-hmm." Imogene set a hand on the doorknob. "Until Veda gets back, I'm in charge of feeding the cat. Are you sure you don't want me to stay and help clean up? Nothing more you want to talk about?"

A low buzzing sound drew our attention to the floor. Penelope came into view, riding Spot, my Roomba robot vacuum. She lifted her chin, a queen on her throne, leading the cause to remove dirt and debris from my wide floor planking.

"No. We're fine. Go on." I shooed her outside. "Enjoy your evening."

I moved to the window display and sprayed cleaner on the glass. "It's just you and me," I told Penelope, "and as soon as your ride is over, we're out of here."

I cleaned until I heard Spot play his victory song and redock to charge, then tucked Penelope into her soft-sided carrier for the ride home. I tried Eva's cell phone on my way to the car. Maybe I could arrange for the committee to take her out for dinner or drinks. Anything to put an afternoon at the local police station behind her.

The call went directly to voice mail. I frowned at the screen. Why would her phone be turned off?

I flipped through my contacts and dialed my mom. If

CAT GOT YOUR CROWN

anyone would know what was happening with a Welcoming Committee lady, it would be her.

"Violet Conti-Crocker," she answered.

"Hi, Mom."

"Oh, thank goodness," she gushed. "Tell me you've gotten through to Jack and have Eva with you now. Bring her here. I'll make hot toddies."

I shook my head despite the fact that she couldn't see me. "I can't reach her. I was calling you to see what you've heard."

"I've heard that Jack and his men are detaining the poor thing overnight," she squeaked. "You need to get down to the theater and give your detective friend a firm crack on the head."

"He's not at the station with her?"

"No. He's combing the crime scene." She spewed the words as if they were ridiculous.

I hung my head. Sweet Eva would be traumatized for life after a night in a stinky jail cell with every manner of drunk, hooligan, and miscreant in the city. "Okay, Mom. I'll see what I can do."

I disconnected and dropped behind the wheel, wiping sweat from my brow after a whopping ten seconds outdoors. "Come on, sweetie," I told Penelope as I powered down all the windows and cranked up the air-conditioning. "Grandma says we've got a head to crack."

Chapter Four

*Furry Godmother protip: Heavy stitching can
ruin a look—and your night.*

Jack was on the sidewalk outside the theater, surrounded by local reporters, when I arrived. He looked hot, bothered, and fresh out of patience, an unfortunate trifecta considering I'd come to argue with him. His gaze jumped to mine the minute I joined the fringe of onlookers, and he lifted his chin infinitesimally in acknowledgment. I raised my fingers waist-high in return. His eyes narrowed on the gesture, but he didn't miss a beat in the delivery of his canned cop statement. "National Pet Pageant MC, Viktor Petrov, fell from the balcony at lunchtime today and was pronounced dead at the scene. An investigation is under way. Yes, I've taken point on this. No, there are no further details at this time. Mostly because that is all I am at liberty or willing to share." He ended with a sweeping glare, and the crowd broke away in muddled complaints.

I hurried in his direction, Penelope swinging contentedly in her carrier at my side.

He caught me by the elbow when I neared and steered me into the shadow of the building. "What are you doing here?" he asked, gaze traveling the length of my new outfit. "I thought you went to work."

"I did."

He gave the pleated skirt and camisole top another look. "This is new." It was hard to tell if he had an opinion on the look or was simply stating facts.

I rolled my shoulders back and cocked a hip, pulling out my inner debutante. "I couldn't wear clothes doused in cream sauce all day," I said.

Mom had forced me into every class on poise and grace she could find until I was too old to stay where she left me. I'd hated everything about the lessons at the time, but I'd found more and more use for them lately. Specifically when insecurity was getting the best of me or I needed to hold my ground. Both situations normally involved Jack.

He wiggled his fingers through the front door of Penelope's carrier and clucked his tongue at her in greeting. She purred in response. "How are you holding up?" he asked, dragging his gaze back to mine.

"Not well," I admitted, inching my chin higher. "I've got plans for a total breakdown later, and I'm thinking of bothering my therapist in Tahiti, but for the moment I'm on a mission from my mother."

"Oh yeah?"

"She sent me here to crack your head. That's threatening a police officer, and I feel like you could haul her in for that."

Jack's lips twitched. "She's mad I sent Eva Little to the station."

I tapped the end of my nose. "I'm here to convince you to release her."

Jack widened his stance and folded his arms. "How are you planning to do that?"

"Brute strength?" I guessed.

His lips wiggled, probably considering the eight inches and fifty pounds he had on my five-foot-four, size-eight frame, but he tamped the smile down before it could arrive. "No."

"Please?"

Jack hiked a brow. "I'm disappointed, Crocker. Usually you do better than this."

"I'm off my game," I admitted. "It's been a long day, but we both know Eva didn't kill Viktor, so why not let her go?"

"Can't."

"I just heard you say you're running point on this investigation. You can do anything you want, and you already know she's innocent. Don't make me prove it."

Jack's expression turned droll. "First of all, I don't want you trying to prove anything. You just about get yourself killed every time, and I've got no patience for that nonsense right now. Secondly, I have justifiable cause to hold Eva, even if you don't like it. If nothing else, she might've seen something useful for finding Viktor's killer. So she's right where she belongs. Down at the station, going over every detail of those final minutes with my team."

My heart fluttered. "She's not a suspect? You think she can actually *help* the case?"

"Maybe."

"Maybe?" I gave him my best business face. "Stop talking in circles, Jack Oliver. Are you planning to charge her with something or not?"

Jack stiffened. "Eva Little doesn't strike me as a killer, but she's a strong lead, and I've been doing this long enough to know that killers come in all shapes and sizes, so I'm not ruling anyone out. I'm following the facts."

"Maybe Viktor fell," I suggested. "Have you thought about that?"

"Based on Viktor's height and the height of the balcony railing, he would have had to climb over intentionally or be pushed. Eva was seen having a heated argument with the victim this morning, and she admits to slapping him. Her hair was on his jacket. She was in the balcony."

"Her hair was probably on his jacket because he was a handsy creep," I said, "and you already know she was standing close enough to slap him."

Jack pressed his lips into a thin white line.

I used the break to circle back through my argument and find another approach. "Slapping him for his unwanted advances doesn't make her a murderer. That wouldn't even make sense. She didn't need to be here. She was a committee volunteer, like me, and if he was such an enormous problem that she'd consider killing him, why wouldn't she have simply stepped down? The whole thing will be over in five days. Besides, women deal with weasels like Viktor all the time. We just chin-up and move on. If we killed every man who ogled, catcalled, or groped us, there'd be a lot fewer men walking around."

Jack's brows knitted tight. "People do that to you?"

"Me and every other woman between fourteen and seventy."

He scanned the horizon, head shaking, jaw locked.

"Hey." I stroked a hand down his arm, and his attention snapped back to me. I dropped my fingers away. I had more important things I needed to tell him before he had to get back to work inside the theater. "I went to Viktor's dressing room while you were in the lobby with Eva earlier. I needed the playbook with his detailed daily itinerary so that Mom could get started moving the event to a new venue without losing pace."

"You removed evidence from the dressing room?"

"Not evidence. Just the playbook, and I locked the door on my way out because I found an envelope with money inside. Thirty-eight thousand dollars," I said, raising my brows. "All one-hundred-dollar bills, tucked neatly in his top desk drawer."

Jack cast a glance at the building beside us, brows furrowed. He dipped his head lower, rolling his shoulders in and creating a small space between us that was just our own. "I went to Viktor's dressing room when you left. The place was trashed. There was no money. My guys went over it piece by piece, tagging everything."

"What?" I whispered back, working his words through my crowded head. "Someone took the money? How did they know it was there?"

Jack didn't answer, careful as always not to give me more information than absolutely necessary.

"That kind of money is a stronger motive for murder than what you're holding Eva on," I said. "Viktor wouldn't have told anyone he had money like that laying around his dressing room, so whoever took it is probably the same person who gave it to him. That couldn't have been Eva, because she was already with you when I left there, which means she was with your people at the time the room was tossed."

A glimmer of pride flashed in his eyes. "True."

"Thank you. So, Eva can go home?"

Jack smiled. "No."

"Why not?"

"There's no rule that says the money and the murder have to be related. Eva could easily have been involved with Viktor's death somehow without knowing that money existed."

I puffed out a sigh. "You think it's more likely the poor guy was robbed by one criminal and murdered by another in under an hour?"

"Like I told you," he said, "I'm not ruling anything out. I'm following the facts, and I'm making calls on evidence, not emotion."

"Heaven forbid you ever act on your emotions," I grouched.

Jack crossed his arms in a cocky cop pose. "If I acted on my emotions, *I'd* be in jail." He dropped the attitude to dig a roll of antacids from his pocket.

"Fine. I'm going home," I said. "If my mom asks, tell her I was here, but you won't listen."

"That's not—" His phone buzzed on his hip, and he

pressed it to his ear, scowling at me as he answered. "Detective Oliver. A what? No. This is a pet pageant."

I stepped away, lifting a hand in goodbye. Jack needed to get busy finding a killer so poor Eva could go home. "Think about what I said," I whispered.

"Stay away from Armstrong Park," he called after me. "People are calling in a bear sighting."

I turned on my toes and paced backward a few steps, smiling. "I'll let Chase know."

Jack lifted his arms like an airplane. "What?"

"It's not a bear," I called, putting more space between us. "It's a massive honey-hued Tibetan mastiff."

"Of course it is."

* * *

I called my best friend, Scarlet, on my way home. Scarlet and I had met when we were in diapers and our mothers got us together regularly at their coffee dates. We'd been fast friends just as our parents had hoped, but never quite the little ladies of society they'd planned. Scarlet and I had always been more along the lines of double-trouble. Given our steadfast, headstrong maternal origins, I was never sure why anyone had expected differently.

When I'd fled to college, Scarlet had stayed and married the eldest Hawthorne brother, Carter, straight out of high school. They had four babies now, and Scarlet was deeply involved in our district's policies, community outreach, and social affairs. So it seemed Scarlet had eventually made her mother proud. I, on the other hand, was terminally single, hadn't produced a single grandchild for my mother, had gained four pounds since moving home last year, and couldn't bring myself to care about any of it.

"Is this a wine or chocolate situation?" Scarlet asked in lieu of hello.

"Both." I gave her the day's rundown, some of which she'd already picked up through the local grapevine, which was how she'd known I was stressed out before asking, and the rest she couldn't wait for the details on.

"I'll be there in twenty minutes."

Scarlet lived in a proper Garden District mansion with her family, only steps from my parents and a collection of the South's independently wealthy, from old-money aristocrats to modern-day movie stars. I lived a few streets over in an area where homes were a touch newer and within my budget. My one-story shotgun home, for example, was a New Orleans classic. Originally intended as bland utilitarian housing, the rectangular structure had been built for laborers and their families. Now, however, homes like mine had become one of the Crescent City's cultural treasures, each as unique and inviting as the owners themselves. Mine was currently in a state of renovation while its owner figured out who she was.

I set Penelope's carrier on the wide planked floorboards of my living room and kicked my shoes onto the shag rug beneath my coffee table. White wood trim ran the circuit through my home, outlining floors and ceilings, doors and windows. I'd painted the rooms in a muted palette, all various shades of the sunrise. There was something about colors like apricot and amber that warmed my insides and made me smile.

Penelope lumbered out of her carrier when I opened the door, stretching and yawning.

"Dinner," I said, hurrying to the kitchen to refill her bowls and feed Buttercup, my little beta fish. "Auntie Scarlet is coming to help me brainstorm ways to prove Miss Eva's innocence," I told them as they each took a run at their meals.

I popped my phone onto the charging dock on my counter, then unloaded the contents of my refrigerator. Baking kept me calm, but the longer I stood in the safety of my beautiful home and newly renovated kitchen, thanks to the added income from Grandpa Smacker, the closer I came to having that long-overdue emotional breakdown.

A man had been murdered in front of my eyes today.

He'd landed close enough to splash cream sauce on my T-shirt. That was about as traumatic an experience as most people could imagine, and it was hands-down the worst thing that had happened to me in months. I deserved a cry, but I didn't want one. I wanted to *do* something.

I wiped my eyes and piled cubed cheese onto a tray with olives, crackers, and grapes. Besides, I refused to have a meltdown with company coming.

I flopped my secret-recipe cookbook onto the marble countertop and flipped through the pages of things I already made regularly for my shop and special occasions, looking for something I could build upon. The board of representatives at Grandpa Smacker had suggested I divine a new product to be sold at the upcoming Fall Food Festival, specifically, something that could be enjoyed equally by humans and their pets. It was a tricky request, because instinct told me the simplest answer was to provide apple and banana slices with peanut butter for dipping, but I knew that wasn't what the board wanted. They wanted something potentially proprietary, and the Fall Food Festival was a great place to create a test market. Problem was, I didn't have any new ideas yet, and I'd hoped to bring some samples with me to this week's early-morning meeting.

The doorbell rang, and I started, having nearly forgotten Scarlet was coming. I laughed at my foolish reaction, then headed for the door.

"Hello! Come in!" I sang, pulling the door wide to usher her inside. "I'm so glad you came. This has been a day from h—"

A startled bike messenger stared back at me from beneath a pointy red helmet. "Lacy Crocker?"

I yanked my chin back. "Yeah?" He was definitely not Scarlet, but I admired his bravery for wearing a skin-tight, bright-yellow knee-length onesie at his age. Since when had messengers needed to be so aerodynamic?

He handed me a clipboard. "Package."

I signed beside the X. "What is it?"

He shrugged, then traded me a big envelope for his clipboard and pen. "Have a nice evening." He climbed back on his bike and pedaled away.

I shut the door and ripped the bulbous package open. There was a stuffed National Pet Pageant Pet from my shop inside. I turned the big envelope upside down and shook the kitten out. A flyer for the event fluttered out with him. "Weird." I lifted the kitty first, and my heart kicked into overdrive. Someone had taken heavy black thread and stitched a pair of large, poorly crafted Xs over his eyes and a series of smaller ones across the mouth.

Block letters on the back of the flyer spelled STOP.

I didn't need to ask what the sender wanted stopped. I knew from experience. This was a warning to leave Viktor's murderer alone.

Chapter Five

Furry Godmother's words of warning: If you keep your head down, you'll never see what's coming.

I worked to steady my breathing, then took photos of the note and the ghastly stuffed cat's face. I sent both to Jack before heading into the kitchen for a glass of wine. Someone knew not only my name and address but where I worked, and had been inside my store, *today*, to buy one of my products for mutilation. Then the lunatic had had my ruined kitty delivered to my doorstep with a warning. It was hard to believe any of that could be true when Viktor hadn't been dead ten hours, but there it was anyway.

I poured my first glass of wine to the rim, leaned over it, and sucked it down halfway, keeping one eye on my phone. Jack was the worst at returning calls and texts, except when I needed him. Then, there was no stopping him.

The phone lit with Jack's face and a text message on the screen. ON MY WAY. STAY PUT. LOCK THE DOORS. BAG THE CAT.

I tipped the wine glass back and finished round one with

a sigh, then poured a second just as liberally. Before I got goofy in an attempt to settle my nerves, I needed to bag the cat. I hunted through my kitchen drawers for gallon freezer bags to stuff the cat, note, and delivery envelope inside. I felt better as I sealed the bags shut, securing the threats.

My front door swung open with a creak, and I nearly swallowed my tongue.

"Sorry I'm late," Scarlet said, letting herself in. I'd given her a key to my place last Thanksgiving and a code to my alarm in case of emergencies.

She locked up behind herself while I watched from the open kitchen archway. "I have red and white wine, plus two kinds of chocolate," she said, bustling through the room. She dropped a large quilted bag onto my coffee table and raised a smile. Her satin emerald tank top and white shorts were adorable against her freckled porcelain skin and fiery red hair. Her crimson nails matched her parted lips as she took in my nearly empty again wine glass and likely bewildered expression. "Whoa."

I lifted the freezer bags in my opposite hand. "I had a delivery a few minutes ago. Bike messenger. Mutilated NPP kitty."

She took the clear packages, eyes widening as she turned them over in her hands, then read the one-word note aloud. "Stop."

I cringed.

Scarlet sucked air, attention snapping back to my face. "Did you call Jack?"

"He's coming."

"Sit." She pointed to the couch, then marched into the kitchen and returned with the bottle opener and a second glass. "Start from the beginning."

I didn't think the words would come out when I opened my mouth, but they flowed. I couldn't stop. I talked until I'd unloaded every detail I could recall and every scary thought that went with it. Mostly, I couldn't understand how I'd become the target for a threat before I'd even made it home from work.

The doorbell rang, putting me on my feet. I froze halfway to the door, hoping it wasn't another delivery. Three steady thumps set my heart into a sprint.

"It's Jack." The familiar tenor rumbled through the door, unwinding my muscles.

I pulled him inside with bone-melting relief. "Thanks for coming."

"Are you okay?" His eyes searched mine, probably seeing more in my unsteady stare than I was willing to say.

For example, I wasn't fine. I was terrified. "Yeah."

He greeted Scarlet, then scanned the room. "No Chase?"

"Nope, but there's plenty of wine," I said.

Jack turned a heated look on me. There was a question in his eyes I couldn't read.

Scarlet handed him the bags. "This was delivered before I got here." She reached for the wine, and I watched, stunned, as she poured a refill. Scarlet hadn't enjoyed more than one glass of her favorite cabernet since she'd gotten pregnant with Poppet almost two years ago.

Where is Poppet? I'd been so focused on my own trauma, I

hadn't even noticed Scarlet was practically missing an appendage.

Scarlet studied me. "I'm not nursing anymore."

My brows went up. "Is that okay?" I asked. How had I missed such an important transition in my best friend's life? She loved nursing. Loved babies, and Poppet was going to be her last. "How are you doing?"

She gave me a sad smile. "I'm okay. It's how life works, right? She and the boys need me less and less all the time. It's you I'm worried about."

Jack snapped a pair of blue gloves over his big hands and shook the contents of my freezer bags onto the coffee table. He took snapshots with his phone and tapped the screen for a long while before returning the items to their bags and stuffing both into the black shoulder bag he'd brought with him. "I'll see what the crime lab can get from these, contact the messenger service who made the delivery, and try to work backwards to identify the sender. Is that toy from your store?"

I rubbed the creeping chills off my arms. "Yeah, and assuming this is all about Viktor, I can narrow the date of purchase to today." Though, busy as my store had been, I'd still have hundreds of sales to comb through, and if the buyer used cash, it would all be for nothing. "I'll check the receipts tomorrow."

"Any idea who might've done this?" he asked.

"Viktor's killer?"

His lips pulled down on both sides. "Anything more specific?"

"No." I took my seat beside Scarlet on the couch. "But the culprit should be easy enough to find. We know he or she was in the building when Viktor died. You put the place on lockdown right afterward," I said. "That alone narrows our suspect pool to roughly one hundred and fifty people if we include pet owners and trainers, assistants, pageant staff, and security. I like those odds better than we've had in the past, when the killer could have been anyone in New Orleans."

"*My* suspect pool," Jack corrected. "You don't have a suspect pool, and the suspect is rarely a random person in the city because murders are rarely random. The killer usually has some connection to the victim, and most people have a lot fewer than one hundred fifty relationships, which makes this more complicated, and these suspects are about to scatter across the country in a few days when the pageant ends."

I wrinkled my nose. I hadn't thought of it that way. "Are you on duty?"

Jack scraped a heavy hand over his face. "No."

Scarlet went to the kitchen and returned with another wine glass. She poured it to the top. "Here. Drink this. You'll feel better."

Jack gave the glass a wayward look but accepted and took a seat on the armchair beside the couch. "You should probably bow out of this event and lay low until it's over," he told me. "Maybe take a vacation."

Tahiti came to mind. Maybe my therapist could fit me in between mai tais.

Jack sipped the wine and fixed an appreciative gaze on Scarlet. "Thanks. I ran into Carter last week. Congratulations on the sleeping baby."

She beamed. "You're welcome. I'm thinking of hiring a

nanny so I can get more involved in things. Maybe volunteer at the boys' school, help Carter at the office or Mom with her community stuff. I used Poppet as a cop-out for a long time, but I think I'm ready to see what the next stage of my parenting life will be like."

"You want me to run a background check on anyone?" Jack asked.

"Not yet, but I could use some input on the interviews," she said, swinging her eyes back in my direction.

"Of course," I said. "Anything you need. You know I can use the distraction."

Her eyes lit, and a sneaky expression crossed her pretty face. "Great, then maybe I can help you with something."

Jack paused midreach for the chocolates. He gave us each an appraising look.

I wasn't sure if he knew she'd just offered to help me find out who'd killed Viktor and threatened me, but I did, and I accepted with a tiny nod.

Scarlet lifted the box toward Jack with a sweet smile.

His eyes narrowed, and he turned them back in my direction. "Can you get off this committee of your mother's? Tell her about the threat; she'll understand," he said. "If she doesn't, I can talk to her."

I didn't want to burst Jack's bubble, but his badge meant a total of jack-squat to my mother, especially where community service was concerned. My mother served the district like armed forces served our country. She would bleed and die for the cause, but unlike our military heroes, she'd cheerfully take me with her. "I have to help find a new venue, then reroute everyone and everything," I said. "There's a million things to do, and I can't just quit. She needs me." I paused to let the words sink in. A year ago I would've jumped on an excuse to avoid Mom's goofy committees. Now I truly wanted to help.

Jack and Scarlet looked as stunned as I felt.

"I have to head over to the theater after work tomorrow and help transport everything to the new destination, wherever that will be. Between work and the pageant, I won't have any downtime until the winning pets are crowned in a few days."

Scarlet made a face and set her glass down. "No downtime at all?"

"I'll make time for the nanny interviews," I promised. "Just tell me when and where."

"I was actually going to ask if you wanted to help me with something in the French Quarter Wednesday morning."

"The Quarter?" Jack asked, sitting forward once more, his wine level now at a normal pour.

"Jackson Square," she clarified, biting into another chocolate.

I smiled. I loved the French Quarter as much as I loved any part of my city, and I never said no to a visit or an opportunity for shenanigans with Scarlet. "What time?" I asked. "I'll ask Imogene to open the store."

"Early," Scarlet said. "Carter's law firm is setting up a water booth during San Fermin en Nueva Orleans. We should probably be there by seven."

Jack frowned. "The running of the bulls?"

"Absolutely," I said, smile widening.

San Fermin en Nueva Orleans happened every July and

coincided with the running of the bulls in Pamplona, Spain. Except, in New Orleans, the bulls were roller derby girls dressed in red with whiffle bats and set loose on the streets of the Quarter, where they chased down hordes of paying men and women dressed as bullfighters and gave them a whack. There were lots of parties before and after the event, with Spanish wine, sangria, and tapas galore.

"Count me in."

Jack rubbed his eyes. "I don't think a large-scale event in the Quarter is where you should be this week."

I felt my smile fade and the enthusiasm slip from my limbs. I needed this escape with Scarlet. Time away from the pageant, my shop, my mother, *the killer.* "It's not as if I'm going to announce I'll be there," I said. "Only you and Scarlet will know, and I won't exactly be standing alone on a corner. I'll be at Jackson Square with hundreds of other people, and the Quarter will be stuffed to the gills. I'll blend in and disappear."

"And I'll be with her the whole time," Scarlet said. "I carry mace and a stun gun now."

"And I have my whistle," I told him. I was licensed to carry a concealed weapon, and I'd had a lifetime of target practice at Dad's club, but I wasn't a fan of shooting people, so I'd never seen a good enough reason to have a gun outside the range. Jack knew that, and he'd given me a whistle to help draw attention if I ever needed help. That whistle had saved my life once, and I never left home without it.

Scarlet's phone rang, and she excused herself to the kitchen to answer.

Jack took her spot on the couch at my side and hooked an

elbow over the backrest. Depth and urgency raged in his eyes. His jaw clenched and released. His cologne reached across the small space between us, igniting memories of other times we'd been so close I'd thought I'd collapse. Just like then, he didn't speak.

"What are you thinking?" I asked, feeling the warmth of the wine in my head and stomach.

"I'm wondering how I'm going to keep you safe." His voice was low and his expression grim. "I don't have a great track record when it comes to keeping you out of harm's way, and I don't know how to change it."

I scooped his heavy hand in mine and squeezed his fingers. "You do," I argued. "You always save me. You'll figure this out too, and I'll be fine."

Jack turned his palm beneath mine and laced our fingers together, a look of pain written on his brow.

The gesture was small but intimate, and my heart skittered and jumped in my chest. I was an affectionate person by nature, but Jack was not, and it made the easy, comfortable way he'd begun to touch me lately all the more meaningful. I curled my fingers over his and tried to look one hundred percent calmer than I felt.

"Don't go back to the pageant," he said. "Let your mom handle it. She's got a whole committee of socialite minions at her beck and call. She can get by without one."

If only it were that easy. Even if I hadn't minded telling Mom I couldn't help her anymore, I still had a job to do. "I'm in charge of costumes," I said. "No one else can mend and repair on the fly like I can. I've got everything I need to fix any problem in my tackle box. I even keep extra costumes in my car in case something is damaged beyond repair and a pet needs a new outfit in a hurry."

"Leave that stuff with your mom," he said. "Let someone else dress the pets and sew the buttons. I know this pageant is important to you, Lacy, but returning puts you in close proximity to someone making threats against you, and *you* are important to me."

My heart clunked to a standstill. I wanted to tell him I'd call my mother immediately and let her know I wasn't returning. I wanted to tell him I trusted him to figure this out, release Eva as a suspect, and catch the true killer. I wanted to tell him, but the words piled on my tongue until I was sure I'd choke on them. I wanted to make Jack happy, but I also knew how these scenarios turned out. I'd lived through more of them than anyone should have, and the fact that I'd lived had had nothing to do with sitting back and waiting and everything to do with me getting involved in this investigation while the trail of evidence was still warm.

I had to find the killer before I wound up just like Viktor.

Chapter Six

Furry Godmother's hard truth: Life isn't perfect and
neither is your outfit.

Penelope and I arrived at my parents' house an hour early the next morning. Dad had promised me pancakes via text message before bed, but I suspected the invitation was a ploy to get me there and check me for signs of a nervous breakdown. Either way, I loved pancakes and my father, so I wouldn't have missed it. Most people knew Dad as Dr. Crocker, the locally adored veterinarian. To me, he was infinitely more, but most specifically a confidant, hero, and friend.

I pulled my Volkswagen onto the driveway behind my family's modest five-thousand-square-foot Victorian and pressed the shifter into park. Mom's great-grandfather had commissioned the home, complete with scrolling gingerbread woodwork and muted mauve-and-olive color scheme, in the late nineteenth century. I'd grown up here, reared in the shadow of my mother and grandmother before me, but it was Dad who'd made my childhood fun.

He strode into view as I unbuckled and climbed out, crossing the lawn to my side from the renovated barn on their property, which had served as his veterinary practice all my life. "There's my girl." He kissed my cheek.

"Hi, Daddy."

He rounded the hood of my car to retrieve Penelope's carrier from the passenger seat. "I'm so glad you ladies made time for an old man and some pancakes."

I followed him onto the porch with a smile. "You're not old." He was barely fifty-five. "You're younger than George Clooney, and when have I ever turned down pancakes?"

A wild squawk turned me around on the porch. "What on earth was that?" The sound came again, this time louder and with a series of naughty words at the end.

"Parrot," Dad said. "He's got a broken wing and a potty mouth. I just hope none of my other patients bring anyone under eighteen with them today."

"When did you get a parrot patient?" I asked.

"Yesterday. He's from the NPP, actually."

I took a moment to kick the notion around. "Chase thought Big Splash might've followed a parrot outside."

Dad released Penelope in the rear hall, then locked the back door behind us. "I'm not sure what a Big Splash is, but the parrot definitely left the pageant unsupervised. He was collected from Armstrong Park with an injured wing." Dad gave me a careful once-over, expression turning parental and sad. "How are you doing? Your mom said you were fine, but I know what you saw yesterday was awful, and sometimes things like that can take a little while to sink in and take hold."

"I'm okay," I promised. I wasn't sure that was completely true, but it was true enough for the moment.

I still had to fess up about the threat I'd received last night by courier, and that was bound to change my emotional status. Dad would hate to hear it. Mom would wonder what I'd done to provoke it, and I didn't particularly want to relive it.

He slid an arm across my shoulders and steered me into the dining room, where my mother sat with a cup of coffee and the morning paper. She took her glasses off to look at me. "What are you wearing?"

She was wearing a baby-blue blouse and pearls.

Dad kissed my cheek. "Good luck." He ducked into the kitchen, presumably to avoid the line of fire, but there was no hiding necessary today. Today was a day of truce for me.

"I'm glad you asked," I said, doing a slow twirl for her. I'd intentionally chosen something to wear that Mom would have to love. "This delightful number is a designer, butternut-yellow silk wrap dress that my mother saw in a shop window last month and suggested would look delightful on me." Hopefully it would cushion her response to my bike-delivered threat.

"You went back and bought it?"

"Yes, ma'am." And I'd kept it in my arsenal for the next time I needed to deliver bad news. Now I needed to go back for a few more because, in my experience, threats to my safety rarely ended after just one.

Her lips formed a small smile. "Your mother is clearly a genius. You look stunning."

I performed a curtsy, then took a seat across from her at the elaborate, hand-carved antique table for twelve. Per the usual, only three seats had settings. Dad at the head and Mom and me on either side. "How's it going with locating a new venue?" I asked.

"Fine." Mom stirred her caramel-colored coffee with calm confidence. "I'm looking at the Audubon Tea Room today. The committee and I have been invited for lunch and a proper tour. You're more than welcome to join us, though I suppose you're busy."

"I have to open Furry Godmother," I said. "It's just Imogene and me until I get time to hire some help." I bit down on the insides of my cheeks. I hadn't meant to bring up needing help. I'd crossed into dangerous territory. I'd once babysat for the girl who'd helped me last summer while she was home from college. She was unavailable this year because she was getting married.

"I spoke with Paige's mother," Mom said. "She's home again right now, but she doesn't have any free time."

I let my eyelids fall shut. "I know."

"She's planning a wedding," Mom said. "Isn't that nice?"

I forced my eyes open and tipped my head with a bright smile. "Yep."

I poured a cup of coffee from the carafe on the table and sucked in a mouthful. I'd need a little caffeine in my system for the direction this train had taken. "Some man is very lucky," I said. "Paige is a doll."

"Indeed." Mom stared.

I avoided eye contact.

"I noticed you talking with Chase Hawthorne yesterday,"

she said, uncrossing then recrossing her legs. "You two are thick as thieves this year."

I nodded. "We are." I'd always thought Chase was handsome, but we'd lost touch until last summer. Then I'd broken my leg escaping a lunatic in the fall, and Chase had stuck by my side while I'd healed. We'd bonded over weeks of bad television and a lifetime of shared memories. I loved Chase deeply, and I had no doubt he knew that. I was sure he felt the same way. I just wasn't sure the love we had was the kind either of us wanted.

"Well?" she asked. "What are you going to do about that?"

"About what?"

"You and Chase," she said. "I've never seen a pair of adults so close who refuse to so much as go out on a proper date. I can't understand it. Your children would be beautiful."

Dad arrived wearing a ruffled apron, oven mitts, and a semi-panicked expression. These days, the only discussions more heated than the ones centering on my wardrobe were those involving my love life. "Pancakes!" He set the tray between Mom and me, then made a second trip for toppings.

The disruption didn't faze Mom. "I saw him on his veranda last night when I got home. He said he went by to check on you, but Jack Oliver's truck was there. What was that about?"

I let my head fall forward. It was nearly impossible to buy a home in the Garden District, but Chase had somehow managed to buy the one right next door to my parents' five months ago. I hadn't even known the home was for sale.

Now I had to segue from my tragic love life to the other

topic I didn't want to discuss. "I had to call Jack because a bike messenger delivered a threat to my doorstep. I even had to sign for it."

Dad nearly collapsed onto his chair. "What?"

I passed my phone to him. A picture of the stuffed cat and note was centered on the screen. "Jack is looking into it."

Mom gaped. "Is this about Viktor Petrov?" She craned her neck for a better look at the image in Dad's hands. "He's barely cold."

Dad grimaced, his pale face whiter than his dress shirt. "You aren't looking into that man's fall."

It wasn't a question.

"I didn't do anything," I said. "All I did was go to Viktor's dressing room to get his playbook." *And find thirty-eight thousand dollars. And see a pet owner arguing with a PA. And vow publicly to get to the bottom of things and save Eva.*

"Jack was at your house on official business?" Mom asked. "Nothing more?"

Dad dropped my phone onto the table and stabbed a pancake with unnecessary aggression. "That's hardly the most important part of this conversation."

"Jack was off duty when I called," I said, helping myself to a stack of warm buttery pancakes, "but he came anyway when I sent him the photos."

"I know you like him," Mom said, "and he likes you. That's painfully evident to everyone in this district. More painful to some than others," she added under her breath, "but you should think long and hard before you jump into anything with a cop."

"Why?" I clamped my mouth shut the moment the word was out, hoping uselessly that my mother would show enough grace not to answer.

"Is that really what you want for your life?" she asked. "A significant other who may or may not come home from work every night? Someone who could leave you a widow at any moment?"

I stuffed my mouth full of pancake so I couldn't respond. Anything said in my mother's presence could and would be held against me until I died.

"A life like that is bound to give you premature grays, wrinkles, and stress weight," she continued.

I shoved another hunk of carbs into my mouth. The conversation was irrelevant. Jack had never given voice to any feelings he had about me beyond frustration and, occasionally, entertainment. So, as much as I liked Jack, and as much as I thought he liked me too, until he told me how he felt, what I thought I knew didn't matter. People didn't start relationships on hopeful speculation.

"Chase would make a lovely husband," Mom said. "He's handsome, charming, witty, and he puts up with your tomfoolery. Even starts some of it, I imagine. You're perfect together, and he believes in you, Lacy."

Chase also believed the French Quarter was haunted, but I doubted Mom wanted to hear that right now.

I waved my white linen napkin in surrender.

"Fine," Mom conceded. "Did Jack stay long after he took the stuffed cat and note?"

"A little while," I said. "Scarlet was there, and the three

of us talked until after midnight before they both headed home."

"Scarlet," Mom said. "There's a girl who has her head on her shoulders."

I concentrated on my breakfast while Dad fumed silently over my recent threat and Mom sang Scarlet's praises.

I'd been up until nearly dawn researching the National Pet Pageant by skimming pet owner blogs and newspaper articles from around the country. Most of the material I'd found was overblown and grossly sensationalized, but I was shocked at the number of scandals involving Viktor Petrov. More peculiar still was the fact that the online pet community seemed to have accepted his misogynistic tyrannical ways. Instead of him being kicked off the pageant for his horrible behavior, ticket sales had increased every year. The public loved it. It was just as Mrs. Smart had said. Fans couldn't get enough of his spectacle.

I couldn't help wondering what the people on the receiving end of his wrath thought of him. Even Eva had slapped him, and she was the most mild-mannered human on earth.

"Well, are you ready?" Mom asked, standing over me and clearing my empty plate.

"What?" *When did I finish all four pancakes?*

Mom huffed. "You need to adjust the hem on the gown you made me. I've chosen my shoes, and the dress needs to be taken up or it won't fall along my ankles properly." She hiked one perfectly sculptured brow. "We talked about this last week. Or have you forgotten already?"

I followed Mom to the master bedroom. The world beyond her spotless glass doorknobs was exquisitely decorated with plush wall-to-wall carpeting and soaked in the powdery scents of makeup and Chanel No. 5. A stretch of sensored lights flashed on as we entered her personal closet, illuminating rows of dresses, blouses, and jackets alongside shelves of sweaters, jeans, and shoes. I smiled at the jeans. She hadn't owned a single pair a year ago, but she'd admitted in the spring that I was having an impact on her fashion choices.

"I'll just be a minute," Mom said, slipping behind her screen to change. She emerged in the pastel replica of a gown I'd made in college. I'd recently worn the original to a fancy dinner party, and Mom had fallen in love. She'd requested one of her own, in lilac, and I'd agreed.

"Beautiful," I said, lending her my hand as she stepped onto the small pedestal set before her mirrors.

"Thank you. You do marvelous work," she said. "Which reminds me, your store has been open a year now, and it's time we marked that milestone with a party."

"Oh, no thank you," I said, lining her hem with pins. I had enough going on without worrying about the details of a party.

Mom, on the other hand, never tired of details. Mom was a party-throwing machine. Her events were lavish and frequent. Invitations were coveted, and despite the significant amount of time she'd devoted to the NPP, she'd still managed to host three luncheons and two dinner parties this month.

"I don't need a party," I repeated, in case she'd missed my previous response. The faraway look in her eyes suggested she had.

"You have to do something to commemorate the milestone," she scoffed. "It's a big deal."

"I know. I was thinking of offering a discount on merchandise or BOGO pupcakes and tuna tarts."

Mom grabbed handfuls of her skirt and whipped the material out of my hands. She glared down at me. "Be serious."

"I am," I said. "I don't need a party for staying in business. The fact I'm still in business is reward enough." I tugged her skirt back over her ankles and slipped the final few pins in before she had another outburst.

Thankfully, her ringing cell phone diverted her attention while I double-checked my work. "What do you think?" I asked when she hung up.

Mom twisted at the waist before her mirror. "Very nice. Thank you." She grabbed her original outfit and headed for the screen to change again. "Aren't you going to ask who I was talking with?"

"No. That would be rude."

She frowned. Probably because she always asked who I was talking to. "It was Mary Jean. She said Jack released Eva last night. Did you know that? Are you the reason he let her go?"

"No," I answered honestly. "We barely talked about Eva last night, and when I tried to discuss her with him earlier in the day, he blew me off."

Mom made a sour face, then stepped behind the screen.

I left the closet.

Voodoo was on her four-poster cat bed near the window in my parents' master suite, tail flipping lazily as she sunned herself.

Penelope had a pink cushion in my bedroom in Uptown but preferred to sleep on my head.

A few minutes later, Mom led the way back to the dining room, listing things that needed to be taken care of for a smooth transition of NPP venues. "Don't be late tonight," she warned. "We'll need all hands on deck if we're going to pull off a relocation of this magnitude. And be sure to wear what you have on. It's perfect. Also, try not to act surprised when I call you forward. We're down by a judge now that Mackey has stepped into the role of MC, so you're up."

I stopped moving, and Mom went on several steps without me. "Up where?"

She turned back, looking exasperated. "It's an expression. It means you're the replacement judge."

"I can't judge," I said.

Mom turned forward once more and marched on.

"I'm serious. I'm not qualified," I said, hurrying after her. "This is a national pageant. There's a lot at stake, and I don't know anything about pets except how cute they are."

"You know as much about pets as anyone. You grew up watching your father care for every pet in the district. You own a shop where you bake for and dress them. There are always five judges. We're down one, so you're up."

"Stop saying that."

Mom stopped in the dining room and hiked her bossy eyebrow.

I pressed a fingertip to the twitching skin beneath mine. "Great."

"Good."

"Fine."

Dad stood to greet us with Penelope purring happily in his arms. "I was going to crate her for you when I heard you coming."

"It's no problem," I said. "You've already caught her, and that's sometimes half the battle."

He smiled. "I didn't crate her because I know you've got a full schedule, and I thought I could keep her with me at the office instead. There's no need to tote her to work, then over to the theater, then off to the Tea Room when she can spend the day with Voodoo and me."

I gave Penelope a long look. He was right. All that running around amounted to a lot of time in her crate, and she couldn't run loose at the theater or the Tea Room, not to mention the commutes. "You don't mind?" I asked.

"I wouldn't have volunteered if I did."

* * *

I parked at the end of the block farthest from Furry Godmother and hurried along the sidewalk toward my shop. The searing summer sun and suffocating humidity baked my skin and aggressively accosted my wrap dress. The most I could hope for was to reach the cool air-conditioning of my shop before there were permanent sweat stains on the silk.

Meanwhile, the Garden District was hard at work earning

its name. Bees buzzed around bountiful baskets of seasonal flowers hanging from streetlamps overhead. Every corner, every windowsill, every grassy knoll was alive with an eruption of color, and the air was scented with its bouquet. I jumped a little river of water leaking from a gardener's hose as he watered the city's landscaping and hustled toward the crowd outside my still closed shop door.

A woman in a flowy skirt and a peasant top smiled up at me from the bench outside my window as I passed. Big gold-framed sunglasses covered her eyes and mounds of wild blonde hair hid parts of her face as the wind blew. I ushered the customers inside, flipped the lights on, then poked my head back through the open door to admire the sleek black cat on her lap. He was a dead ringer for Voodoo. The woman, however, looked a little lost.

"Are you waiting for someone?" I asked, scanning the street in either direction.

"No. I'm just thinking," she said.

"Well, do you want to come inside where it's cooler? I have cold water in the fridge, and I'd love a closer look at your cat."

The woman stood on long legs and platform wedges, then pulled a big canvas bag onto her shoulder. "Sure. Thanks."

The cat stayed on her heels as she walked inside. I held the door for them both.

"He's not my cat," the lady said. "I have no idea where it came from, but it's been following me since I got into town yesterday." She shoved a stiff arm in my direction, and a pile of bangle bracelets jingled from the move. "I'm Willow."

"Lacy," I said. "You're not from New Orleans?"

"No." She pushed the sunglasses onto her head, securing mounds of golden beachy waves with the weight. Her eyes were the color of the sea, warm and enchanting. "I'm from everywhere. My parents were kind of hippies. We traveled through my childhood. Now I travel on my own."

"Well, welcome," I said.

"Thanks. I've always wanted to visit New Orleans," Willow said. "Dad would never agree to it, but Mom loved the city, and I should have known I would too. I'm pretty excited to finally be here."

I filled Penelope's bowls with kibble and water for the cat, then grabbed a cold bottle of water from the mini-fridge behind my counter for Willow. "Are you staying nearby?"

"I got a room in the French Quarter. I'm actually in town to see my great-grandma, but she wasn't home last night, so I found a place on Royale. From what I gather, it's a miracle anything was available. There's something going on this week."

"There's something going on every week," I said. "It's one of the things I love."

She nodded approvingly. "Hopefully my great-grandma is back soon. I don't know how long I'm staying, but I'd hate to leave without getting a chance to say hello."

"Was she expecting you?" I asked.

"I thought so. I ran into a sexy man outside her door this morning who seemed to know her. He had this accent." She fluttered her eyelids and made an appreciative sound. "It was this thick, southern-Louisiana sound."

I smiled. That was one of my favorites too.

"I could plant roots here for that accent alone," she said. "Once I told him who I was looking for, he told me to check up here, so I came right over, but I haven't seen her."

I wrinkled my nose. "He sent you to the Garden District or to my shop?" I couldn't imagine searching an entire neighborhood for one old lady. I also couldn't imagine anyone finding their great-grandmother at Furry Godmother, unless their great-grandmother was Imogene, and I already knew Imogene's entire family. Willow wasn't one of them.

"Lacy Marie Crocker," a familiar crabby-sounding voice barked. Mrs. Hams, a portly middle-aged woman and my mother's archnemesis, beetled in my direction. Her faux-leather fanny pack bounced against her brown culottes. Her pink T-shirt had a giant red heart in the middle and the word LLAMAS embroidered across the center. Mrs. Hams and her plantation-owning girlfriends called themselves the Llama Mamas and lived to provoke my mother. They frequently challenged Mom and her rival group, the Jazzy Chicks, to charity fund-raising competitions. In keeping with my overly complicated life, Mrs. Hams had me on retainer.

"Hello." I smiled, unable to imagine what had her in the district and a foul disposition so early in the day.

"I'd better let you work," Willow whispered. She gave a small wave before slipping back into the sun, black cat trailing in her wake.

Mrs. Hams set her dimpled hands on the counter and harrumphed. "I spent a small fortune on Llama Mama labels, swag, and giveaways for the National Pet Pageant, and now the news is saying someone died and the show is canceled.

What am I supposed to do with seven hundred Llama Mama lapel pins?"

"The pageant isn't canceled," I said. "The news reporter was supposed to make that clear. Which channel said it was canceled?"

Mrs. Hams looked at her fingers. "I didn't stick around for the whole cart and pony show. I called my car as soon as I heard the teasers; then I came right here to get my information from the horse's mouth."

I frowned, less than thrilled with being the horse in any scenario.

"Is it true?" she pressed.

"There was a death, yes."

"What's your mother going to do about it? Surely the show won't go on in a place where someone just died."

"Mom's moving the event," I said. "There's no practice tonight, but we'll move forward tomorrow at a new location, possibly the Audubon Tea Room."

"That place is too small," Mrs. Hams complained. "Where will everyone go when it isn't their turn on stage?"

"I don't know, but we're lucky she found anyplace with such little notice," I said. "Mom's having lunch at the Tea Room today for a closer look."

Mrs. Hams peeked around the room, then pressed her torso to the counter between us. "I heard it was the MC who died. Is that right? Viktor Petrov?"

I nodded, slightly confused by her sudden look of conspiracy. "That's right. He fell over the balcony."

"Doubtful," she said. "I've been watching him and this event for years. Everyone hates him."

"The world loved him," I said. He was the reason people kept coming back to an event as long and dry as a pet pageant. Viktor made it interesting.

"The world, yes," she said, "but I'll bet one of those PAs finally had enough of his bullying and did him in. That man was always yelling. Belittling. Humiliating someone. I'm a little shocked at the end of every show where no one has dropped a row of stage lights on his head."

I tapped my thumbs on the counter, considering her words. "Do you think he was really that awful, or could his behavior have been faked for ratings and attention?"

Mrs. Hams stared. "Who knows why anyone does anything?" she said. "All I know is, if I'd been the butt of his belligerence day after day, I'd be fit to toss him off a balcony too."

I cringed.

"I'll go home and wait for my relocation instructions from the committee. Make sure your mother knows our competition is still on. I've prepared far too long to quit now."

"Will do," I said.

Mom and Mrs. Hams had an ongoing game of *who can raise the most money for charity*, and they both played for blood. The game never seemed to end, but they always set stakes and time limits to make it interesting. They spent their time between rounds either gloating or plotting and sulking. The whole thing was borderline ridiculous, but it diverted Mom's attention from me, so I stayed out of the way as much as possible.

"And tell the police to speak with the assistants," Mrs. Hams called on her way to the door.

"I'm sure the police already have," I assured her.

And I'd have plenty of time to ask a few questions of my own while I helped move everything to the new venue tonight.

Chapter Seven

Furry Godmother protip: Silence is golden, especially when you're hiding.

I arrived at the Saenger Theatre in time to see Mom and several of the committee ladies pull away in a town car, presumably on a trip between venues. They'd likely be back, so my timing was perfect but my time limited.

I hurried inside and down the long narrow backstage halls toward Viktor's dressing room. I wasn't sure what I expected to find there, but my conversation with Jack the previous afternoon had plagued me. I'd left Viktor's dressing room neat as a pin and locked up tight. How had someone gotten inside? Why would they have torn the place apart? I'd found the money with no effort at all. If the intruder had wanted the cash, then why make a mess? Certainly not to lash out at a man he or she had already killed.

Viktor's dressing room door was open but roped off with crime scene tape. I ducked my head beneath the flimsy yellow line and rapped my knuckles against the jamb. "Hello?"

I slid inside when no one answered and tiptoed through the space, careful not to touch or disturb anything. The room was tidier than the disaster Jack had described, but it was still in serious disarray compared to the state I'd left it. Toppled books had been neatly stacked and tagged but left on the floor. The contents of Viktor's desk seemed to have been arranged across the top, also tagged. The lingering aroma of a half dozen policemen had replaced the soft scents of ginger, stage makeup, and turmeric I'd noticed earlier with a competing compilation of colognes, aftershaves, and sweat.

A second door stood open at the back of the room, and curiosity pulled me inside. As in the dressing room, everything in the closet had been bundled and tagged. Suits. Shoes. A row of plastic heads topped with toupees. "Ew."

A floorboard creaked in the dressing room, and a sharp chill ran down my spine.

I pressed my back to the closet's interior wall and held my breath. Had the killer returned for a piece of evidence that would connect him or her to the crime? Would the killer find me inside? Would they try to kill me too? The building had bustled with wall-to-wall people and pets yesterday, but today, even Mom and her swarm of committee ladies were gone.

The world went silent, and my ears began to ring.

Had the one who'd sent me the note last night also seen me sneak under the crime scene tape today? A dead giveaway that I hadn't listened. Hadn't obeyed. *Hadn't stopped.* Maybe I could say I'd been looking for someone and seen the door open, then simply hoped I'd find the person inside Viktor's closet. I mentally kicked myself for not being a better liar.

A long shadow appeared outside the closet, and my head spun. Was there even anyone around to hear me scream? I grabbed a pint-sized parasol, ready to defend myself by any means necessary as the shadow stretched through the space at my feet.

The soft *snick* of a gun dropped my eyelids shut. The quiet cuss that followed peeled my eyes back open.

Jack holstered his sidearm and glared. "What are you doing in here, Crocker?"

I dropped the parasol and heaved a sigh. The last few cases like this had taken an emotional toll, and maybe I needed the vacation Jack had suggested more than I realized. I pressed my lips together to swallow the budding whimper, but it arrived anyway, and Jack's expression softened.

"Hey." He stepped inside the closet with me and gripped my shaky elbows in his steady hands.

I leaned into him briefly, resting my cheek against the cool metal of the detective shield hanging proudly from a beaded chain around his neck. "I was just looking," I said, pulling back to gather my marbles.

"I don't want you getting involved in this. I thought we agreed on that last night."

I craned my neck for a better look at his face in the tight quarters. "Really?" I hadn't meant to give that impression.

Jack's jaw set and his stormy blue eyes fixed on mine. "I don't want you putting yourself in danger again. I've got this covered. You can stand down."

"Have you made any progress on finding the person who sent me that threat?" I asked, hoping to change the subject and remind him why it was so important that we find the killer quickly. Viktor was already dead, but I wanted to live.

"No." Jack released my elbows but didn't move away. He shoved his fingers into the front pockets of his jeans and spread his feet further apart, reducing our height difference by several inches, something I'd noticed him doing more and more, especially when I was distressed. "I called the courier company, but the sender's name and contact information turned out to be bogus. The fee was paid in cash, and the camera over the register was a dummy meant to dissuade robbers. No actual feed to review."

I rubbed the place above my heart where a deep ache had begun to form. I had held out a senseless hope that Jack would make a phone call and this would all be over before it started. That maybe this case would be different. The threats would stop instead of escalating, and the killer would make a stupid move that put him or her in jail sooner rather than later.

"What about you?" he asked. "Any luck with yesterday's receipts?"

"No." I'd spent every spare minute reviewing register receipts from the day before and found nothing useful. "The NPP-edition stuffed cats were almost all paid for with cash. The few that weren't were families unrelated to the pageant."

Jack's concerned gaze dropped to my hand on my chest. I curled the trembling fingers into a fist and dropped it to my side. "I couldn't sleep after you left, so I researched the pageant," I said. "I watched news clips and read through forums until almost dawn. It was eye-opening."

Jack dipped his chin in stiff agreement. "Me too."

"It's a tough competition," I said. "There's a lot at stake." I'd been told as much, but it hadn't truly sunk in until I'd seen past competitors interviewed. "It's expensive just to enter, and that doesn't include the cost of travel, airfare, hotels, rental cars, food. Some people have come thousands of miles to participate. They hire trainers before the event, buy ridiculously expensive animals, custom costumes, hire managers. They empty their life savings and mortgage their homes. It's like a weird form of gambling, putting everything they have on the line with the hope that five random judges will choose their pet as best in show."

"People do it with their children too," Jack said. "Think of all those stage moms and the kiddie talent shows or beauty pageants, hoping their kid's going to be the next Top Model, movie star, or American Idol."

"The winner gets fifty thousand dollars," I said, forcing my tongue off the roof of my suddenly dry mouth. "That might not seem like much at first, but the top contenders will come away with endorsements and sponsorships for everything from pet foods to product placements, and the winner earns a spot in the commercial for next year's pageant."

Jack nodded.

"Given all this, don't you think a competitor has more reasons to shove Viktor off the balcony than Eva?"

Jack watched me carefully. "What I think doesn't matter, and I'll bring her back in if I have to."

"You won't have to," I said. It was one of the few things I was certain of, and the pet owners weren't my only suspects. "Mrs. Hams stopped by Furry Godmother today. She's a fan of the NPP and watches all the televised coverage. She said all the PAs hated Viktor and suggested that one of them might've had enough of his constant badgering and snapped."

"I'll be sure to take that into consideration," Jack said, looking as if he had no intention of taking Mrs. Hams's opinion into consideration. "We've got statements from everyone who was in the building yesterday, except you," he said.

"Sorry." I'd run off to help Imogene with the crowd. "I can swing by the station on my way home." I swallowed a knot of emotion as Viktor's lifeless body registered in my mind's eye once more.

Jack furrowed his brow tightly and narrowed his eyes, a look I'd once interpreted as anger but Jack had claimed was his thinking face. His shoulders rolled slightly forward.

I held my tongue and gave him time to come out with whatever he was working on behind the cranky expression. It was in my nature to rush to fill the silence, but Jack chose his words. It was one more thing I'd grown to appreciate about him. Anything he said was heavily vetted by his toughest critic before it left his mouth. "You don't have to go all the way to the station," he said, "if you don't want."

I puzzled. "But what about the written statement?"

"Maybe you'd like to stop by my place instead." His gaze flicked quickly away before returning to me with a mix of emotion I didn't begin to understand. "You can complete the statement, then we can talk about how best to break the news of your committee resignation to your mother over dinner."

"Dinner?" I parroted.

"Anything you'd like."

Jack was an amazing cook. I knew firsthand because I had a habit of showing up at his door unexpectedly, often without a plan or reason to be there, and he was usually in the kitchen.

My head began to nod before the words were out. "Okay, but I can't quit the show."

"You really can," he assured me. "I'll help."

"Mom made me a judge."

Jack's mouth fell open, then snapped shut. His hands jumped free of his pockets, and one landed on the butt of his gun.

A slight overreaction.

The floorboard creaked outside the closet before I could ask if the gun was for me or my mother.

Jack flicked the snap on his gun holster open with one thumb. He pressed a finger on the opposite hand to his lips, as if I might have been capable of breathing in that moment, let alone making an actual noise.

A young brunette came into view outside the closet door, walking slowly toward Viktor's desk.

Jack stepped across the threshold, and she squealed.

I stepped out behind him.

"What are you doing here?" he asked the frightened PA I recognized as Veronica. The same girl I'd seen arguing with a pet owner outside Viktor's office door yesterday.

"Nothing," she panted. "Looking."

Jack gave me a quick side eye. I'd told him I was just looking too.

I wiggled my fingers in a wave. "Hello, Veronica," I said.

She pulled wide eyes from my face to Jack's. "What were you two doing in there?"

I blushed as a number of pleasant possibilities bombarded my mind. None of which were remotely based on reality. "Talking," I said.

Jack ignored her question and stepped forward, shoulders square, hand still on the butt of his gun. "What are you looking for?"

"Nothing."

He had her whole attention again, and she squirmed under his scrutiny. Jack refastened his holster and crossed strong arms over a broad chest, emphasizing his height, build, and shiny New Orleans detective badge now pressed against his navy T-shirt. "Something," he said, casting a pointed look at the crime scene tape she'd crossed. "Something motivated you to intentionally enter a space I've made off-limits, and I want to know what it was."

Veronica looked at me.

I baby-stepped forward. "Did you forget to mention something during your interview with the police yesterday?"

"No." She shook her head in the negative. A tear slid from the corner of her eye. "Yes."

"Which?" Jack barked.

Veronica and I started. I'd forgotten how intimidating Jack could be when he was in cop mode and talking to anyone other than me.

"I sent Viktor some things that I want back," she said, folding her arms and sinking onto a nearby chair. "I'm such an idiot."

Jack stared, unmoved. I bit my tongue against the urge to fill the silence.

Veronica rolled red-rimmed eyes up to meet Jack's no-nonsense expression. "I sent Viktor a few very personal emails and photographs. I hoped his computer was still in here so I could delete them before the police printed them for a case file or posted them on the Internet. I was sent home last night before the team finished in here, so I thought I'd take a look now while everyone's at the other place and see if I could find them."

I was physically ill on her behalf, and extremely thankful the era of social media and selfie-sending hadn't been so popular when I was younger. At least none of my teenage misdeeds or dalliances had been photographically documented for all eternity. When I got rid of a letter or photo from my past, it was never seen again.

I couldn't imagine why a pretty young girl like Veronica would send anything like she was describing to a mean old man twice her age, but people were strange, and my life decisions hadn't always come from a place of sound logic and reason either, so who was I to judge?

"How well did you know Viktor Petrov?" Jack asked. "You must've been close to send him personal emails and photos."

"No," she said. "I only knew him peripherally. We had short conversations every day. Nothing more substantial than his schedule, but we had these moments. These brief flirtations I thought meant something more. I read into the exchanges like a fool. He never responded to the emails, which was humiliating, and of course I couldn't unsend them, so he knew I was trying to start something." She dropped her face into her palms and groaned. "I'm such an idiot."

"Did Viktor have a specific beef with anyone in the pageant?" I asked.

Jack turned a warning face on me.

I lifted my brows and shoulders. "I thought we were doing a good cop/bad cop thing," I whispered. "I saw her arguing with a pet owner outside this room yesterday right after Viktor fell. Maybe that guy was an enemy of his."

Jack swung his attention back to Veronica. "What was the fight about?"

"He wanted into the room," she said, "but I needed inside to look for the emails and photos while the security staff was in the theater dealing with the fall. Then Mr. North showed up and stopped me."

"Why did Mr. North want in here?" Jack asked.

"I didn't ask and he didn't say," Veronica said, "but we saw Lacy leaving, and then the door was locked. Neither of us could get inside. Security showed up a few minutes later and escorted us to the theater, where we waited to be questioned."

"Well, someone was inside before the police came to investigate," I said. "Who else had access?"

She shrugged. "Everyone I know was in the theater."

"Did any of the other PAs want to hurt Viktor?" Jack asked.

"I don't think so."

So much for Mrs. Hams's theory.

I moved to Veronica's side and crouched before her chair. "I wish I could get those emails and photos back for you," I said. "I can't do that, but if there's anything else you can think of that might help close the case quickly, maybe the police won't have any reason to look too closely at your private correspondence with him."

She looked to Jack, who bobbed his head in vague agreement.

"Veronica," I said, "can you think of anything else?"

Her brow wrinkled in thought. She stuffed a thumb into her mouth and chewed the skin along her nail.

"What about Miles Mackey?" I asked. "He stepped into the MC role pretty eagerly. Can you think of a reason he was in such a hurry?"

"MC is the most prestigious position at the pageant," she said. "He'll get paid more, get more airtime, more interviews, more of the spotlight and fanfare. Judges blend into the background, but there are a lot of bonuses to being MC if you're an attention hound."

I couldn't help wondering if the position's pay increase also came with a hefty cash bonus.

Or bribe.

Chapter Eight

Furry Godmother's advice on life: Never tell your age, your weight, or your mother no.

I arrived at the Audubon Tea Room about thirty minutes after Mom called to demand my presence. She and the committee had approved the venue over lunch, and everything for the NPP was currently in transition and acclimation, including one hundred pets in need of their Furry Godmother.

I hurried toward the row of glass front doors, my little pink tackle box of seamstress supplies bouncing against my thigh with each step. The Audubon Tea Room was on Magazine Street, like Furry Godmother, but instead of being surrounded by cafés and boutiques, it was tucked neatly in with the Audubon Zoo, a place I'd visited dozens of times in my life, often for fund raisers, frequently for weddings, but never as part of an event's staff.

I flung the large glass door open, feeling both strangely out of place and slightly empowered. I wasn't just here for the refreshments this time. I was needed, and I had a job to do. Two jobs if I counted my new judgeship.

The ballroom was a magnificent rotunda with polished hardwood floors, whimsical art on the walls, and an enormous chandelier suspended from an impressive domed ceiling. An extensive bank of windows offered fantastic views of the veranda and garden beyond. The veranda was spacious and well landscaped, perfect for an open bar, buffet, or band and often where the bride and groom exchanged vows before enjoying a grand reception inside. The surrounding gardens were lush, picturesque, and private. I especially enjoyed the ancient sprawling oaks, all bearded in moss like the ones outside my bedroom window when I was growing up.

"There you are." My mother's voice stopped me before I'd managed to get both feet inside the ballroom. She and the committee ladies strode forward in tight formation. Mrs. Smart strode along at Mom's side, swinging her duckhead cane smartly as she kept pace. "Where were you?" Mom asked.

"I stopped at the Saenger to talk with Jack," I said.

A few of the ladies exchanged bashful grins at the sound of his name. I'd missed Jack's return to the Garden District after the death of his grandfather, but according to Scarlet, he'd thwarted a constant flow of female advances before my return, and none of the district do-gooders or debutantes had made it past his front door with their store-bought casseroles and overeager ovaries. Shamelessly, that was one of my favorite stories, though Jack admittedly hadn't liked me either at first. He'd actually accused me of murder, but that was before he got to know me.

"Has he found the killer?" Mrs. Smart asked, her voice low but hopeful. "I'd love to have this mess cleaned up before the show begins. Otherwise the reporters will focus on Viktor's death instead of the lovely animals and humans that make my husband's pageant special."

"Soon," I said. "Jack's working hard, and I'm doing all I can to help."

Mom rolled her eyes. "I'm sure that's true," she told Mrs. Smart. "Lacy frequently goes above and beyond, so long as I haven't asked her to do it."

I pointed a droll expression at my mother.

"What do you think of this place for the NPP?" Mom asked, ignoring my look. "I think it will do, don't you? We can use the space outside for the larger animals' performances. The gardens will make for fantastic photos."

"I like it," I said.

Mom smiled. "Thank you." She clasped her hands together at her waist, looking more pleased than I'd seen her in some time. "I've invited Mrs. Smart to join me for breakfast at the Ruby Slipper Wednesday morning. Maybe you'd like to join us," she said.

Mrs. Smart smiled. "Oh, please do. I'd love to hear more about your adventures as an amateur sleuth."

I narrowed my eyes at Mom.

"Don't look at me," she said. "You're the one who insists on being the Garden District's Nancy Drew. Now, can you make it to breakfast or not?"

I sighed. I loved the Ruby Slipper. They had a dish called Shrimp Boogaloo Benedict that made my mouth water. *Sautéed gulf shrimp and a creole tomato sauce served over fried green tomatoes and a buttermilk biscuit.* I moaned a little at the thought. The dish also came with two poached eggs, and I made myself sick trying to finish it all every time. Sadly, I already had plans for Wednesday. "I wish I could, but Scarlet asked me to help out at a booth for Carter's law firm that morning."

"A booth?" Mom asked. I could see the wheels in her brain spinning in search of something she'd forgotten. "Have the Hawthornes decided to get involved with the NPP?" Her gaze rose over my head several inches as a pair of long arms curled around my middle.

I relaxed easily against him, not needing to see his face to recognize my sneak hugger's gentle hold or enchanting presence. "Chase Hawthorne," I said in my slowest southern drawl. "Are you following me?"

"No, ma'am, Miss Lacy," he answered with obnoxious formality, "I do believe I'm simply drawn to you."

Mom squeaked with pleasure, then patted his cheek. "You are still full of mischief, I see. Has been since he was a little nugget," she told Mrs. Smart, who looked less than enthusiastic.

Chase moved around to my side and scooped one of my hands into his, knowing I wouldn't jerk away or pinch him in public. He lifted our joined hands and kissed my knuckles.

I shook my head at him, but couldn't stop the smile budding on my lips, so I rolled my eyes instead.

Mom beamed. "So, Chase, tell me all about your family's

plans to get involved this week. I hear you're setting up a table and Lacy's helping Scarlet with the details."

Chase's eyes widened. A sly grin curled over his lips. "Is that so?" he asked me.

"Yes." I answered Chase but looked at Mom. "I'm helping with the table, but we won't be here. Scarlet's running a water station in Jackson Square for San Fermin en Nueva Orleans."

Mom's smile fell flat. "The running of the bulls. Tell me you're kidding."

"You know I can't say no to Scarlet," I said, wiggling my hand free of Chase's grip. I curled my fingers around the crook of his elbow instead.

"You just said no to me about breakfast," Mom complained. "Would it kill you to say no to someone else for a change?"

"She tells me no all the time," Chase said, "if that makes you feel any better."

Mom narrowed her eyes on me. "It doesn't."

"I only said no to you because I'd already said yes to Scarlet," I argued.

Mrs. Smart frowned. "Did you say bulls?"

Chase grinned. "Yes, ma'am. Though these bulls aren't like the ones in Pamplona. These are roller derby girls. They dress in red with little horns on their helmets, and they carry whiffle ball bats."

I squeezed his elbow, hoping to silently communicate *shut up* before my mother blew a gasket. She was already mad that I would miss her breakfast to be there. She didn't need Mrs. Smart to hear the details.

"The event raises a lot of money every year," Chase said,

smoothly changing gears. "This year's proceeds will go to the Animal Rescue of New Orleans."

Mrs. Smart turned a curious expression on my mother. I wasn't sure if she had any more questions, but she wouldn't find answers with Mom. I could see in Mom's flat expression that she wouldn't say another word on the subject. She'd simply pack this information away with all the other unpleasant things she pretended didn't exist.

I hung back when Mom led the group away.

Chase swung around to face me. "How are you holding up?"

I could see the deep concern in his eyes. Scarlet must've filled him in on last night's threat. "I'm okay. Is that why you're here? Checking in on me?"

He squinted. "Would you be impressed if I was?"

I smiled. "Why are you really here?"

"Well, your tip about the bear in Armstrong Park paid out yesterday. Big Splash was down there with a parrot that had escaped. Witnesses say he tracked it all the way to the park, where it eventually collided with a big office building window. The bird's wing was damaged, and he won't be able to perform in the pageant, but he'll heal in time. Your father patched him up last night, and the bird is staying there another day or two. Meanwhile, Big Splash is back on track for tomorrow night."

"The bird's a cusser," I said. "I heard him when I stopped by my folks' place for pancakes."

He lifted his gaze in the direction Mom had gone. "You guys had pancakes?"

I laughed. "So, you're here to check on the dog?"

Chase's smile opened wide. "Actually, I'm here on business. It seems that Sue Li told everyone what a great job I did bringing Big Splash and the parrot back and how much I'm helping her with her custody issues, and now I've got pet owners calling the office and asking for me by name. They all want me to represent them in pet custody cases or to draw up wills with instructions for the care and provisions of their animals in the case of their deaths."

I barked a laugh. "Chase Hawthorne, Pet Attorney. Almost makes those long painful years at that fancy Ivy League school worthwhile."

"Almost," he said, "and it ticks my dad off, so that's nice too."

I slid my palm back over the crook of his arm and turned toward the sounds of howling cats and bird chatter. "I need to make sure everyone in need of a costume adjustment gets it before tomorrow's big opening ceremony," I said. "Then I need to figure out where I'm supposed to go and what I'm supposed to do when I get here tomorrow night. Walk with me?"

He bowed his head and smiled. "Anywhere."

We made our way through the clutch of humans and animals, some practicing their acts, others enjoying a bit of downtime before the dress rehearsal began.

I helped cats with hats and shih tzus with tutus. Repaired the seams of sequined flapper dresses on felines and buttoned pinafores on poodles while Chase handed out his business cards with reckless abandon and a heaping helping of old-fashioned Louisiana charm.

Just before my fingers went completely numb from the endless hand-stitching, I reached the end of my work and moved onto the veranda to wait for Chase. A pair of raven-haired twins had latched onto him, and they seemed to be interested in more than his legal representation.

The gardens were eerily quiet outside the busy building. Five chairs had been erected before a long glass-top table with a little sign taped to the top. JUDGES was written on the paper in hectic black scrawl.

I pulled out the middle chair and took a seat, enjoying the muggy heat of evening as it warmed my skin and loosened the tension in my muscles.

An extra-large easel stood on the far side of the beautiful brick patio. The paper attached to it simply said VIKTOR. Massive marble urns in various heights flanked the easel, and I could only assume there would be a giant portrait of him on display for the opening ceremony tomorrow night. I was wildly thankful to know he wasn't in any of the urns. More likely, the body hadn't even had time to be looked at by the coroner yet. I'd learned over the past year, with great disappointment, that unlike on my favorite television shows, details were slow coming back from labs, especially when I was in a hurry.

The chair beside me scraped over fancy brick pavers as Chase took a seat and passed me a bottle of water. "It's beautiful out here."

"Indeed." I cast a smile at him and uncapped the water. "Thanks."

He winked.

"Mom made me a judge," I said, tapping a fingernail to the paper sign on the table. Part of me still hoped it wasn't true, but being there, sitting at the judges' table, made it impossible not to think about.

"I heard," he said brightly. "Nervous?"

Considering I knew nothing about the pet pageant world and some of the owners had put their entire life savings on the line in hopes of winning? "Yes."

Chase laughed softly. "Come on now. You don't give yourself enough credit. You're probably thinking you're not qualified for the job and you don't know what to do, but I've got some news for you."

I turned my chin slightly, daring a look in Chase's direction. "Yeah?"

"Yeah." He fixed me with the easy smile I envied. "You might not realize it, but you're a bit of a celebrity around these parts. Half the district's pets are wearing your designs and the others are damn jealous that they aren't. You love animals. Always have. You know enough about their health, safety, training, and general well-being to take over this pageant, and you are more than qualified to be a judge. Just read the little information packet they're passing out so that you'll know what to score the acts on specifically, and you're golden. Remember how great we did at judging that dance competition last fall?"

I'd been a total mess judging that competition, but no one had died or ever mentioned my ineptitude, so when he said it like that, it didn't seem like I had as much to worry about.

I tipped my head against him. "Thanks, Chase."

He wound a long arm around my shoulders and dragged my chair against his, then leaned down to press a kiss to the top of my head. "Anytime."

Jack strode into view and stopped on the other side of our table. "Hawthorne," he said. "Lacy."

I jerked upright, stunned speechless by his ridiculous stealth despite his size. "Hello."

"Your mom's looking for you," he said. "She's gathering the judges inside to start the dress rehearsal."

"Okay." I nearly knocked my chair over as I stood with all the grace of an injured elephant. "Thank you."

My ankles wobbled, and Chase's big hand snaked out to steady me. "You're going to do great. No worries."

His smile was contagious, and I felt my cheeks rise in response. "Thanks." I gave his fingers a quick squeeze, planning to let go, but he held on for an extra beat.

"I'll come by tonight with champagne to celebrate your new role."

The air seemed to heat, and I kept my eyes off Jack. He and Chase had a strange and tense relationship that I tried to stay out of, though I suspected the circumstances of their friendship had a lot to do with me.

I'd told Chase what I thought about him and me as a couple last Valentine's Day. It had been hard for me to say because I'd had a feeling it wasn't what he'd wanted to hear. I didn't want to hurt him or lose a friend, but in true Chase Hawthorne form, he'd cheerfully accepted my rejection as an invitation for another time. He seemed to still be running on that idea.

I nodded in acceptance of the champagne offer. "That sounds really good," I admitted. Something told me I'd be ready for a drink by the time I got home tonight.

My phone rang, and I jumped, breaking my connection to Chase. I used the distraction to rush inside, away from the testosterone-filled nightmare behind me. "Hello?"

"Miss Crocker, this is Richard Hemsel, your Grandpa Smacker Product Placement Coordinator. I'm sorry to call outside standard business hours and on such short notice."

"It's no problem," I assured him, though I wasn't thrilled with the words "short notice." "Is everything okay?"

"Yes. Fine. Thank you. However, the board has called an early-morning meeting to settle details for the Fall Food Festival, and we'd like you to be in attendance. Will that be possible?"

"Tomorrow? I suppose. What time?"

"Seven sharp."

Seven worked. I could easily open Furry Godmother by ten with a start that early. "All right, I'll be there. Thank you for the call." I disconnected in time to fill the last open seat at the makeshift indoor judges' table before my mother took the podium.

A white nine-by-twelve folder was on the seat. My name was written across the top in the same messy scrawl that was on the notes outside.

Mom tapped the microphone at the center of the large round room, and competitors formed a broad semicircle as she began her speech about everything that had happened in the past twenty-four hours and what would come in the next four days of competition and celebration.

Pet owners, PAs, trainers, and crew stood along the bowed walls, drinking in her words.

I scanned their faces, surprised not to see Miles Mackey anywhere. This seemed like the kind of spotlight moment he would have loved to hijack. I twisted in my seat, checking everyone in the crowd. Chase and Jack were still outside, face-to-face and visible through the glass patio doors behind me. I would have loved to hear what they were talking about, but there were no signs of Mackey anywhere and that had my attention.

I imagined him falling onto my new table from the chandelier, then scanned the domed ceiling overhead.

Nothing.

The top of his head came into view outside a window across the room. His body was blocked by a couple in matching black polo shirts with embroidery on the pockets, probably the name of the pet they were representing. I leaned over the arm of my chair until I thought it would tip over, seeking a better view. What was keeping Mackey from the chance to take Mom's microphone and spotlight position?

Suddenly, hands began to clap, and the couple in black shifted, revealing Mackey and another familiar face, Mr. North, the pet owner who'd fought with Veronica about getting into Viktor's dressing room yesterday.

"No way," I whispered, leaning impossibly further in my chair. *What are they talking about?*

"Lacy," Mom said a little too loudly into the microphone.

I snapped upright and smiled.

The crowd applauded again, and Mom waved a hand, encouraging me to stand.

I obeyed.

Beyond the window, Mr. North passed something that looked like an overstuffed white envelope to Mackey. Was it possible? Could it be the same envelope from Viktor's desk at the Saenger Theatre? The stolen money from the destroyed dressing room?

"You can be seated now," Mom said.

I jerked my attention back in her direction. The crowd had traded clapping for staring, and Mom looked as if she might die of profound embarrassment. I forced my wooden legs to bend and fell back onto my seat.

The barrel-chested judge beside me sniffed and turned his face away.

I considered texting Jack about what I'd seen through the window but thought better of it. Truthfully, I wasn't sure what I'd seen. Maybe Mr. North had only passed Mackey a handkerchief or a party invitation. Maybe I was continuing to snoop after I'd been told to STOP.

Miles Mackey marched through the parted crowd and into the center of the room. He greeted Mom with air kisses, then accepted the microphone with a bow.

She attempted to dismember me with eye daggers all the way back to her seat.

"Lights," Mackey instructed.

The lights dimmed, and a projector sent the image of a score sheet onto a screen lowering from above.

"These are the items our judges will be looking for tomorrow and all week long," Mackey began.

Beside me, the other judges had their sample sheets pressed

to the table in front of them and were making notes on the lines and in the margins.

I looked at the white envelope in my hands. The score sheets must be inside. I tapped the envelope's contents half-way out, then thumbed through the papers in search of the one shown on the overhead display.

Mine was marred with dark lines on the back side that were bleeding through and making it difficult to read. "Jeez," I muttered, flipping the page over to see what was wrong.

My heart rate spiked and my lungs constricted as I took in the three simple words written across the back of my sample sheet.

YOU'RE NOT LISTENING.

Chapter Nine

Furry Godmother suggests counting blessings instead of calories; the latter will only make you cry.

I snapped a photo of the note with sweaty hands before stuffing it back into the envelope with the other papers, then sent the pic to Jack, who appeared like Batman seconds later. He moved into my line of sight and offered a simple nod but didn't approach. Instead, he moved silently through the crowded room as Mackey's presentation went on, scanning faces, hands, everything in sight.

I watched him work with a mix of hope and terror.

A sudden intake of air ripped painfully through my chest, and I realized I'd stopped breathing at some point. I panted in response, suddenly starving for air. My slippery phone slid out of my hand and clattered onto the floor, sending my heart back into a sprint.

How is this happening again? Why so soon? It wasn't my first time being threatened by an unknown person, probably a killer, but the others had given me a little breathing time in between threats. *Didn't they?*

I ducked my head and scooped the device off the floor, then took my time sitting up. The panic spooling in my chest was quickly growing out of my control, like a tropical storm just off the coast. I inhaled long and slow, pulling air in through my nose before releasing it just as steadily through my mouth. I applied all the tricks and methods my therapist had taught me for times like these. I blocked out the noisy room and pictured my dad instead. I visualized Penelope, my store, and Imogene. Moonlight on the Mississippi and piles of warm beignets beneath a heaping mound of powdered sugar. Slowly, my heart rate fell back to something I could manage while surrounded by strangers.

"Miss Crocker?" Chase's voice blew into my ear. He'd crouched beside me and covertly taken my hand while I regained myself. "There's been a mix-up with the Siamese's sweat suits. Would you mind lending a hand right now?" He leaned across me and whispered an apology to the table of judges. "I won't keep her long. Very sorry for the interruption."

I let Chase lead me outside, where I immediately doubled over at the waist, sucking mild night air in deep steadying breaths. "Thank you," I whispered.

Chase rubbed my back. "You looked like you needed an escape hatch."

I straightened and pressed my palms to my hips, continuing the long breaths. The white envelope was sticky and wrinkled from my sweat-slicked hands. "I did."

"What happened?" He pulled me further into the shadows, away from the nearest window and prying eyes.

"Jack didn't tell you?"

He shook his head. "No. He just took off. Did something happen?" Concern marred his handsome face. He seemed to see the truth in my eyes. Something *had* happened. *To me.* "Lacy, what's going on?"

I handed him the envelope. "Another threat. This one was at my seat when I got to the judges' table. It even has my name on the outside." Which meant the killer was there, in the building with me. Sharing my space. My air. Lurking far too close and utterly undetected. My cheeks and ears flamed hot with the realization I was right, and it was scarier than any other scenario I could imagine. I might've already spoken to the nut today. We might've had a casual conversation about snaps verses buttons on feline fedoras or how much we enjoyed the iced lattes from French Truck Coffee in the Lower Garden District. All while I was clueless and the other person was planning to deliver threat number two at first opportunity. I pressed a palm to my mouth, the other to my rolling stomach.

Chase shook the papers out of the envelope and fanned through them to the page in question. He raked a hand through his hair while overenunciating some classic swears. *My sentiments exactly.* "Where's Jack?" he asked. "Why isn't he with you? Why didn't he pull you out of there as soon as he knew?"

"I think he's looking for who might've done this. He went into panther mode in there and started slinking around, watching." I rubbed the knotted muscles at the base of my neck and walked nervously in small random patterns.

"Well, I'm done watching you be threatened," Chase said, catching me midloop on my path to nowhere. "Let's go home."

"I can't." I planted my feet as Chase tried to tug me away. "No, Chase. Stop. I'm safer here with all these people than I am alone at my place."

"Really?" he asked, brows up. "Like Viktor was?"

My mind swam. *Good lord. The killer is here and could kill me in front of everyone exactly like he killed Viktor.* I leaned forward again and did some more deep breathing.

"All these people didn't stop what happened to Viktor," Chase said. "Home is better. We can lock up and control who comes in the door. Plus you won't be there alone. I'll stay with you, or you can stay with me." His expression turned pleading. "If you don't want to be with me, then at least let me take you to your parents' house. The security system over there beats Fort Knox."

"I think I saw Mr. North hand Mackey an envelope," I said. "What if he's the one who stole the money from Viktor's room, and now he's giving it to the new judge?"

The telltale sound of a lighter drew my attention away from Chase before he could answer. A little golden glow appeared several yards away in the night.

Chase reached for me and pulled me close. "Be calm," he whispered in my ear. "You're safe."

I nuzzled against his chest on instinct, not wanting to know if the smoker who'd appeared was really a killer who'd hoped to find me alone. I wrapped my arms around Chase's middle, thankful for his calm, strength, and sanity when I wanted to collapse, cry, or pack my bags for Indonesia.

"Hey," Chase said, projecting his voice congenially. "How'd you get out here?"

I lifted my eyes in curiosity.

Miles Mackey puffed a long skinny cigarette in the darkness. Creeping tendrils of gray smoke climbed like gnarled fingers into the air as he meandered in our direction. "Even the MC gets a break from time to time," he said, looking every bit as pompous as he sounded. "I see you two are having a little break of your own." His beady black eyes trailed over me in an icky leer that knotted Chase's fingers into the material of my dress and pressed me impossibly closer.

"We're just getting some fresh air," Chase said. "Miss Crocker has run herself ragged these last few weeks preparing for the show, and the last twenty-four hours have been especially difficult, as you know."

Mackey seemed confused. "I suppose moving an event this size takes some effort, but everything always gets done, now, doesn't it? No need to fret."

"I witnessed a murder," I said, unexpectedly and with more venom that I'd intended. "One can hardly blame me for my fret."

Mackey took another drag on the cigarette. "Of course."

I wanted to tell him he couldn't smoke here. That smoking was a terrible, potentially deadly habit and that I didn't want to breathe in any more of his toxic mess, so he should kindly leave, but that was just my adrenaline kicking in. None of my upbringing or debutante training would allow that sort of outburst anyway. What I'd actually say would be much less honest and forthright. "Did you know Viktor Petrov well, Mr. Mackey?" I asked, much more sweetly. "You've worked with him for several years, haven't you? I'm sure this has been especially hard on you."

Mackey tossed his cigarette onto the stone pathway and crushed it underfoot like a disgusting piggy litterbug. "I knew Viktor well. He was a cad and a pill, and he knew it. He didn't care. Why should he? He was the star, after all." Heavy emphasis on *was*. The bitterness in Mackey's tone and words was strong enough to taste on my own tongue.

"And now you're the star," I said.

"Indeed." Mackey smiled, turned, and strode away with a jaunty whistle.

"I don't like him," I whispered, stepping away from Chase. "He has motive," I said.

Chase hung his head forward. When he'd righted himself a moment later, he seemed to have aged. "We're not leaving, are we?"

"No."

"And you're doing this again?"

"What?"

"Meddling. Poking bears and such. Probably putting yourself in danger unnecessarily and trying to give me ulcers."

I let my mouth form a little O. "No. Of course not." I stroked the sleeve of his dress shirt, then caught his gaze with mine. "I would never try to give you ulcers."

He smiled.

"Let's get back inside. It looks as if everyone else is still on a break in there." I pointed to the closest window, where the lights inside put the people on display. "Let's see if we can find Mr. North."

I explained the exchange I'd witnessed from my seat at the judges' table while we maneuvered through the throngs of animals and people inside, searching for one man in particular.

"No wonder Mackey's in such a good mood," Chase said. "He just got thirty-eight large in cash. Do you know how much fun we could have with that? What we could do?"

"Open a cat shelter?" I asked. "Remember, I can't be sure of what I saw. There were people in the way, but it would make sense given everything else I've learned so far." North had wanted into Viktor's dressing room the day he was killed, then the money went missing, and now North had passed something that looked a lot like the cash envelope to the new MC.

"No cat shelters," Chase said. "You and I could take a private jet to Paris for the day or rent an island for the weekend."

"What would we do with a whole island?" I asked, stopping to consider the possibility.

Chase wagged his eyebrows.

"Be serious." I smiled and moved on, searching the crowd of faces for Mr. North. "No one needs a whole island for that."

Chase laughed. "Maybe I do."

I turned to ask a few follow-up questions on that, but North's familiar profile caught my eye. "There." I lifted a finger toward the refreshment table, and we wound our way across the room, then pinched ourselves into line behind North.

I grabbed a disposable cup and pretended to wait my turn

at the coffee dispenser. "Oh, hey, Mr. North, right?" I asked innocently.

His smile fell a bit when he saw me. "Hello." He filled his cup with hot water, then opened a paper tea packet and popped the little bag into the water.

I pushed my cup under the coffee dispenser and pulled the tab. The heavenly aroma of liquid energy soared into my nose, and I smiled. "How are you doing?" I asked, pressing the full cup to my lips.

"Fine, thank you." He moved away to stir his tea, but I followed.

"I just wanted to see if you were okay after what happened yesterday," I said quietly.

Chase had a plate of fruits and cheeses behind me, moving as inconspicuously as he could at my back.

"Well, it was unfortunate. Mr. Petrov was a nice man," North said, seeming not to have noticed the six-foot lawyer attached to my rear.

I held back a snort. North was officially the first and only person I'd spoken to who thought Viktor was a nice man. "I'm actually referring to the fight I saw you having with that PA, Victoria."

"Veronica," he corrected.

"That's right," I said, "it's just so hard to keep everyone straight. I guess I have a lot to figure out. For example, are the PAs usually difficult to get along with? It doesn't seem like they should ever argue. They're here to assist. It's right there in their titles. Personal *assistants*."

"That sort of thing never happens," he said. "It was completely my fault we argued. Tensions are high and all." He glared at his tea bag, then checked his watch, probably wishing he could speed up the steep and escape the refreshment area and me.

"What were you arguing about?" I asked.

He raised nervous, angry eyes to me. "I just told you. I was stressed out. I needed a break from the hoopla in the theater, and I snapped at her for no reason."

"She was just walking by and you yelled at her?" I asked, sipping coffee with a smile. "That is some serious stress. How does that work exactly?"

"What?"

"You just saw her there in the hall and yelled at her about nothing specific? Did you say something like, 'Your shoes are offensive, and your face makes me angry'?" I asked.

He frowned. "Of course not."

"How did it go, then?" I pushed. "Did you ask her for something and she denied the request?"

His expression went cold. He plucked the tea bag from the water and tossed it into the trash. "I'd better go and check on my cat."

"I'll come with you," I said, falling into step behind him. "I heard that the MCs get cash for giving some of the pets special attention or treatment. Is that true? I need to get caught up on pageant culture as quickly as I can before opening night."

"That's tomorrow."

"Exactly."

North stopped suddenly and turned on me. He stepped into my personal space and lowered his voice. "You want some advice? I know you've been following me, and I don't like being followed. So, you need to knock it off immediately and find someone else to answer your questions."

I pulled my chin back. "I'm not following you," I said, "besides now, I mean. I wasn't following you before you made your tea."

North narrowed his eyes. "I saw you coming out of Viktor's dressing room yesterday. You stopped and stared. That's how you know I argued with Veronica. You were already there, but why? What were you doing in Viktor's dressing room when we were all supposed to be in the theater?"

"I had to get the playbook so we could keep the event on track. Why were you in the hallway?"

"Taking a walk to cool down," he said. "Stress." He worked his jaw. "Why are you following me now? What do you really want?"

"Nothing." I stepped backward and bumped into Chase. "I was just being friendly. I'm trying to figure things out around here."

"Yeah, well do yourself a favor and stop." He scanned the crowd, then turned and left.

This time, I let him. I didn't like the way he'd said *stop*.

The screech of microphone feedback quieted the masses, and Mom reappeared. She gave us a two-minute warning. Dress rehearsal was about to begin.

I spent the next two hours staring blindly through mini-performances of everything we'd see again over the next few days in full. I delivered everyone a mental ten since we weren't giving actual scores. This was only a dry run.

Jack had stopped briefly at the judges' table when I'd returned to my seat. He'd swapped my envelope for another, untampered packet so stealthily that I'd barely seen it happen, and I'd been watching. He kept moving from there, I assumed to drop the envelope into an evidence bag, but I couldn't be sure, and I couldn't ask because he hadn't been back.

Chase had stayed in the audience where I could see him, and I appreciated that more than I could explain.

Mr. North was notably absent from the rotunda, except for the sixty seconds he and his cat marched around a tiny obstacle course designed to look like an outdoor garden. The full-white cat wore a collar of pastel roses and followed North's commands through a series of small feats. She weaved between little poles painted to look like birds. Jumped through a tiny hoop covered in faux vines and walked a narrow ledge over a miniature waterfall at the flick of North's wrist or finger. The cat's work was spectacular, but my mind was on her trainer. *Is it possible that North killed Viktor? Was the murder somehow related to the money? Was it bribe money? Did the MC's opinions influence the judges? How and why? Will I eventually be offered some dirty money too? Will it be enough to rent an island?*

I gave the crowd another careful scan, but no one appeared especially guilty. Maybe I was completely off the mark and wasting time by worrying about North. Maybe I hadn't even thought of the real reason or killer yet. *Could a past pageant loser have wanted revenge? How many of these faces fit that bill?*

I suddenly realized that Jack had been right. Most people didn't interact with a hundred people on a regular basis. Despite the closed community we were working in this time, there were actually more suspects than there had been for any of the other murders I'd poked around in.

By the end of the night, I was mentally and emotionally exhausted and desperate for my bed. Unfortunately, I still had a ton of baking to do if I wanted to fill my display case in the morning. Not to mention, I needed an idea worth presenting to Grandpa Smacker at the early-morning meeting. So far, I had nothing to bring to their table, and I couldn't go to work empty-handed too.

I made my rounds saying goodbye and searching for my pink tackle box of sewing supplies. Eventually, I gave up on the latter and Chase walked me to the parking lot, sans tackle box.

"You're sure you're okay to drive home?" he asked. "I don't mind taking you. I can come back with Carter to pick up your car and bring it to you later."

"I'm okay," I said. "Rain check on the champagne?"

"Sure." He smiled. "In the meantime, I'm going to find that tackle box and be your hero."

I rose onto my toes and kissed his cheek. "You will always be my hero, Chase Hawthorne. Thanks for looking out for me tonight."

* * *

I beeped my car doors unlocked, and Chase jogged back to the Tea Room.

I opened my driver's side door and nearly had six consecutive strokes when the interior light bulb lit the area in front of my car and a tall shadow peeled its way off my hood and moved in my direction. Jack had been leaning motionless near my mirror, and I hadn't even noticed him. My cheeks flushed hot. It was the second time tonight he'd seen me being sweet with Chase, and I felt strangely guilty.

"Hi," I said.

"Hi."

Silence gonged around us alongside chirping nighttime bugs and the occasional round of frogs in the thick garden foliage.

"Everything okay?" I asked.

"I was going to ask you the same thing, but I see you've already got a confidant."

My chest and neck heated to match my cheeks. It was ridiculous to feel as if I should explain myself to Jack, but I did. Though I would never admit it if he asked. "A girl can never have too many confidants," I said, smiling awkwardly. Was he implying that he'd like to be mine? *Does he not know he already is?*

"I heard you put a pin in the champagne," he said, looking more at ease. "Lots of baking to do."

"Yep."

"Would you like some help?" he asked, flashing me a killer smile. "I'm an excellent baker, and I carry a gun that I'm trained to use in your defense if needed, which is also nice considering that letter we still need to talk about."

I blew out a long thin stream of air. "I could use a little

help in the kitchen, I guess, but you have to promise to use your words and fists before you pull that sidearm. If needed."

Jack seemed to think it over. "Deal." He extended a hand, and I placed mine in his. The tough-guy expression melted slowly into a teasing, youthful smile that reached all the way to his eyes. "Your place or mine?"

Chapter Ten

Furry Godmother's easy cure for ants in your pants:
Wear a dress.

I woke with a headache at five o'clock the next morning. Sleep deprivation was getting the best of me, and I vowed to take a nap as soon as humanly possible. At the moment, however, I had to get over to Grandpa Smacker's for my seven AM meeting.

My limbs were stiff with fatigue as I dragged myself upright and shuffled toward the shower. Jack had stayed only until midnight, but we'd covered a lot of ground in that time, and I'd provided the written statement he needed for Viktor's murder file. I'd tried to think of every detail that could be useful later, but I'd been mildly distracted by the fact that there was a hunky detective in my kitchen.

I stepped into the steamy shower, praying for an epiphany about snacks that people would want to share with their pets while I washed as much sleep as possible down the drain. I didn't have an epiphany, but I did look great in my new navy slip dress with a modest neckline and flirty hem. Once I'd added oversized white-framed sunglasses, a structured white leather handbag, and matching pumps, I was channeling my inner Jackie O. I headed for the front door with a stack of bakery boxes. "I'm sorry you can't come," I told Penelope, "but I have to visit Grandpa Smacker's offices first, and I can't bring you inside. No cats." I made a sad face to show solidarity. "You're a perfect kitty, but food manufacturers aren't big on people seeing cats go inside, so you'll be on your own today. Keep an eye on your little sister, Buttercup." I gave the fish bowl a big smile, and Buttercup lowered slowly behind her little pink castle.

I paused at the home security keypad, where a small piece of paper had been wedged behind the panel's edge.

> Baking was fun, but I still owe you dinner. My place.
> Very soon.
>
> —Jack

My smile grew as I tucked the note into my bag. Jack's help had been priceless. He'd wisely suggested preparing all the doughs and batters while we waited for the first few rounds of things to bake, and it had worked perfectly, streamlining the process and accomplishing more than I'd imagined possible in just a few hours. Chase would have suggested we drink until the timer went off between batches, and left to my own devices, I probably would have spent the time rehashing everything I knew about Viktor Petrov and the moving pieces surrounding his murder. With Jack's advice, all the prep work had been finished when he left at midnight. All I had to do was stay awake and swap trays in and out of the oven until everything had been baked. He'd even loaded and set the dishwasher before saying goodbye.

I opened my passenger door and stacked the bakery boxes onto the floorboards in front of the seat, where they would receive less direct sunlight and had no chance of flying everywhere when I turned a corner or got carried away with my gas and brake pedals.

My phone rang as I rounded the hood to the driver's side. Mom's face centered the screen.

"Cluck in a Bucket," I answered.

"What?" Mom asked. She paused. "Lacy, I know this is you. I just checked my screen, and I didn't misdial."

I smiled as I dropped behind the wheel and cranked the air-conditioning.

"Lacy?"

"Good morning," I said, still pleased at how easily I had flustered her.

"It's your mother."

I laughed. "Yes. I know. Hello, Mom. How are you?" I pulled onto the street with an even bigger smile and pointed the Volkswagen toward Grandpa Smacker's offices.

"I don't know why you do that," she said. "It wastes time, and I don't have any to spare. Do I hear traffic? Where are you? It's six thirty in the morning. I didn't even think you'd be awake."

"How can you possibly hear traffic through my closed

windows? And why are you calling if you thought I'd be asleep?"

"A mother knows," she said, "and probably for the same reason you've started answering my calls with ridiculous accents and business names."

Touché.

"You're not the only funny one in the family," she said. "You get your humor from me."

I laughed. A genuine happy sound that rattled in my chest and wet my eyes. I hit my blinker and headed out of Uptown. "Is that right?"

"Quite," she said flatly. "I'm hilarious."

I swiped tears off my cheeks beneath my glasses. "What's up, Mom?" I asked. "Or were you just calling to wake me up?"

A long beat of silence stretched across the line.

"Mom?"

"Oh! I remember," she said suddenly. "Did you know there's another group of chickens planning to set up a booth in the Tea Room foyer and collect donations? I couldn't believe it when I saw them on the list last night. I thought I'd screened better than that."

"Who are they?"

"A local chapter of the FFA. How am I supposed to compete with a bunch of kids in overalls?"

I rolled the cuckoo question around a few times before answering. "For starters, you aren't competing with them. This is all for charity, remember? Secondly, why will they be wearing overalls, and can I get in on that option?"

"Lacy," she scolded. "Be serious. You're a lady. They're the Future Farmers of America. Of course they'll be wearing overalls."

Apparently my mother's knowledge of farmers ended with the copy of *Click, Clack, Moo* that one of Scarlet's kids had left in her parlor. I took a left through the Central Business District.

"I know I'm not competing with the FFA," she said finally. "I'm competing with that dastardly Hams and her Llama Mamas, but think about it. If you walked into the event, planning to make a donation to some adorable chickens, who would you give your money to? The group of adorable young-sters in pigtails and cowboy boots, or a group of middle-aged women? Meanwhile, Hams will get all the money from people who love llamas. There are no other llamas, Lacy."

I rolled my eyes until it hurt and affected my driving. "So, rent some decoy llamas," I suggested. "Or better yet, let it go this time. You already have your hands full, and it really doesn't matter who collects more money."

Mom gave a raspy exasperated sigh. "You don't under-stand me at all."

Truth.

"Maybe we can put glitter on their beaks," she suggested.

"No." I shook my head at the windshield.

"It can be nontoxic glitter."

"Let me think about it and get back with you," I said. "Also, is there any chance you saw my pink tackle box before you left last night? I misplaced it while we were there, and I had to leave without it."

"No, but I'll have the girls look for it after breakfast."

"Thanks." I beat my thumbs against the steering wheel. "You know, maybe it's not about making your chickens or yourself more appealing than the FFA group. Maybe you just need to make the collection process more fun or interesting. Like those giant funnels people love to put coins on and watch them go around until they meet their doom. I think you just need something too cute to pass up sitting beside your chicks. Then folks would have to stop to see it, and while they're there . . ."

"They'll put their money into my collection contraption. That's brilliant," Mom gasped. "We can make it so that people have to give to the Jazzy Chicks if they want to see the thing work. Then I'll get all the potential chicken-lover donations and beat those blasted Llama Mamas."

I appreciated her enthusiasm, but I wasn't sure how I felt about plotting to steer donations away from children in overalls and pigtails. "Hey, I'm getting on the highway. I have to go, but we can talk when I get there after work. I'll give the potential contraption some more thought when I'm not driving."

"Perfect," she said, "but promise me that you'll be careful out there. Some drivers are maniacs."

I agreed to her terms and disconnected.

I pulled into the lot outside Grandpa Smacker's offices with hope in my heart. Maybe no one would ask me about the recipe I had yet to create for the Fall Food Festival. Maybe this would be more of a brainstorming meeting where the marketing team pitched ideas to one another while I ate fresh-baked breads smeared in Grandpa Smacker's homemade preserves and drank coffee. Then no one would know I had nothing to offer them.

The receptionist buzzed me in, and I hurried through the Disneyesque waiting room, heavily decorated to look as if I'd stepped into another place and time, specifically onto a mid-twentieth-century farm, complete with bird songs piped through hidden speakers and apple pie–scented diffusers sweetening the air. A white picket fence was painted along the walls with tall grasses and wheat blowing in the background, while wide-paddled ceiling fans slowly churned the heavenly apple aroma through the building.

I stopped at the heavy-laden table of refreshments before entering the boardroom. Fifteen minutes later, ten sets of eyes were on me while I tried to swallow a hunk of apple I'd dragged through Grandpa Smacker's organic peanut butter, then dunked in fresh-from-the-hive honey. The staring posse wanted to know all of my ideas for the Fall Food Festival.

"Um," I said, fumbling to wash the apple down with a swig of insanely good coffee. "I didn't bring any samples," or ideas, "but I'm working on something organic and naturally sweet or savory so that pet owners can pack a picnic basket and have a date with their pets," I said, rubbing my sticky fingertips against a napkin.

Ten serious faces lining the big conference table nodded.

"We like it," the man with a pear-shaped head said. He was the new director of marketing, but I'd immediately forgotten his name. "We can work with that. A date with your pet." He shoved to his feet and rubbed his wide chin. "We can build a nice campaign around it. Man's best friend. Take your best friend to the park or on a hike." He looked at the ceiling as he began to pace. "What sorts of ingredients will we need to create a shelf-stable version of these products?"

I crossed my legs and took my time thinking up the answer. I had no idea what products we were even talking about. "All the basic ingredients we're already using on the pupcakes and tuna tarts," I said confidently. "The flours and fruits are safe across the board, but I'll have to prepare some samples and find some willing test subjects to run the pet-friendly options past a more discerning human palette." I didn't envy the ones in charge of putting that test group together. *Excuse me, sir, would you be willing to taste-test some dog treats for potential human consumption?*

I left the meeting feeling heavier, both from the gluttonous breakfast I'd enjoyed and the renewed pressure to perform. I couldn't show up empty-handed again. The sales and production team needed samples the next time I came, preferably ones they wouldn't spit back into the wrappers.

Jack was at the coffee stand with a small blonde and two redheads when I arrived in search of a refill to go. One of the redheads was a natural strawberry blonde. The other had the kind of fiery vixen red that came only from the hands of a professional colorist. I admired her bravery. I rarely cut my pale blonde locks, and I never colored them. Too many bad things happened in the beauty parlors of my mind, like errant dye jobs that resulted in unchangeable wicked-witch green and bangs that barely reached my forehead.

Jack's eyes crinkled at the corners when he noticed me,

and the women all turned to see what had caused his sudden smile.

I waited while he brushed them off and made his way in my direction, looking like a million bucks in his tailored suit and black silk tie. "Good morning," he said. "You look nice."

"Back at ya." I gave the tip of his tie a gentle tug. "I don't think I'll ever get used to the rich-guy look on you."

"I'm always a rich guy."

"Yeah, but there's normally a badge right here." I smoothed the tie against his chest where the detective shield usually hung and smiled.

"You prefer that guy?" he asked, a distinctly serious look in his eyes.

I chewed my lip, making a show of choosing my words, though they'd been ready since the moment he'd posed the question. "I think I just like you," I said with a noncommittal shrug of one shoulder.

Jack rubbed a broad hand over his smiling lips. "Back at ya," he said, repeating my words in a voice that made my knees weak. "How are you feeling this morning? You said you were fine last night, but a second threat in twenty-four hours is a lot to take in, and I didn't want to press you. Sometimes things are a lot clearer in the morning."

"I think that expression is supposed to mean we realize things are not such big deals once we sleep on them."

He stared. "This is an enormous deal."

I rocked my head side to side. "I know, but as far as threats go, I've had worse, and technically the notes aren't threats. The first one only said STOP, and the second said I'd been warned, which wasn't wholly accurate, and it also wasn't a threat, just an incorrect statement." I forced a tight smile, hoping the false bravado fooled Jack, but I knew it wouldn't. Very little ever did. "I'm more worried about what to prepare for the Fall Food Festival than those notes right now. I've got zero ideas and the board wants to use the festival as a testing ground to gauge interest and opinion on a new line of pet-friendly products. I'm not convinced that anything I come up with will be as good once it's been mass-manufactured, bottled, freeze-dried, or frozen. And if the flavor is lost in translation, I don't want my name on it. Grandpa Smacker shouldn't either. So, that's a ton of pressure."

Jack stepped a little closer. "You don't have to worry about any of that anymore. I roped you into working here so we could catch a bad guy, and we did. You don't have to stay. Your life is already busy enough without this place, and these guys can figure it out on their own."

"I know," I said, "but I like giving people safe nutritional options for their pets. In that regard, I'm helping to make animals healthier, and if I don't make these products, someone else will, and the next person might not care as much about what goes into them."

A warm smile graced Jack's face. He'd told me once that it was my passion that had drawn him to me, even before we'd officially met. He'd seen me admiring my artwork on the window at Furry Godmother and taken notice. *Of course, it's that same passion that has put me on his bad side regularly these days.* "Have dinner with me."

I smiled. "I thought the dinner invitation was a lure to get me to come over and give you a written statement. I already did that."

Jack's steady gaze raked over me. "Have dinner with me," he repeated.

My toes curled in my vintage pumps. "Okay." The answer came more softly than I'd intended, but his smile inched a little taller on each side.

"Okay," he said, eyes heated with pleasure. "It's a date."

I tucked a long barrel curl behind my ear and traded my coffee for a bottle of water because it seemed to be getting warmer in the narrow hallway. "How's your investigation coming along? Anything new come up since you left my place last night?"

"Actually, yes," he said. "I was planning to share the details over dinner, but since you asked, I doubt I can keep it from you that long."

I grinned. "Go on."

"I missed your marketing meeting because I was on the phone with someone from my team down at the station. They pulled Mr. North in for questioning first thing this morning."

"North?" I felt my eyes go wide. "What did he say? Was I right? Was there money in that envelope?"

Jack nodded. "It was a bribe. North called it 'padding palms' and confirmed bribery as part of the pageant culture. Apparently, he and Viktor had an arrangement for special treatment and placement of North's cat. So, when Viktor

132

died, North knew the money had been wasted, and he needed it back to try to make a similar arrangement with someone else."

"North tossed the room because he was in a hurry to find the money before someone caught him in there," I said.

"Yep, and he claims not to have known how much was in the envelope when he took it. He'd only expected to get the five grand back that he'd given Viktor."

"Five? So others were paying Viktor too." I'd assumed the whole thirty-eight large had come from Mr. North, but it made sense that no one owner would pay so much for the fifty-thousand-dollar prize, now that I thought about it. Though the sponsorships and opportunities that came with the win would've amounted to much more. How many other owners had Viktor lied to? "Wait a minute. There will only be three finalists, and one of those gets crowned as the pageant winner, but if each briber gave Viktor five grand, then why did he have more than fifteen in his desk?"

Jack watched me as I worked it out for myself.

"He was taking advantage of people," I said. "As if taking bribes isn't bad enough, he let more than three people bribe him knowing full well they couldn't all be finalists, and no one could tell on him because what they'd done was illegal. This pageant is totally corrupt," I said sadly. Why couldn't people just be honest, do their best, and accept the results?

"I agree," Jack said, "North and his cat were pulled from the lineup. They've been disqualified for unsportsmanlike behavior and banned for life. It's a good start toward cleaning things up over there."

"I'm glad," I said. "Mrs. Smart will be happy to know that kind of thing won't happen again, though I think she'll be brokenhearted to know it happened at all. She's nearly as uptight as my mother when it comes to her husband's pageant." I checked my watch. "I bet one of the more than five people who tried to pay Viktor off found out what he was up to and lashed out. I want to stay and talk, but I have to go. I need to fill the bakery display at Furry Godmother before I open, and I'm sure traffic has picked up by now."

Jack wet his lips and shifted his weight. "There was something else I'd planned to talk to you about later," he said, "but it's probably best I let you know in case something happens between now and then."

I froze, unable to imagine what had made Jack look so uncomfortable. "What?"

"The case we have against Eva is getting stronger the more we dig, and she's not talking, which makes her look like she has something to hide. If she doesn't fill in the blanks or find someone to corroborate her claim that she walked onto the balcony after hearing the crash, I might be forced to arrest her. Right now, all we have in her defense is her word, and it won't be enough much longer."

"I'll talk to her," I said.

Jack nodded. "See you later?"

"Yeah." I capped my water bottle and hurried back through the lobby and into the beating sun. I'd been so preoccupied with the personal threats, the increased business at my shop, and my promotion to judge that I hadn't taken the time to talk to the one person who could shed some light on what the heck had happened in that balcony.

My daily to-do list was already filled to capacity, but I was suddenly itching to add one more thing to the schedule.

I needed to talk to Eva.

Chapter Eleven

Furry Godmother encourages good posture; otherwise the crown slips.

I had to park around the corner from Furry Godmother, but I managed to snag the last spot on the block, so I called it a win. I'd hoped to arrive in time to fill the bakery display and tidy up after yesterday's crowds, but I'd spent more time talking to Jack than I'd realized, and it was nearing ten when I landed on Magazine Street. Instead of having my pick of parking, I had to outmaneuver every other business owner and employee who was also running a bit late for a ten AM opening. Early-bird shoppers were already drifting through the doors of local cafés, toting iced coffees and pastry bags with their leftover breakfast items inside. I had to hustle if I was going to make my shop presentable before it got too busy to bother.

Much as I wanted to grumble about people who rolled out of bed ready for a public appearance and a little shopping before noon, I could appreciate the benefits. Like being able to breath the air instead of bathe in it.

My meticulously blown-out hair was stuck to my neck, cheeks, and forehead before I rounded the corner at the Frozen Banana smoothie shop. I stopped in front of the open glass doors, and the arctic blast of air-conditioning called to me. Sweet scents of spun sugar, fresh-baked waffle cones, and homemade fudge rolled out and tugged me closer. Frozen Banana was delicious any time of day and my favorite place to go when I was in a mood. For two extra dollars, they'd add a shot of coconut rum to my pineapple-and-orange smoothie. No judgment. And it was amazing. I slowed at the threshold, debating a frozen coffee but unsure how I'd carry it with the stack of bakery boxes already in my hands.

"Do you think I'm pretty?" a scratchy voice asked. The sound was about three octaves lower than any I'd ever heard pose the question.

I stepped back a few paces and twisted at the waist in search of the person that went with the voice. A homeless man under a pile of coats despite the raging heat sat beside the Frozen Banana's door. I craned my neck for a look at him around my stack of boxes. I hadn't noticed him until he spoke, but now he had my full attention. "Actually, I do," I answered, leaning in for a better look at the shiny crown on his ratty hair. The little silver accessory was strikingly familiar, and the design pattern of its Swarovski crystal accents bore an uncanny resemblance to a crown I'd had inside my little pink tackle box last night. The thought made no sense because I'd lost the tackle box at the Tea Room near the zoo, a long way from here. Though he certainly could have taken a walk in that direction, it seemed strange that he'd wound up on the sidewalk so near my shop.

"I like your crown," I said.

"Thank you." He stuck his hands out at me, as if to show off a new manicure. "Do you like my new rings?"

I squinted against the sunlight and dropped into a squat just out of the man's reach. His breath nearly knocked me over, more from the sharp tang of alcohol than poor hygiene, which was another issue all its own. From my new vantage point I could clearly see a row of sticky-backed gems clinging haphazardly to his dirty forehead and a shimmer of glimmer paint across his bronzed skin. I'd used gems exactly like his to decorate Penelope's hard plastic carrier. They'd been in my tackle box too, along with a matching bottle of shimmer.

The man's eyelids drooped, then his head, and he began to snore.

"Sir?" I said. "Excuse me, sir?"

He didn't respond, so I stood and nudged him with the toe of my white leather pump, lightly at first, then a little harder.

"Hey!" I gave his thigh a series of little kicks until his eyes opened again.

"Do I look pretty?"

I put my foot securely back under me and baby-stepped away. "Yes. Very pretty. Can you tell me where you got your beautiful tiara and makeup?"

"They were gifts from Her Highness."

"Who?" I scanned the street for signs of someone fitting the regal description. All I saw were tourists. "Who is Her Highness?"

"The paper lady," he said, swinging an arm in the direction of my store.

"Paper lady?" I took a few steps in that direction, and my overturned tackle box came into view on the ground beside the bench outside my shop door. The shadow of someone just inside sent a rush of panic through me. "Thank you," I told the man as I speed-walked toward Furry Godmother, trying not to topple my bakery boxes in the rush.

I stopped, speechless, a moment later and stared.

There was no one inside like I'd thought. The shadow I'd seen was only a near life-sized paper cut out in the shape of a person taped to my door. She was covered in sticky beads, wore a scribbled-on paper crown, and had dark-black Xs for eyes, like the ones stitched onto the stuffed cat I'd been delivered. Unlike the cat, the paper lady had a lolling red tongue hanging from the straight line that represented her mouth, and she'd been thoroughly hosed over with red craft paint.

The part of me who was still grasping at straws insisted this wasn't a threat either, it was just really bad art, but the rest of me wasn't listening to the lie.

My knees knocked painfully as I lowered the boxes onto the bench and freed my phone from my handbag. I took photos of the threat, as was my new daily routine, and sent them to Jack, then sat beside my bakery boxes. I wasn't sure if opening the door and going inside would contaminate the crime scene.

What I knew for sure was that it was going to be a long day.

Jack arrived nine minutes later and drove partially onto the sidewalk instead of looking for a proper parking space. He jumped out in jeans and a T-shirt, detective badge in place, mirrored aviators hiding his eyes. "You okay?"

I nodded to assure him I was, but my mouth still said "No."

"You're smart to sit out here and keep watch," he said. "You're safer in public, and your presence probably kept some derelict from taking any of the evidence."

I went along with the idea I was "keeping watch" instead of what I really was, too scared to move.

He crouched by the toppled tackle box. "This the one you were missing?"

"Yep."

"Any witnesses?" he asked, looking at the curious faces all around. No one spoke up.

I pointed to the heap of coats by the Frozen Banana. "That guy is wearing one of my crowns, and he told me about the paper lady. I don't know if he saw anything or if he helped himself to the bling."

Jack stretched onto his feet. "All right. I'll bag this up, then you can go ahead and open for the day, if that's what you want to do. I'll talk to the guy with the crown when I finish. Doesn't look like he's going anywhere."

I watched while Jack returned to his truck and pulled his black shoulder bag out with a yank. He snapped on blue latex gloves and bagged the items on the sidewalk first, smoothing yellow labels over each and scratching his initials in the corners.

Imogene stepped through the little cluster of people at the corner beside Jack's truck and gasped long and loud when she saw the mess. She grasped the pendant on her necklace as she inched closer to the door. "Have mercy," she whispered. The paper lady was about Imogene's height, and the two seemed to stare one another down. "This meant for you?" she asked, flicking her gaze in my direction.

"Unless you've got a crafty enemy," I said hopefully.

Imogene looked into the sky, closed her eyes, and mumbled something incoherent with one hand raised overhead. Then she got busy digging through her mammoth handbag.

Jack peeled the paper lady off the window and rolled her carefully. "This paint is getting all over." He looked at me as he stuffed her into a large bag. "Paint that hasn't fully dried in this heat couldn't have been here too long."

That sparked another question in my mind. "How'd you get here so fast?" I asked. He must've left Grandpa Smacker's right behind me to have changed and gotten here so quickly. My search for parking and chitchat with the homeless prince hadn't amounted to more than ten minutes.

"I left right after you. Got the texts that you needed me when I was already en route to the Tea Room."

"You were in a suit thirty minutes ago. How'd you have time to change? Do you keep an extra detective costume at the office?"

He looked down at himself and frowned. "I keep a couple of suits at the office. I like to come and go in my detective costume."

I smiled.

Jack stuffed the evidence into his black shoulder bag and rolled his shoulders. "You're going to need to lay low until I can get a handle on who's doing this," he said. "I know you're going to argue, but please don't."

"How am I supposed to lay low?" I asked.

He blew out a gust of frustration.

"I'm a judge at the pageant that got this nut's attention to start with."

"Quit."

"Can't. My mother will kill me." Better to take my chances with the murderer.

He smiled.

Imogene pulled a stick of wood from her handbag, then flicked a sliver lighter to life and lit the stick's end.

Jack and I watched, dumbstruck.

"You carry sticks in your purse?" I asked.

She waved it at me. "This isn't a stick. It's a plane of Palo Santo, holy wood. It'll help clean up all that bad juju you've got going on right here." She dropped the lighter back into her purse, then swung her empty palm in giant circles, indicating my entire self.

I choked on the string of stinky smoke coming off her stick as she marched around me.

"Stop," I whined, gagging on the cloudy air.

Jack stepped out of her way as she went for a second pass.

Imogene stopped on the third trip and stood in front of me to blow out the stick. She held it across her palms like an offering. "Spit on it, then keep it under your pillow and light it as needed to defend your juju."

"I'm not spitting on anything," I said, pinching my face into a knot. "I love you, but that's just bonkers, and why would I want to keep something I spit on under my pillow? Hard pass."

She moved the gaze of her forlorn brown eyes from my face to the stick and back.

"Jeez." I reached for the stick. "I'll keep it under my pillow, but I won't spit on it, okay?" If someone managed to get the jump on me while I was sleeping, I could always club them in the head.

Imogene gave me the stick, then hugged me tight while the smoke cleared.

Mom popped into view over Imogene's shoulder, looking as if she was ready to club someone already. "What's going on?"

"You called my mother?" I asked Imogene. I wasn't completely surprised. I just hadn't seen her use her phone, and she'd been here only a few minutes.

Mom headed for Jack. "How could you let this happen?"

"I called as soon as I knew," he said.

My jaw dropped. *Jack called my mother?*

I made a face at him.

"You and I had an agreement," she barked at him. "You're supposed to keep her safe, and you're supposed to keep these sorts of things from happening."

A man in the crowd raised his phone in Mom's direction and held it there.

Jack pointed a finger at the man's face without taking his eyes off my mother.

The man put the phone in his pocket.

I reached for the door to my shop. "Why don't we take this inside?" I asked, before footage of my usually poised mother berating a New Orleans detective went viral.

Jack nodded, and I turned the deadbolt to let us in.

I locked up behind us, then spun on Mom. "What are you doing? Jack is not my keeper, and it's completely unfair of you to task him with something so ridiculous. He has an entire city to keep tabs on already, and I'm a grown woman. I don't need a babysitter."

Jack, Imogene, and Mom muttered a jumble of words that sounded a lot like agreement on all sides. They all thought I needed a babysitter.

I dropped my head back and growled at no one, then refixed my attention on Mom. "I've told you before. You can't just assign a local detective to be personally responsible for my safety," I said.

She and Jack exchanged a look.

"She didn't," he said. "I offered."

"What?" When had Jack and my mother spoken about me? Why hadn't either of them mentioned it?

Jack's jaw went stiff and his stance rigid. The air around us grew uncomfortably thick.

Mom clapped her hands softly. "Enough of this for now," she said, dragging a pointed gaze to Jack. "I would like to know what's going on with Eva. I'm having trouble reaching her, but I'd like to ask her to return to the committee, if that's okay."

"It's fine with me," he said. "She was released after making her official statement, but she remains a person of interest.

She's free to do as she pleases, but she's still our strongest suspect at this time."

"Great," Mom said through gritted teeth and a forced smile. She turned on her toes for another look at me. "What are you doing about it? Don't say nothing, because I know you're lying. People who are doing nothing don't get bloody-looking paper ladies glued to their door."

"I'm going to talk to Eva as soon as I can," I said, forcing the image of the dripping red paint out of my head. "Maybe she's remembered something else since giving her statement, or maybe she'll be willing to open up to someone she knows personally."

"Good idea," Mom said. She lifted her chin at Jack. "I have to go. Try not to let anything else happen to my little girl, or I'll be forced to make good on our agreement."

"Mom," I started, having no idea where to go from there.

She turned back to me with narrowed eyes. "What are you wearing? That is not what I asked you to wear," she said. "I swear if you were any more stubborn, you would've been born a bull."

I tugged the short bell of my skirt in both hands. "It's blue."

"It's navy. Navy is not pastel, and I'm done with this song and dance. My stylist will deliver a rolling rack of appropriate outfits to your dressing room immediately. Choose from there."

"I have a dressing room?"

Mom rolled her eyes in a heated tizzy, then pointed two fingers at Jack's eyes to let him know she was watching him, or might poke them out Three Stooges style, while I gaped after her.

"What agreement?" I asked Jack when Mom had made it out of sight on the sidewalk beyond my window. "She said you have to keep me safe or she'll make good on your agreement. What does that mean?"

"It means she vowed to kill me in my sleep if any harm comes to you. Ever."

"She called that an agreement?"

"Yeah," he said, "because I agreed."

I groaned. "You really are my keeper."

"Yep."

I fell against his chest and wrapped my arms around his middle. "I'm so sorry."

Jack laughed. A few beats later, he hugged me back.

Chapter Twelve

*Furry Godmother's advice for life: Never look a
gift horse in the mouth, especially if it comes
dressed as a bull.*

Imogene walked Jack out a few minutes later while I helped a customer choose a dress for her Chihuahua. Imogene brought the bakery boxes back inside with her, and I said a silent prayer of gratitude that they hadn't been stolen, because even after all the trouble I'd gone to baking and hauling them to work, the paper lady had made me forget they existed.

I rang the woman up for the dress while Imogene set my boxes onto the counter and began filling the bakery display. Imogene had paired a teal pantsuit and white camisole with a purple head scarf wrapped exotically around her salt-and-pepper hair. She looked exquisite, confident, and ready to lecture when the line at my register disappeared. "I don't envy Detective Oliver," she said as an opening. "Keeping you alive and out of trouble is a full-time job. I should know. I did my time."

I smacked my lips at her. "Well, don't make it sound like a jail sentence," I said. "I wasn't *that* bad."

She raised her brows. "You were worse, and at least if I'd been in jail, I could've eaten a warm meal and watched my programs. Instead, I chased you around this district with my heart in my throat for eighteen years while you and that red-headed friend of yours tried to tear the place down."

I smiled. "We have had some good times, haven't we?"

Imogene clucked her tongue.

"Besides, Mom only said Jack has to keep me out of harm's way, not out of trouble. Those are different." I let the concept sink in a bit further. "I don't understand why Jack offered to do such a thing, anyway. And I can't decide if it's gallant or controlling." It would help me decide if I knew how the whole conversation had come about between him and my mother and why no one ever told me these things.

"Speak of the devil," Imogene said, "here she comes now, and she's gone and dressed like him."

Scarlet's smiling face flew along the windows and pivoted at the door. Little red horns protruded from a bulbous red helmet on her head.

Imogene grabbed a bottle of glass cleaner and a rag, then headed toward the sticky door where the paper lady had hung. She pushed the barrier wide and held it while Scarlet skated inside. "What are you dressed up for?" she asked. "Does your mother know you're out looking like that?"

Scarlet spun in a circle on high-end roller blades. "I'm no longer my mother's problem," she said. "I'm thirty years old.

I'm my husband's problem now." She smiled at Imogene's sour look. "Carter likes my outfit," she continued, striking a pose in her red-and-black roller derby ensemble. "What do you think?" she asked me, skating to the counter.

Aside from the skates and knee and elbow pads, Scarlet wore little black spandex bike shorts under a red crinoline tutu that stood out in every direction and what appeared to be a shiny red leotard under a red cut-off shirt that had the Hawthorne law firm logo on the back.

"My mother would die," I said. It was the first and only thing that came to mind for a long while. A few seconds later, I managed, "It's really cute."

"Thanks."

My tired brain caught up with the situation a minute later. "Are you going to be one of the bulls tomorrow? I thought you would be standing around the water table with me." If Scarlet wasn't going to be there, who was I going to talk to? Who would check out the best costumes with me, nosh on vendor sweets, and rehash my murder investigation drama?

"I'll be at the table until it's time to line up," she said. "Then I really want to run down some men with my whiffle bat." She mimed swinging a bat a few times, then grabbed the strap of her black cross-body bag and pulled it over her head. She slid the bag onto the counter. "I skated over to make sure I still knew how, and to bring you your outfit."

"You mean T-shirt," I said.

She nodded and grinned. "There's a T-shirt."

I looked at the box, then Imogene. Imogene stopped working midwipe on my window and turned to watch. I felt the intense flutter of anticipation in my middle as I opened the box with bated breath. There was an entire outfit inside, and it coordinated with Scarlet's, minus the skates. I lifted the pieces one by one.

Imogene made a disapproving face from across the room. "That shirt is too small," she said. "You can't fit half your blessings in that little scrap of fabric, and that skirt had better come with some long pants, not those little booty shorts like Miss Thing is wearing over here. Your mother will kill you twice for that."

I gave Scarlet a sad look and held the shirt up to my chest. "She's not wrong about my blessings."

"Braggart."

I smiled.

I fished a bottle of water from my mini-fridge and passed it to Scarlet. "How's life?"

She sucked down half the bottle before stopping. "Better than yours at the moment, I think. I heard about the paper lady on your door."

"Well, the rumor mill is still spinning," I said, slightly impressed by the speed the news had traveled.

"Actually," Scarlet said, "I heard it from the man on the corner wearing glitter paint and a crown."

"Did you think he looked pretty?"

She cracked up. "I did." She twisted the bottle cap back on with a sigh. "I wish I could help you with this investigation. Usually I hear all sorts of interesting things at times like these, but whatever's going on with the pageant seems to be internal to the event, and all the people are from out of town, so none of my sources know them. The details are sealed up tight behind the Tea Room doors." She leaned her elbows on the counter and set her water aside. "Maybe I can rent a pet and go in posing as a contestant."

Imogene headed back our way with the glass cleaner and paper towels. The shop door and windows sparkled from her touch. "Maybe you can put your connections to work finding your friend some more help. I didn't sign on to work all these hours," she said. "The place was dead when I stepped in. Now I have to request time off and coordinate my schedule with hers like this is my job. I don't want a job."

"Can I stop paying you?" I asked.

She made a mean face. "You know what I mean. I like helping. I don't want to be all tied down like this. I'm about to die of exhaustion."

I rolled my eyes. "And you call me dramatic."

Scarlet skated around the counter and gave me a quick hug. "I'm on it, but I've got to skate home and change for Pilates now. Don't worry another minute about looking for help here. I will find you help that you will love."

"Thank you," Imogene and I responded at once.

Scarlet waved and skated away.

I took my time folding the pieces of my new outfit and returning them to their box.

"I see you smiling at those," Imogene said.

I jumped, then stuffed the box under the counter.

* * *

The walkway from the parking lot to the Audubon Tea Room was lined in fat pillar candles stuck inside fancy glass vases. Strings of bistro lights wound through the canopy of tangled, reaching limbs overhead. I admired their wispy beards of moss and the enchanting effect that had been created.

A pair of men in black suits opened the double doors to the Tea Room foyer with practiced precision, as if they shared one mind. They held their respective door with one of their hands while bending the other behind their backs and bowing slightly. I stopped to curtsy.

Mom shook her head at me, apparently waiting in the foyer to complain about something immediately upon my arrival.

"Hello, Mom," I said, smacking air kisses on each side of her grouchy face. "I know you're mad about earlier, but look." I turned in a slow circle, showing off the petal-pink, knee-length dress I'd picked up on my way home to check on Penelope and Buttercup after work. "The saleslady assured me this is pastel."

"You know that's pastel," Mom said sharply, though her eyes gave her away. She loved designer chiffon as much as she enjoyed complaining about me.

"You look amazing," I said, admiring my custom-made gown on her narrow, youthful frame. "Smoking hot."

She blushed. "At fifty-two, I'm grateful for *not frumpy*, but I'll take the compliment."

"Please. You barely look old enough to be my mother, and you know it," I said. It was true. She'd had me at twenty-two and looked roughly fifteen at the time. These days, I saw the question in strangers' eyes. We could easily have been sisters, me at thirty and her looking ambiguously forty.

She held my gaze for several silent seconds before hooking her arm in mine. "I'm not happy about what happened to you earlier," she said. "I should've handled the situation with more dignity and grace. I'm sorry. I was angry, and I let it get the best of me, but I'm not angry with you."

"You're mad at Jack?" I guessed. "It's not fair to hold him to his offer, even if it was his idea. There's no way he can protect me from everything without putting me in his pocket and keeping me there."

Mom sighed. "I think he would try that if he could, and I wouldn't stop him if I thought it was possible."

My chest warmed at her words. I didn't want people worrying about me, especially Jack and Mom, because they both had so much to take care of already, but it was nice to be reminded that I was important to them—not just my general existence and safety, but my happiness. I was blessed beyond measure with a family, blood related and otherwise, who wanted the best for me, and the truth of it swelled my heart.

"When did Jack make the promise to babysit me?" I asked, "and why didn't you tell me?"

"He came to me after the first time you were threatened last year," she said, turning sad blue eyes on me. "Back then, your father and I knew him better than you, and we were doing the best we could to convince you both to play nice, Jack with his suspicions about your sudden return to the area and you with your intolerance of his general disposition. His tune changed when you were put in danger, and he's come to us consistently over the year since, namely after each of your subsequent near-death experiences. He blames himself, and I don't try to dissuade him." She looked almost guilty as her gaze shifted to the floor. "Whatever keeps you safe is all that matters, and I doubt he minds the challenge."

I hugged her arm tighter as we continued through the busy space and leaned my head against her shoulder. "Do you know about Jack's past?" I asked carefully, unwilling to give away anything personal about him that she didn't already know.

"We do," she said softly. Of course she would. It was her business to know everything remotely related to her district.

"Then you realize," I said, "that he probably thinks of you as family, and that means a lot because he doesn't let people in."

Jack's teenage mother had run off and left him to be raised by her father, who had been busy building a condiment empire and had sent Jack abroad to be raised in elite boarding schools instead of in a home with his next of kin. He'd become understandably guarded.

Mom slid her eyes to me as we walked. "He lets some people in."

She stopped at the entry to the main hall, then turned to look back through the foyer.

"There. Do you see?" she asked, tipping her head slightly toward the empty table with a large FFA logo on the skirt. "They put their cage of chicks right there on the end and let people hold them."

"Oh my goodness. I forgot." A stab of regret punched through me. "I was completely off balance after the paper lady incident, and I didn't have time to think of a cute way to draw attention to your table. I'll make a list of ideas when I get to the judges' table. I swear."

"No worries," Mom said. "I've got it handled. That was where I hurried off to this morning after I left your shop. I spoke with an old friend who makes hideous metal sculptures and charges a fortune for them. I figured if anyone I knew thought outside the box, besides you, it was him." A small prideful smile curved her lips as she shifted her attention to the Jazzy Chicks' table. "I told him what you said I should do, and he had something that fit the bill perfectly. He rents it for weddings and graduation parties."

I took a step in that direction. A large medieval-looking contraption sat front and center on the Jazzy Chicks' display. The thing was made of glass and metal, almost like a snow globe, except instead of snow, the bottom was littered with paper money and checks. A braid of tiny light bulbs wrapped the glass like a vine. I probably could have fit two Penelopes inside if I tried. "What is it?" I asked.

"It's your idea," she repeated. "Here. Try it." She opened her clutch and handed me a twenty-dollar bill. "The slot is in the metal at the top. The metal hides the hole, so it looks magical and not like a cheap piggy bank."

I positioned the money over the slot and fed it inside. When the tip of the bill breached the glass, a fan started beneath the base, and all the money on the ground swirled to life like a game show tornado machine. The vine of lights illuminated, and jazz music played. "Holy cow."

"There's a sensor," she said, crossing her arms and beaming.

My money was sucked into the tornado. It joined the little party for another two or three seconds before the globe fell still and silent once more.

"Isn't it marvelous?" Mom asked. "Now, if you wanted to give some money to a table with adorable chickens, would you put your cash in the stenciled burlap sack of a pigtailed yodeler, or would you bring it here and make magic happen?"

"I don't think you understand farmers at all."

She ignored me. "Okay, enough dillydallying. Let's get you into position before the show begins."

"I think you did great, Mom," I said with a squeeze of her hand. "No one will be able to resist your donation collector machine."

"Thank you."

I made my usual circuit to check seams and stitches on contestants' hats and gowns before letting Mom lead me to my seat at the judges' table. Everything looked impossibly more beautiful from the new vantage point. Audience chairs had been set in arched rows and draped in black linen. Cameras were strategically positioned around the room, their operators at the ready. Speakers and wires were perfectly hidden. The center space was open for performers, and the judges' table lined the rear wall of windows, with lush green gardens just outside. It was hard to believe anyone could have pulled this off in two days, but Mom was a force of nature. Pride filled my chest as she took the stand to announce Mackey and kick off the opening ceremony of the National Pet Pageant–New Orleans.

One by one, the feline competitors and their owners showed

off their stuff, sometimes to music, sometimes in silence. The costumes were fantastic on pets and owners alike. I gave every act a ten because anyone who could get a cat to perform deserved a pat on the back, but my favorite of them all was a local group called the NOLA Lolas.

The NOLA Lolas were a tabby trio wearing the equivalent of giant scrunchies for collars. Purple, green, and gold. Lola, Lola, and Lola. I'd never heard of them before, but I would absolutely never forget them. My foot began to tap with the first measure of a familiar jazz tune. The trainer, dressed in a black suit with a purple fleur-de-lis tie, began to bounce in little timely bursts, perfectly choreographed to the tune. His cats took notice and began a game of leapfrog, hopping over one another in a crisscross pattern until the trainer took a bow. They ran for him then, one by one, and were tossed onto a broad platform several feet off the ground. From there, they drove a cylinder across the plank, each cat on two legs, front paws on the prop ahead of them. When the cylinder hit the short wall at the end of the plank, fleur-de-lis flags popped up, and the crowd went crazy. The cats ran down a set of padded steps and began a flurry of varied activities. I didn't know who to watch. One spun on two legs. One ran a big colorful ball around the floor. One walked a little tightrope. It was a three-cat circus, and I was on my feet, whistling with the audience as the music climbed to a crescendo. The cats unified, climbed a row of carpeted columns, and grabbed the thick purple ribbons on top. When they jumped back down, fancy white letters became visible on the rich satin material. Together, they announced: NEW ORLEANS STRONG. The crowd exploded in applause and a set of tiny confetti rockets burst with the final note of the song.

I couldn't have been more excited if it had been Penelope on stage. Those cats were fantastic! My heart raced as I pounded my hands together while the trainer led them in a series of bows, all three cats cradled in his arms.

I was thankful for the small break while the stage was cleared so I could catch my breath.

By intermission, I was eager to get out of the spotlight and slouch a while. I moved slowly "offstage," toward the green room with private refreshments set out for judges and pageant staff only. The spread was gourmet and elaborate, and once again, Mom had outdone herself. I found a place against the wall and watched as people trickled in. Unease crept over my skin, never far away these days. One of the people filling the room could be the same one who had threatened me this morning and for the third time this week. Worse, one of them was a killer.

I rubbed the gooseflesh off my arms and willed my coiling stomach to still. Jack was on the case. If anyone could find the culprit, it was Jack. *And the pageant will be over in a few days anyhow*, I reasoned, *so either way, the danger will soon be gone.*

Chase inched along in my direction, surrounded by a gaggle of giggling women. I recognized most of them as pet owners and PAs, though one was a member of my NPP Welcoming Committee. I also recognized Chase's smile as the one he used in court while facing off with a witness from the opposing side.

I fluffed my hair and refreshed my smile. "There you are," I said in a gush.

"Here I am," Chase repeated with the quirk of a brow. "Everything okay?"

I reached for his hands and pulled him to me, forcing the women at his sides to fall back. I rose on my toes and kissed his cheek.

Chase's arm snaked out and held me in place. His lips found my ear. "Help," he whispered.

Behind him, the ladies ogled and giggled.

I slid my arm through his and beamed at his pursuers. "Ladies, thank you so much for looking after him for me." I snuggled tight to his side, "but I think we're going to sneak off and get some fresh air."

A woman at least twice our ages raised her hand before we could escape. "Is it true he was a professional volleyball player?" she asked me. Her gaze slid over Chase thoughtfully.

He squirmed at my side.

Two of the other ladies began to tap the screens of their phones. Googling, I guessed, and I knew what they would find. A wide assortment of photos from past competitions where Chase wore nothing but sunglasses and board shorts. I'd looked too when he'd first come home, and suddenly I felt a little creepy for it. "I'm sorry," I said, ignoring the question. "I don't mean to rush off, but we only get a few minutes, so I'd better make haste while I can." I slid my hand down to take Chase's, then led him away. I didn't stop until we'd found a quiet piece of the hallway where we were alone.

"I feel dirty," he said with a full-body shiver.

I shook my head. "You know women go through that every day, right?" Did the men in my life really have no idea? He turned his mouth down and his expression softened.

"It's life," I said. "Though women are normally more discreet about our appreciation of a nice physique," I told him. "I guess this is the price you pay for being sexy, young, and fabulous." I nudged him with my elbow. "Are you going to be okay?"

"You think I'm sexy?" he asked.

My mom came into view, and I stepped away from Chase with a laugh. "I need to catch Mom before intermission ends. I want to see if Eva's here tonight. I haven't spoken with her about Viktor yet, and I really need to."

Chase lifted his palms. "Go on, Crocker. Do your thing. I owe you one for the save."

"Darn right," I said, slipping into the mix of people heading in and out of the private hallway.

Mom looked up as I drew near. The ladies and Mrs. Smart turned in my direction as well.

"Hello," I said to the little group. "Everything is going well. Yes?"

Mrs. Smart nodded. "It's all very beautiful," she said. "I think New Orleans might be one of my new favorite cities. Your mother has been spoiling me. Showing me around. Making sure I have everything I need, sometimes before I know I need it."

"That's my mom," I said, "selfless and giving."

Mom forced a tight smile.

I scanned her group for the mousy brunette. "Eva?" I said,

locking gazes with my quietest committee sister. "I'm so glad to see you. Do you want to get a little air with me before intermission ends?"

She nodded, then looked at Mom, presumably for permission.

Mom gave a slow blink of approval, and I dragged Eva through the closest exit door.

Night sounds chirped and croaked around us. The area was unlit, oddly dark when compared to the endless lights on every other side of the building. "How about a walk to the bridge and back?"

We turned up a wide cobblestone path that glowed warmly beneath the extensive outdoor lighting at the Tea Room.

"I'm glad you're here," I said. "We need to talk about what you saw in the balcony the day Viktor fell."

"I told the police everything already," Eva said. Her wide brown eyes searched mine as we came to a stop on the high, arching bridge that separated the gardens from the zoo. "I don't know what you think I'm hiding, but I assure you I've reported every detail from the time I spent in the balcony, and I didn't see anything. By the time I got there, he was already gone." Her normally gentle tone was clipped, the words rushed, and she chewed her lip when she finished.

Maybe Eva was just nervous about being cornered and led into the night to be questioned, but I couldn't help thinking she was nervous for another reason, one I wouldn't like.

"I'm not suggesting that you lied," I said. "I'm just trying to put the pieces together, and you're our best chance at finding Viktor's killer. Everyone else seemed to be in the theater or otherwise accounted for at the time of his fall." *Except Veronica and North*, I realized. *Where were they before I found them arguing?*

"I know you mean well," she said, "and that this is the sort of thing you're known for doing, but I don't have anything else to say." Eva leaned against the narrow stone ledge and stared into the water far below.

I wasn't sure if I should feel offended by her words or her tone, but I did. "If there's anything you forgot to mention when you gave your official statement," I suggested, "maybe something you remembered after you left the station or something else has happened since then, I could help you get those details to the detective in charge."

"No." She tucked thick brown locks behind one ear and turned to face me. "It's just like I've told everyone else who has asked. I heard a commotion, and I went to see what was happening, but by the time I got there, there had already been a loud crash and there was screaming coming from below. I stretched onto my tiptoes to see what was happening, and that's when you saw me." She blinked back fresh tears, composure quickly slipping. "I didn't kill him, Lacy. I know I'm the easiest one to point fingers at, but I didn't do it, I swear."

I gave her a short hug. "It's going to be okay," I said, casting my gaze back toward the lights glowing softly in the distance. "I'll figure this out."

Eva hadn't killed Viktor, but someone in there had.

Chapter Thirteen

Furry Godmother's words of wisdom: Life is short; eat the fruit dip.

I drove home with the windows down. The rush of wind in my hair was freeing after a long, tense night in the spotlight. It was unnerving the way audience members scrutinized the judges as carefully as they watched the contestants, as if they could intuit our thoughts, guess our scores. My scores were usually tens, so maybe that was true. Still, the fact that one of the onlookers was likely a stalker and cold-blooded killer tested my antiperspirant's promises.

I slowed at the next intersection and smiled as Willow's face came into view beneath a streetlamp. Her eyes were closed and her chin was up as she seemed to savor the firm rush of summer wind. I pulled against the curb across the street and waved from my open window. "Willow!"

Her eyes opened. "Lacy?" The same black cat wound around her ankles. She held her cross-body bag against her middle as she jogged over to see me. Wedge-style sandals peeked from beneath the flowing material of her patchwork skirt with each long stride.

"Where are you headed?" I asked.

"Just walking. Enjoying the city. I got on a green trolley near my hotel and it brought me all the way here."

I laughed. "That was the St. Charles streetcar," I told her. "It's a historic landmark, the oldest continuously operating line in the world and my personal favorite." I'd ridden the St. Charles Streetcar dozens of times before I'd had a driver's license or money for a cab. The rush of climbing on board and leaving my life behind had been intoxicating, and I'd gotten hooked fast. In fact, most of my early teen adventures had begun with a ride on that streetcar, and shockingly, my mother had never stopped me. As long as I was back in time for dinner.

"Cool," Willow said. "Where are you going all dressed up? Hot date?"

I gave my new dress a look. "Home. I was judging a pet competition. Cats tonight. Dogs tomorrow. Birds and other pets on day three, and the last night is for crowning the winners."

She puckered her brow. "That sounds like fun, so why do you look distressed?"

"It was fun," I said, working up a better I'm-fine face. I considered how to put everything that had happened to me these last few days into words, then decided not to burden her with the mess that had become my life. "I saw a man fall to his death from a balcony," I blurted.

My jaw dropped, and I slapped a palm across my open mouth. "I'm so sorry." I apologized. "I didn't mean to say that." I bit the insides of my cheeks in embarrassment.

"The guy from the paper?" Willow asked. "Oh my gosh. I just read about that in the headlines this morning. He was with the National Pet Pageant." She bounced the heel of her hand off her forehead. "Of course. Oh my goodness. You must be so shaken. I hope you didn't have to see the aftermath." She shivered.

"I did. Up close," I said. "He nearly fell on me." My eyes went painfully wide.

"No wonder you're distressed. That's enough to ruin anyone's week."

"It's not just that," I rambled on. "A friend of mine is a suspect in the murder, so I've been trying to prove her innocence, but now I'm on my third death threat since Sunday. Well," I paused, "they aren't literally threats, but the threat is implied." Holy cow! Why couldn't I shut up? Did I need to talk to someone so badly that I'd unload such horrific and personal details on a virtual stranger? When was my therapist coming back from vacation? *I need her.* "I'm going home to pour a glass of wine and bake. Do you want to join me?"

I slammed my mouth shut. Since when did I ask people I'd met once at work to come home with me? I forced my smile in place as I searched my head for what had possessed me to make the impetuous offer but came up empty. I dug deeper for a polite way to redact and had the same result.

My passenger side door opened, and Willow poked her head inside. "I love to bake!" She lowered onto the seat, pulling the fabric of her skirt safely inside with her and tucking it under her thighs. The black cat jumped on her lap. "No," she said, gripping him around the middle and attempting to lift him off.

The cat stretched his legs toward hers until they seemed to thin into four black strings, reaching for her lap. "Mew!"

"It's fine," I said. "Penelope loves company, and I don't mind if you don't."

Willow groaned but shut the door and put the cat back on her lap. "This cat is obsessed. I ate lunch at a café having open-mic poetry readings today and lost track of time. When I left the place two hours later, the cat was still sitting outside the door. Waiting. He just fell into step beside me when I passed, as if I'd only been gone a few minutes."

"Wow. He's really attached." I angled back into traffic and motored onto my block a few minutes later. The streets were quiet in my neighborhood, beautiful and calm. A couple held hands in the distance, swinging their arms between them, and a jogger rounded the corner as I pulled into my drive. I felt a pinch of panic as I looked at my front door. Was my house clean? Would I die of embarrassment when she saw ten discarded outfits strewn over chair backs and couches or fifty pairs of shoes piled near the door? Was Willow possibly dangerous? Had I invited a lunatic inside to kill me privately behind closed doors?

"Sometimes baking is the only way I can work out my thoughts and frustrations," she said, slowly stroking the cat's fur. "It's a good plan for tonight. It'll clear your head and help you refocus yourself after the week you've had. What are you baking?" she asked as we climbed out.

"Pupcakes, tuna tarts, pawlines, and canine carrot cakes." Three dozen of each, and they'd probably all be sold out before lunch tomorrow.

Willow spouted a whimsical laugh. "I've baked just about everything, but I've never baked for animals. This will be fun."

"You've baked everything?" Was she for real? "Like what?"

She shook her head, looking truly joyful. "You name it. I was baking before I could reach the countertop without a step stool. My mom used to tell me to always bake happy because I had the power to bake my moods right into the dough."

I opened the front door feeling lighter and let my new friend inside. "I love that." The warm feeling I got when I saw my dad suddenly enveloped me, and I was thankful my path and Willow's had crossed. I didn't know any other bakers, and I really liked the idea of working side by side with someone as passionate about it as I was.

Penelope eyeballed the new cat, then ran for a seat on Spot, the robotic vacuum I'd recently purchased for home. The one at work made her so happy that I'd finally broken down and ordered one for the house too, but she wasn't usually as interested in this one. I'd always assumed she'd simply had enough vacuum riding at work and had other things to do at night, but now I wondered if it had more to do with showing off. There was rarely an audience at home.

"I love those," Willow said, stepping nearer to the vacuum.

Penelope pawed the big round button, and Spot played his

get-up-and-go song, then disembarked the dock and headed for the nearest wall.

Willow laughed. "Excellent." She gave my home an appreciative scan. "Your place is beautiful."

"Thanks. Wait until you see the kitchen. I just remodeled it, and I still get goosebumps." I did a mental kick to my head for bragging. What was wrong with me?

Willow's jaw dropped as she took in the newly renovated space. "Wow." She ran her fingertips over the white marble counters and across the stovetop before turning to admire the double oven and wine fridge. "This is right out of a magazine."

"I went a little overboard, I know, and I'll never get the money out of it if I move, but I have no plans of moving and it makes me so crazy happy."

"I bet." She pressed her palms to the island countertop and pulled her backside up to sit. Her feet dangled against the cabinets below. "I saw your store name on a billboard by the aquarium today," she said. "You must do really well."

"Business is better since I got a few of my products in the Grandpa Smacker lineup," I said. "Did you go inside the aquarium?"

"No. I was down that way catching the ferry to Algiers."

"Really?" Algiers was a nice little community across the Mississippi from the French Quarter. Lots of people commuted back and forth from there for work and play. "What's going on in Algiers?"

"Nothing special. I just wanted to ride the ferry and see the New Orleans cityscape from a new perspective. I took a few pictures, then rode back. It was fun."

I sighed, appreciating her free spirit and trying to recall the last time I'd had a day without responsibilities and obligations dictating my every minute. "I'm glad you're enjoying my town," I said, then selected a bottle of Crescent City Merlot.

"I love everything about it here," she said. "Everyone I've met. Everything I've seen. Everything I've done. I'm a traveler at heart, but something inside me can't imagine leaving this place. Isn't that bizarre?"

"Not really," I admitted. I was intimately familiar with the feeling. "Have you seen your great-grandma yet?" I uncorked the bottle, then freed two glasses from the rack and poured wine into each.

"No. I tried her again today, but she was out. A neighbor said she just got back from a trip, but that can't be right. She was the one who sent me the letters asking me to come here." Willow sipped the wine and shrugged. "Maybe it's good that we've missed each other these last couple days. By the time we meet, I will have already seen the city, and I can focus on getting to know her instead."

I lowered my glass midsip as Willow's plight began to sound familiar. "You've never met your great-grandma, but she sent you letters asking you to come to New Orleans, and she was gone when you got here."

Willow nodded. "That's it."

The proverbial hamster began to fumble his way around his creaky wheel in my head. "You like to bake," I recapped. *Her mom said she could bake her emotions right into the dough.* That sounded downright magical to me. "Is your mailing address in Ohio, by chance?"

Her eyes widened. "Yes. How did you know that?"

"Okay." I set my glass aside and gave Willow a closer look. "This is going to sound completely bizarre, and I'm probably a nut for asking, but your story is so close to another one I've been following peripherally through a friend."

"Go on," she said, a wide, expectant grin on her face. "What is it?"

"Is your great-grandma's name Veda, by any chance?"

"Yes!" She patted the counter with her palm. "That's totally crazy! You know Veda? And I keep running into you? It's cosmic."

Her enthusiasm was electric.

My smile widened until it hurt my face.

"How do you know my great-grandma?"

I sipped my wine, trying uselessly to make sense of such a wide and random coincidence. "Veda is my nanny's best friend. I've never met her, but I hear about her all the time."

Willow swiveled on my countertop, dragging her gaze around my kitchen and the adjoining hallway. "You have a nanny?"

"No." I laughed long and loud, and it felt amazing. "She *was* my nanny. Now she's my shopkeep. I still see her and talk with her almost every day."

"Is her name Emma Jean?" Willow asked.

"What? Yes! I mean, it's Imogene, but that's close enough. How can you possibly know that?" My head spun as I gathered baking supplies onto the counter. "I don't normally believe in coincidence, but this is too much."

Willow lifted the beautiful amulet on her necklace and

slid it back and forth over the shiny silver line. "It's not a coincidence. I actually came to your shop because the handsome cop in the Quarter that saw me knocking on Great-Grandma's door sent me there. He knew she wasn't home but didn't have any details, so he suggested I talk to Emma Jean at Furry Godmother, but when I met you and your name was Lacy, I figured he was wrong or pulling my leg."

I dropped a container of yogurt on the counter as another realization hit me. "The guy with the sexy southern-Louisiana accent was a cop?"

"I think. He had a badge." She lifted her necklace. "On a chain."

"Oh my goodness. I'll bet that's my detective's former partner, Henri." I laughed again. "I know him too. Jack has told me that Henri keeps an eye on Veda, and he surely fits the description you're giving."

"Is he dating anyone?" she asked. "I think he's my soulmate. Did you say you have a detective?"

I laughed some more. My side ached. My heart was light. "Yeah. He's not mine, but there's a homicide detective in this district named Jack Oliver who has become a good friend of mine."

Willow swirled her wine and watched me as I ordered things on my counter and preheated the oven. "You like him."

"Yeah."

"He likes you, too."

I snorted. "How do you know? Have you met him too?"

She stilled her wine and studied my face, smile drooping a bit at the corners. "I just know."

The doorbell rang, and I jumped. "Stay here and call 911 if I scream." I tiptoed into the living room and peeked out the front window before opening the door.

Chase pulled me into his arms as he stepped inside.

I arched my back as he curled himself around me and squeezed.

"Sorry I didn't stick around to the end tonight," he said. "I had to run to the office for some paperwork. Sue Li is like my personal marketing department. I had a line of pet owners asking me for pet custody papers, wills, and all sorts of things at intermission."

I pressed my palms to his chest and peeled myself away. "Your dad must be proud." I grinned, imagining Chase explaining the situation to his father. His dad was probably almost as thrilled with Chase practicing pet law as my mother had been when I'd told her I wanted to open a pet boutique.

"He's so mad." Chase smiled. "He's forbidden me from representing any pets or their owners. I agreed, then I stopped charging them."

I laughed again, harder and louder.

"I'd forgotten how much fun it is to irk my dad," he said. His gaze drifted past me, and his brows rose. "Well, hello. I didn't realize Lacy had company."

"I suppose this is Jack," Willow said, standing in the kitchen doorway with a thoughtful expression. "He's very handsome. I'm finding a pattern in this city."

I turned to smile at her.

She looked my way. "Sorry. I didn't mean to be nosy. When I heard all the laughing, I figured we didn't need 911."

My cheeks flamed hot as I led Chase toward the kitchen, hoping she wouldn't bring Jack up again. "Willow, this is my dear friend Chase Hawthorne. Chase, this is my new friend Willow."

Willow bit her bottom lip. "Ah," she said. "Sorry for the mix-up." She slid her gaze from Chase to me, then back. "Lacy mentioned her cop friend, and you look like a cop, so I just assumed."

He smiled. "You think I look like a cop?"

Chase looked nothing like a cop. "Chase is an attorney," I said, rounding my counter to get to work.

My guests shook hands.

"Nice to meet you," he said, taking his time to drink her in. "You're not from around here."

"Totally," she agreed, "but I'd like to be, and I'm thinking hard about staying."

Chase's brows rose. He turned a curious look in my direction. "How did the two of you meet?"

I poured him a glass of wine. "You'll never believe it, but it turns out that it really is a small world. Willow is Veda's great-granddaughter."

Chase took a moment to process, then stepped back, dropping his hands to his sides.

I grinned.

Chase Hawthorne was the single most superstitious, believe-anything man in all of New Orleans, and the great-granddaughter of a woman with an alleged magical cookie shop had just touched his skin. I imagined he was waiting to turn into a frog or frosting. I wasn't sure how his mind worked.

While I'd considered every ghost and witch story I'd ever heard to be exactly that, Chase had internalized and ruminated on them. Even Imogene freaked him out with her talk of juju and such. He'd once bought a spell from her called other-lawyer-be-stupid so he could get out of a Segway-riding-while-under-the-influence charge, and when the charges had been dropped, his weird beliefs had been cemented further. On a scale of one to ten for unusual people, Imogene was a seven and a half. Veda was fifty-two.

Willow chose a bar stool as I tied an apron around my middle.

Chase left an empty seat between them when he sat down. "How's your progress coming on the other thing?" he asked, casting a cautious look at Willow.

"It's okay," I said. "I told her about the investigation." Though not exactly intentionally. "It's going too slowly as usual, and I'm especially uncomfortable with the fact the person sending me threats knows my name, place of business, and home address."

"Not good," Willow whispered.

"Hear, hear," Chase agreed.

The low hum of my robot vacuum registered as Penelope rode by. Her chariot bounced off the kitchen door, turned in a circle four times, then headed back the way it had come.

The black cat leapt onto Willow's legs with ease, and she held him in place, instantly, absently stroking his shiny fur. "If this cat doesn't leave soon, I'm going to have to name it."

"You'd better start thinking of names," I said. "Chase can represent you or your cat in any legal issues you might be having," I teased, pushing a sliver of carrot between my smiling lips.

"Not my cat," she said, turning to Chase. "It's so bizarre. He's just been following me around the city since I got here."

Chase downed the rest of his wine and poured a refill. He was especially attached to the idea of witches having "familiars," or animal-shaped spirits who served their witch as a servant, spy, and companion.

I made a mental note to dress up as a witch for Halloween while I slid the first round of canine carrot cakes into the oven. "If Willow isn't busy tomorrow night, maybe she can go to the pet pageant with you and be your fake girlfriend."

"I doubt he needs a fake girlfriend," she said.

Chase widened his eyes.

I added a little more wine to my glass and hers. "He does. A bunch of pet moms were ogling him today, and it made him uncomfortable."

"Welcome to our world," she said dryly.

I pointed at her.

Chase shook his head regretfully. "I apologize on behalf of all men if I've ever made you uncomfortable," he said, "or if I've ever said anything crass and inappropriate about your incredible figure."

Willow laughed.

I smiled as the wine began to peel layers of stress away, at least temporarily. "You've never made me uncomfortable," I told him.

"Well, then, I apologize for all the wildly inappropriate

thoughts I've had about you. Specifically those about your incredible figure."

I tossed a dish towel at his head.

Willow moved to my side of the island. "Mind if I cut in?"

"Be my guest." I set the timer for a second round of canine carrot cakes, then went to sit on the stool beside Chase. "I'm glad you're here," I said. "Thanks for coming over tonight."

Chase reached for my hand. "You're having quite the week. Where else would I be?"

Willow began to hum as she gathered ingredients from my fridge.

I leaned my head on Chase's shoulder. "You're my best friend, next to Scarlet," I clarified. "You know that, right?"

"I do." He leaned his cheek on my head. "Normally, I'm not a fan of second place, but Scarlet Hawthorne is a worthy number one, and I'm not just saying that because she married my brother."

Willow smiled at us as she hummed. She seemed to float around my kitchen to the enchanting melody. She dropped folded whipped cream, vanilla yogurt, and a box of pudding mix into a bowl and stirred until it was a pretty, cream-colored, sweet-scented cloud.

She filled a colander with strawberries and grapes, ran them under water, then set them in front of us.

Chase leaned slightly away.

Willow dragged a strawberry through the mix and bit into it with a little wiggle of her shoulders.

My stomach growled. "I love fruit dip. This is perfect. Thank you." I grabbed a grape and dunked it in, then tried the dip with a strawberry . . . then another grape. My shoulders began to shimmy like Willow's. "You've got to try this." I dipped a grape and pointed it at Chase's mouth.

He opened reluctantly, and I dropped it inside.

By midnight, the three of us had finished two bottles of wine and all my fruit. The last round of pupcakes was setting out to cool, and Chase was spinning Willow expertly in a move he'd likely learned at cotillion classes.

I scooped the remaining fruit dip into a container and smiled as I pressed the lid into place. The night had turned out to be great. I never would've guessed I'd spend so much time laughing after my stress level had sprung off the charts just a few hours prior.

Chase and Willow bowed and curtsied as the radio changed songs, and I exhaled a sigh of contentment.

I opened my refrigerator to store the fruit dip and felt the worry creeping back into my mind before I could shut the door. My friends couldn't stay forever. Soon, they'd leave, and I'd be alone. The killer might even be waiting outside my door for them to go.

A dollop of dip clung to one knuckle, and I stuck it into my mouth as I pressed the refrigerator door closed.

"Dance with me," Chase said, a brilliant smile on his lips.

"Yeah," I said, feeling the worry slip away once more and wondering why I'd let anything get me down when my friends were still here and I could dance.

Chapter Fourteen

Furry Godmother's words of warning: A bull in a china shop beats four in the Quarter.

I took a cab to the French Quarter the next morning and got out at Jackson Square. The line from Café Du Monde was so long, it seemed like the ladies at the end might be closer to another café than the one they were aiming for. I'd filled up on coffee before leaving home to save time and money. Now I just had to hope the line to the nearest ladies' room wasn't as long as the line for coffee when I needed it.

I smiled at the row of horses waiting along the curb for someone to want a carriage ride. I wished I'd brought them apples.

A sharp whistle turned me around, and Scarlet skated into view, her short red tutu bobbing and bouncing with each flawless glide. The small red horns on her helmet had been replaced since the first time I'd seen them. No longer little cones, Scarlet's new horns were long and curved, expertly crafted and intimidating enough to make any real bull jealous. "You're early," she said, pumping her little bat in the air. "Bless you."

"Anything for you," I said, raising my gaze to her helmet. "Your horns look quite scary."

"Thanks." She laughed and wiggled her head. "Papier-mâché."

Scarlet linked her arm with mine and pointed me toward the far side of the square. "I'm setting up in front of the St. Louis Cathedral."

We passed throngs of people, street performers, and artists on our way across the lush green lawn and gardens, bypassing the statue of Andrew Jackson and a bubbling fountain behind him.

Scarlet stopped at a long, white-skirted table. "Here we go. I just got the table covered. I need to unload the giveaways and load up the water."

"On it," I said, ripping into the waiting boxes and setting out the Hawthorne law firm's swag. Red buttons, bandanas, and foam bats all carried the firm's logo and a tag line declaring that the Hawthornes had been "serving the Crescent City's legal needs for more than fifty years." I set piles of coordinating business cards and flyers in trays with weights and lined them on one side of the table. The other side would soon be covered in water bottles with personalized Hawthorne labels wrapping their middles.

Soft scents of chicory and cinnamon sugar wafted from

countless coffees and beignets in the square, and I took a beat to absorb the moment. The gleaming white cathedral before me. The steady rhythm of horses' hooves behind me. A trio playing "When the Saints Come Marching In" on a trumpet, drum, and saxophone marching across the street at the corner. I loved New Orleans as a whole, but there was no beating the Quarter for ambience.

Scarlet produced a gallon jug from a cooler beneath the table and stacked clear plastic cups beside it. "I know we have the bottles," she said, "but some runners might be in the mood for a drink without having to commit to lugging a bottle around."

"Smart," I said, unloading a case of mini bottles.

The street before us was closed to traffic and teemed with men, women, and children dressed in white. Their ensembles ranged from fancy dresses with parasols to traditional bull-fighter costumes, but they all wore a red sash about their waist, and the men had red bandanas around their necks as well.

The "bulls" were gathered on the narrow side streets that flanked Jackson Square. Thousands of roller derby girls from all around the world were just waiting to be unleashed upon the crisp white-wearing masses. Shoulder-to-shoulder sheets of red, the girls seemed to move in waves as they grew more and more anxious for the run to begin.

Scarlet finished organizing the cups, then looked me up and down, seeming to notice my bull outfit for the first time. I looked a lot like her for a change, minus the red hair, skates, and helmet. "I like what you did with the pieces," she said, casually circling me. "Fierce eyes. Adorable horns."

"Thanks." I'd found a leftover devil's headband in a box

from Halloween and popped it on top of my blonde barrel curls. I'd added lots of thick black mascara to reaching false lashes, smoky black-and-gray lids, and sweeping liquid eyeliner wings in an effort to look like one of the derby girls.

Scarlet grinned, dropping her gaze from my makeup to my T-shirt. "Imogene was wrong about your blessings. Looks like they fill the shirt out just right."

I laughed. I'd stretched the skinny T-shirt over a corset-tight undergarment that whittled my waist and pushed the girls up to my collarbone. It was nothing short of a miracle that the fabric held up. I'd taken the liberty of cutting a V in the scoop neckline to relieve a bit of stress on the material. I'd added a horn-shaped applique to each cheek of the red short shorts I'd slid on over longer Lycra leggings and come to terms with the fact that my midriff wasn't covered. The T-shirt Scarlet had given me couldn't be everywhere at once. All in all, the outfit was thoroughly over-the-top, and I was feeling sassy. I'd needed to cut loose for weeks, breathe, take a break from worries about costume orders, shop sales, baking, Grandpa Smacker, my mother, and everything pageant related. Add the last few days of awful, and I'd never been so glad to get out of my routine.

"You know," Scarlet said, a mischievous smile spreading over her pretty face, "I have an extra pair of skates in my car, in case you change your mind about being a bull."

I hung my head, desperate to do something thoroughly New Orleansy and knowing I'd better not. "I can't," I said, raising my head. There was only so much I could realistically expect to keep from my mother, and if I showed up on camera in this outfit while some news crew covered the event, Mom would have multiple consecutive strokes and die, then come back to haunt me. "Why do you tempt me?"

"Because you're incorrigible," she said. "And you're doing a great job as a committee lady for your mom, but sometimes I wonder what you're doing for Lacy."

"I do things for me," I said. "I love my job."

"Okay," she said. "I just want you to find a balance so you don't wind up resenting her and this place all over again. I just got you back, and I never want you to leave again." Her smile faded. "So, put on the skates."

"I'm not going to leave again," I said, suddenly heartbroken. "I would never. I was eighteen and trying to find myself the last time, but when times got tough, New Orleans was the only place I wanted to be. This is my home. You're my people, and this is where I belong."

Her eyes glossed with unshed tears, and she nodded hard and fast. "Good. No more leaving?"

I drew a cross over my heart.

She lifted her pinky toward me, and I hooked mine with hers; then we bumped our hips together.

A slow clap erupted as Chase headed our way smiling and whistling. "My, oh, my," he said, pressing his palms to his heart. "You look like you just stepped right out of my best daydream."

"In this?" I asked, batting enormous false eyelashes and dragging long blonde hair over my shoulders.

He cocked his head and let his gaze trail over me until I

was half certain he could literally undress me that way. "Damn."

"Language," I said, tugging his red neckerchief.

He looked adorable in his all-white outfit and red sash.

I tried to imagine Jack in Chase's costume but couldn't. I wasn't even sure what he'd think about me in mine.

The back-up beeper of a truck turned the three of us toward the corner where Chartres, in front of us, met St. Ann Street, several yards away. A trailer hauling live bulls was reversing into position, and a group of men dressed in elaborate, sequined bullfighter costumes were locking metal fence pieces into a corral.

"What is that?" I said. "What are they doing? There aren't supposed to be any real bulls at San Fermin en Nueva Orleans."

The derby girls on either side of Jackson Square began to hoot and pound their red and white whiffle bats against the ground.

The bulls in the trailer paced and grunted.

Chase crossed his arms and smiled at the new arrivals.

I ducked behind him and peeked around. "They can't leave real bulls here."

"They're fine," Chase said. "They're inside a fence and there are only four of them with six cowboys. Besides, I thought you loved farm animals."

Cows, I liked. Chickens, pigs, goats—anything that wasn't wearing two big goring weapons on its head while I was dressed head to toe in a color it liked to kill. "Those cowboys can't stop a stampede with their bare hands," I said, rubbing goosebumps off my bare arms. "I can practically feel the heat from their flaring nostrils."

The bulls were offloaded from the truck and into the pen. The bullfighters perched on the railings and spoke with people closing in for a better look.

Next, a pair of oxen pulling a massive wagon of watermelons set up shop near the bulls.

"What on earth?" I asked. "What are all those watermelons for?"

Chase craned his head for a look behind himself, where I hid. He stepped out of my way, then pulled me around where he could see me. "There's going to be a street party here after the run. The watermelons are being cut, sliced, and distributed to anyone who comes back this way."

I turned my head slowly in each direction, keeping my eyes locked on the bulls. It might've been my imagination, but I thought the bulls looked antsy.

I reached for Scarlet's hand, careful not to lose sight of the bulls and trying not to imagine them running me over. "Maybe I'll take those skates," I said.

She pulled them from beneath the table's long white skirt.

"I thought you said they were in your car."

"I thought you said you didn't want them."

"Touché." I took a seat on the lid of her rolling cooler and laced them up, then took a minute to get used to them. It had been at least a decade since I'd been on skates. I stood slowly, finding my balance, then did a loop around the table, dodging tourists, onlookers, and passersby.

Scarlet clapped.

"How's the nanny hunt going?" I asked, pressing the bulls out of my mind.

Scarlet tracked me with her eyes as I got braver on my new wheels. "Not great," she said.

I went a little farther each time before boomeranging back. "Why? What's wrong?"

"I don't know," she said, wiping humidity from her forehead and adjusting her helmet with giant red mâché horns. "There are a lot of weirdos out there."

I spun on my skates and adjusted my horn-appliqued booty shorts. "You're not kidding."

Scarlet squatted near the table and came up with a helmet. The horns on this one were white and doused in glitter. "Here. If you're going to go that far on the skates, you need a helmet."

I skidded to a rough stop at the table's edge and made doe eyes at her before taking the helmet and hugging it to my chest. "You made me a helmet."

"Well, you're no good to me dead," she said, "and you never were the best skater."

"Hey," I said.

She shrugged. "Put it on. I just saved your life. You'll repay me when we sit down to screen all the cuckoos from my inbox full of nanny video applications."

"Done," I agreed.

"How's it going at the pageant?" she asked. "How are Eva and your mom?"

I strapped my helmet over what felt like ten pounds of sticky blonde hair and silently cursed the ridiculous tropical temperatures. "Eva's doing okay, all things considered," I said.

"I'm a little worried about what Mom's going to do with her time once she no longer has a national pageant to orchestrate. She'll still be feuding with Mrs. Hams, but the aggressive fund-raising will be over for five minutes. I'm hoping she goes back to redecorating her house and doesn't turn too much of her attention on me."

Scarlet slid her eyes my way. "Yeah, right. She's going to be on a manhunt for your most suitable future spouse the minute they close the curtain on this thing, and you know it."

I pushed that horrifying idea immediately out of my mind. "You know what she told me about Jack?" I asked.

"I can't begin to guess."

"She said it wasn't a good idea to marry a cop. That I'd spend my life worrying about him, and he could die anytime he went to work, and where would I be besides broken-hearted?"

Scarlet made a face. "I hate to agree with your mother, but . . ." She let the sentence hang.

"Are you serious?" I asked. The heat of betrayal curled in my stomach. Scarlet and I had a standing lifelong agreement never to agree with the other friend's mother, and while I'd never had a serious talk with Scarlet about my feelings for Jack, it was something she was just supposed to know.

"Hey, to each her own," she said, "but there are definite benefits to marrying a lawyer. For starters, they rarely die on the job. They never come home soaked in someone else's blood, don't get stalked by lunatics or put their kids and wives in danger as a result of their work." She started ticking fingers off her opposite hand. "Carter works normal business hours. He's available for school plays and soccer games. We go on a date every Friday night. It's nice."

I gave Chase a long look. He'd wandered off to talk to the sequined bullfighters.

"He'd be good for you," she said, sliding into position beside me.

"I'm not looking for a husband," I said. "I like my life the way it is, possibly more than I ever have."

Scarlet stared at the side of my head until I looked her way. "You're the most die-hard romantic I know. You always have been, and I get that you were burned while you were away in Virginia and that you're hesitant to put your heart on the line again, but tell me the truth about something."

I didn't respond. I couldn't.

"You might not be looking for a husband," Scarlet said slowly. "I can't be sure on that, but you are looking for love. Aren't you?"

My cheeks heated and my heart skipped. I watched Chase laugh and joke with the men across the way. His handsome face and congenial personality, brains, brawn, and money probably made him the world's best catch.

"Lace?" Scarlet prodded.

I wet my suddenly dry lips. "Yes." She was right. I believed in true love. I saw it in my parents and in Scarlet and Carter. They had the kind of love I'd only read about in story books, and I wanted it too.

She pulled her gaze off my cheek and turned her face back in her brother-in-law's direction. "You know he loves you, right?"

"Yeah." Emotion stung my eyes and burned my nose. I couldn't look away from Chase's bright smile, couldn't deal with how incredibly, unfairly stupid my heart could be. "He's basically perfect, but he's not . . ."

"Jack?" she interrupted.

A small gasp ripped free from my lips. "I was going to say he wasn't the one."

"Were you?"

I blinked tear-blurred eyes at my best friend. "Yes, but how do you know about Jack?"

She gave me a sad smile, then slung an arm over my shoulders. "Sweetie, until this moment, I thought you were the only one who didn't know."

Chase broke away from the bull pen and headed back in our direction, smiling wide. He whistled upon approach. "Look at you in your horn helmet and skates. The fantasy is complete."

I rolled my eyes and choked a laugh as Scarlet moved away. "Everything okay over there?" I tipped my chin toward the sequined bullfighters.

"Yeah. Those guys said their bulls are used to a crowd. They do shows with them all the time." He bumped his shoulder to mine and smiled. "If you get nervous, you can grab onto me anywhere you'd like."

"Jeez." I pushed him back with a laugh.

A man's voice interrupted us as it echoed through a microphone somewhere unseen. His words pumped from every telephone pole speaker for blocks, thanking sponsors, runners, and bulls, advising on events to follow the run and how to sign up for next year.

The bat thumping and hooting grew steadily into a crescendo on either side of us as anticipation thickened the air.

The sea of folks in white were suddenly still and vibrating with intent to run.

My heart raced with adrenaline and endorphins as Scarlet tightened her chin strap. She gave my bottom a whack with her bat, then skated over to join the other bulls. I cruised behind the table and brought up the camera app on my phone.

Chase gave me a slow-motion thumbs-up as he jogged backward into the sea of white.

I snapped his picture. "Have fun!" I called.

"Always," he answered.

Music suddenly replaced the man's voice coming through the speakers. Heavy bass echoed and vibrated in my chest as fifteen thousand people joined in for one passionate chorus of "Born to be Wild."

The buzzer sounded. The crowd screamed, and the runners were off.

The roller derby girls were released by a second buzzer several seconds later, their wheels chomping up the pavement as they chased the runners down.

I clapped and waved and hooted until the sharp peal of a woman's scream turned me to face the bulls.

The oxen reared up on their hindquarters, bucking and stomping the pavement underfoot. Their wagon rattled and groaned behind them until the cart's driver was thrown from his seat. He landed on the ground near their feet with a heavy grunt and curled himself into a ball for protection. The wooden guardrails gave way a moment later, rocked loose from the cart by the continued fit the animals were throwing. Watermelons plummeted from the massive pile, crashing and breaking on the street. Skaters tripped, slid, and fell in the mess as they tried to angle around, but there were just too many people. Too little space, and the squealing guitar solo of a classic rock hit long past its time wasn't helping anything as it writhed through every speaker on the square.

The sequined bullfighters rushed to calm the oxen. They helped fallen skaters up and redirected the remaining derby girls like six shiny pieces of tape trying to plug the holes in a dam.

I watched in horror, unsure what to do, how to help or if I could.

The sounds of screeching metal tore through my chest as the unattended bull fence collapsed with a sudden crash, instantly trampled beneath thousands of pounds of angry animals.

I froze as the mini stampede headed right for me.

Chapter Fifteen

Furry Godmother's gentle reminder: A proper lady never swears, unless she has to.

I screamed and fled into the square, looking behind me as often as forward, racing recklessly on borrowed skates. The earth rumbled beneath my feet as the bulls tore through the table where I'd stood moments before, tossing water bottles and cups into the air with a calamitous sound and dragging the table by its skirt, tangled in their powerful legs.

I dared another look behind me, and the lead bull lowered his head and horns. The only word I could think of burst from my lips on repeat as I dove into the circle of grass behind the fountain, and I wished I wasn't in the shadow of the cathedral as I said it. My adrenaline-fueled body crashed and rolled across a row of pristine flower beds, like an actor in an action adventure. Unlike movie stars, I landed roughly on my knees, then fell forward on my head, busting off one glitter-coated horn and scraping the side of my face through black mulch.

The first bull careered past me as I crawled full speed

toward the historic marble statue of Andrew Jackson and pressed my back to the sturdy stone base. I closed my eyes and promised my maker I'd never dress like a bull again if he kept the stampede from killing me.

My phone vibrated in my shaking hand, and I pressed it to my ear. "Hello?" I choked as the next three bulls charged around the circle, allowing me to live another day.

"Lacy!" Jack's voice boomed through the phone.

I made a strangled sound of confirmation.

"Dispatch requested all available units to the Quarter. Are you there with Scarlet?"

"Yeah." I patted myself down with my free hand, checking for fatal injuries or missing body parts while my heart attempted to push itself directly through my rib cage. *Bumps. Bruises. Scrapes.* Nothing that would need stitches, and I'd miraculously managed not to break an ankle or leg on the skates. I turned a reverent look on the towering white cathedral. *Thank you*, I mouthed.

"What's happening?" Jack demanded.

"Bulls!" I screamed as a group of terrified tourists ran past.

"Bomb?" Jack's voice neared red-alert levels. "Where are you?"

"Jackson Square," I said. "No bomb. Just bulls."

"Derby girls?"

"No." I tipped my filthy helmet back until it rested on the stone base of the Jackson statue. The bulls were across the street and headed for the river with a collection of sequined bullfighters and local law enforcement giving chase. The square was suddenly, deafeningly quiet.

Tears began to fall. A small sob broke on my lips before I could stop it.

"I'm on my way," he said.

"Don't." I wiped the unbidden tears away with resolve. "I'm fine. I need to find Chase and Scarlet."

"Where did they go?"

"They ran," I said with immense, chest-filling gratitude. My best friends had gone in a completely different direction than the crazed bulls.

Sirens screamed and bleated in the distance, but aside from me, there were only a smattering of shell-shocked tourists in sight, probably ones who'd arrived after the bulls were long gone, and a bunch of looters collecting unbroken watermelons.

A familiar black Camaro sliced through the congestion and parked smoothly at the curb, custom red-and-white lights flashing behind the grille.

"Henri's here," I told Jack as his former partner slid out from behind the wheel and moved confidently in my direction. Dressed in unlaced boots, black jeans, and a clingy black T-shirt, the detective looked more like someone who should be in handcuffs than someone wielding them. "He's got this," I said, assuming Henri, like Jack, could handle anything.

Jack was silent for several long seconds while Henri approached.

"Lacy?" Henri crouched before me, running a large palm over his stubble-covered cheek. "Are you all right?"

I nodded, a ball of emotion knotting painfully in my throat. I handed him my phone. "Jack," I said, by way of pitiful explanation.

Henri took the phone, then stood with it and moved away, apparently surveying the scene.

I covered my face with cupped hands and concentrated on breathing.

"Lacy!" Chase's voice rent the thick morning air. "Lacy!"

I forced myself upright and felt the tears begin to stream again.

Fear twisted Chase's brow as he examined the ruined table where he'd left me a few minutes before. "Lacy!" he screamed again, louder and more desperately this time.

I watched helplessly through tear-blurred eyes, unable to speak past the lump in my throat, rendering me temporarily mute.

A sharp whistle cracked like a whip from Henri's lips. He waved an arm overhead, catching Chase's attention, then motioning him in my direction.

Chase's terrified gaze landed on me, and he began to run.

I waited, motionless and silent as I replayed the series of events that had led up to the bulls' escape. *So much noise. The panicked oxen. The watermelons. The screech of metal.*

Chase scooped me into his arms, knocking my skates out from under me, and carried me to the nearest bench. He took a seat, then held me against his chest. "I am so sorry," he said, stroking the length of my back and gathering me closer to him with long, careful arms. "I told you I'd keep you safe. I promised the bulls were secure." He pressed his cheek to the top of my helmet and shuddered. "My god, Lacy, I'm so sorry."

"It's okay," I said. "It's not your fault."

"I don't know what happened," he said. "I checked the gate's latch myself while I spoke to the bulls' keepers."

"Something scared the oxen," I said. "The driver fell. The watermelons fell. Then the bull pen fell."

Henri appeared at the back side of the bench, behind Chase's head, my phone pressed to his ear. "He's got her now," he said into the receiver. "You want me to bring her to you?" Henri lifted my sneakers in his opposite palm, or what was left of them.

I took the cloth-and-rubber scraps gingerly. The poor things had been soaked and trampled into filthy pulps. I could only hope it was just water they'd been drenched in.

Chase stiffened, eyes fixed on Henri. "Who is that?" he asked.

"That's Jack's former partner, Henri LaSalle," I explained. "He's on my phone talking to Jack."

"Tell Jack I've got this," Chase said, an edge of warning in his tone. "Are you ready?" he asked more softly near my ear.

I lowered my skates to the ground and let him help me up.

The intersection at the corner of Chartres and St. Ann was congested with ambulances and EMTs aiding fallen skaters. The oxen driver was strapped to a gurney. His oxen were as calm and bored-looking as they had been upon arrival.

Henri disconnected the call and returned my phone. "I had a look at the bull pen," he said. "Talked to some bystanders. I don't think this was an accident. The gate was probably tampered with while the men in the sequins went to help the oxen. I found an air horn near the toppled fencing that might've been used to get the bulls moving. I'm not sure about the oxen."

I nodded, finally pulling myself together. The danger was over. Help had arrived. Everyone was going to be okay. "Is there any chance this could have been directed at me?" I asked, hoping I didn't know the answer.

Henri gave the path of destruction a careful look. "It's too early to tell. Could be that you were just in the wrong place at the wrong time, but I will find out." His phone rang, and he turned away to answer it. "LaSalle."

Chase looped an arm around my shoulders and led me away. "You need to treat all those cuts as soon as you get home. You don't want them getting infected. You should probably see a doctor."

"I just fell over my skates," I said. *And the little iron fence around the flowers*, I thought. *And I rolled on my head in the mulch a little before crawling through some grass . . .* "I don't need an exam."

"I can stay with you while you shower and change, if you want. Maybe keep watch while you settle in for some rest."

"No thanks," I said, hating the imagery he'd portrayed. I didn't want to go home and lick my wounds. "I told Imogene I'd be at Furry Godmother after the run."

"Work can wait." Chase unlocked his car and opened the door for me.

"No," I said, fueled by something I couldn't name. "I don't want to go home and play the victim." If the little stampede really had been orchestrated to scare or hurt me, then I was doubly determined not to let whoever had caused the fiasco get what they wanted. "Take me to Furry Godmother," I said.

I was going on with my life, and I hoped that whoever had wanted to upset me would see that was where his or her power ended. I could be scared, but I couldn't be stopped.

* * *

I thanked Chase, then climbed onto the sidewalk outside Furry Godmother with my chin high. I was getting tired of a lot of things. Being afraid, being threatened, and being treated like someone in need of protection were fast becoming my top three.

I skated into the shop and headed for my counter.

Imogene's eyes went wide, then narrowed on me as she absently tucked a customer's purchase into a logoed shopping bag.

I peeled my borrowed skates off and wiggled my toes, thankful to be back on solid ground and safe in my little slice of paradise. I'd chucked the remnants of my sneakers into a trash bin in the Quarter.

The people in line at the bakery counter moved in my direction and Imogene followed.

"Pardon me," an older man said. His wife smiled at his side. A small terrier in a matching bonnet and bloomers drifted in and out of sleep in her arms. "Are you dressed up for the hoopla in the French Quarter this morning?" he asked. "We heard about it on the news but didn't make it over in time to watch."

I forced a smile. "That's right. San Fermin en Nueva

Orleans," I said. "I'm sorry you missed it, but you should definitely come back next July and get a good seat. It can be a lot of fun, even for the spectators." I left out the part about my near-death experience.

"Is there a way we can get an outfit like yours for Mr. Puddles?" he asked. "We're only staying through tomorrow night, but we don't mind paying you for shipping."

"Of course." I gave the gray-muzzled dog a look. "Is this him?"

The couple nodded.

I grabbed my measuring tape and took some measurements while the elderly Mr. Puddles did his best to ignore me.

The rest of the folks in line behind them wanted the same thing. I sketched a half-dozen variations of my ensemble, mixing the pieces with some even cuter ones I'd seen in the Quarter and writing up work orders for each.

My outfit was an obvious hit with everyone except Imogene, who managed to bite her tongue until the crowd dispersed.

"You're a mess," she said with a sharp cluck of her tongue. "What are you thinking, dressed like that? This shirt is two sizes too small, and so are those shorts."

"I've got longer ones on underneath," I complained, suddenly sixteen and attempting to break school dress code again.

Imogene headed down the short hall to my stockroom muttering something about my longer shorts being too tight and the horns on my heinie.

She returned a few seconds later with a first aid kit. "Come on. Have a seat. You've got scrapes and bruises all over your

CAT GOT YOUR CROWN

arms and legs. The cuts are going to get infected if you don't take care of them right away."

I obeyed, too tired to argue and thankful to sit back and let someone else spray me with Bactine. A few yips and ouches later, I was still filthy, but bandaged.

Jack swung the front door open and moved purposefully inside. He froze at the sight of me.

"Hey," I said, feeling instantly self-conscious about the same outfit that had made me feel so sassy earlier.

Unlike Chase, who swept me into his arms at every opportunity and vowed to make things better, Jack stood back, taking his time on the approach.

When he finally made his way behind the counter, he raised a tentative arm to his side, and I collapsed against his chest. Jack cradled me in his strong arms, stock-still and silent until I pushed away several long moments later.

"I'm okay," I said.

He unbuckled the chin strap of my helmet and set the bulbous one-horned thing aside. "When Henri told me," he began. He pressed his mouth into a hard line and shook his head, seeming to change his mind about whatever he'd planned to say. "Henri's going over footage from local security cameras now, but the crowd was thick, and it's going to take time."

I gathered my sweaty hair in my hands and forced myself not to ask Jack to finish his other thought instead. "Any new leads on who might be trying to kill me this time?" I said with a little smile. "Besides the bulls."

Jack didn't smile back. "No, but that pet pageant is a

cesspool of hatred and corruption. Everyone looks normal on the surface, but get them alone and suggest someone has mentioned them in conjunction with an unnamed wrongdoing, and they lose their minds dishing grievances and throwing one another under the bus."

I frowned. "Don't tell Mrs. Smart. She'd be heartbroken."

"Yeah. I spoke with her too," he said. "She's outraged. It's a shame her husband's pageant has gone so far downhill on the morals front. I feel for her. It's rough being hurt by something you can't change." Emotion flashed over Jack's face, but he shut it down before I could get my finger on it.

"I promised her I'd do whatever I could to keep the pageant operations aboveboard while it's in my city," Jack said. "She shouldn't have to worry about these things."

I wanted to hug him again. Jack worked a dangerous job, facing off with the absolute ugliest of people and situations every day so others didn't have to. He provided safety and beauty for others at his own expense. "Thanks," I said.

His brows crowded. "For what?"

"For doing what you do. For keeping people safe. For dealing with awful things for the sake of others. So we have the luxury of pretending things are fine whenever we want to."

Jack's lips curved slightly on one side before falling back into that same flat line I hated. The flash of emotion I'd seen earlier swam again in his eyes.

"You don't have to worry about me," I told him, guessing he might be torn between making sure I was okay and getting back to work. "You've got plenty of bigger things to think about and more pressing things to do. I'm fine."

The grim set of his jaw reached his eyes. He pulled his lit phone from his pocket and checked the screen before answering. "Detective Oliver." He pinned me with an immobilizing stare as he listened to whoever was on the other end of the line. "On my way." He pushed the phone into his pocket. "I've got to run."

"Go on," I said. "Save the day. I'll see you tonight at the pageant."

The heads of blatantly eavesdropping shoppers turned to track him through the store.

He paused at the threshold and cast a look at me over his shoulder.

"You okay?" I asked when he didn't move.

The muscle along his jaw pulsed. "You come first to me, Lacy. You should know that. Before this city and before this job."

Breath caught in my throat.

Jack stepped into the sunlight, and he was gone.

I watched him move down the sidewalk outside my window with determination on his brow.

"Well, pick your mouth up off the floor," Imogene said in her slow southern drawl. "That outfit is bad enough without your tongue hanging out."

I took a seat on the stool behind me before I fell over.

Or ran after him.

Chapter Sixteen

Furry Godmother's protip for clean living: Cookies crumble; eat dough.

I took a cab home and back at lunchtime so I could shower, change, and pick up Penelope. I hated leaving her alone more than absolutely necessary. I redressed in a strapless peach dress and heels that would adhere to Mom's strict pastels policy, and if the look was too casual, I'd just choose something from the rack of preapproved garments she'd had delivered to my dressing room at the event.

When I finally made it back to work, Willow was behind the bakery counter hugging Imogene like they were long-lost sisters. My heart skipped a beat as I remembered the very important news I'd forgotten to share.

I set Penelope's carrier on the floor and ran over to join the ladies in a group hug. "I found Veda's great-granddaughter," I said against Imogene's back.

The pair separated, and Imogene dotted the corner of each eye with a handkerchief. "I know all about her," Imogene said, shooting me a pointed look as if to say, *no thanks to you.* "Veda called me before breakfast this morning." She squeezed Willow's hand. "Do you know how long Veda's been looking for you or how hard you were to find?"

Willow nodded. "My family never stayed in one place for long," she said. "I guess I was the same way. Though, now that I'm here, I understand why my dad never wanted to come to New Orleans. Mama and I wouldn't have wanted to leave."

"That's because this is where you belong," Imogene said, cupping Willow's cheek in her free palm. "Veda must be absolutely beside herself."

Willow's eyes went wide. "She is!" She looked at me and bounced on her toes. "Veda said she was looking for me because she had something for me, and when we met for breakfast this morning, she gave me this!" Willow handed me an official-looking piece of paper.

"A deed?" I scanned the lines in search of the property address, then tried to imagine its position in town. "Is this in the French Quarter?" I asked. "She gave you a home in the Quarter!"

"It's not a home." Willow's head was wagging in the negative before I finished my guess. "It's a cookie shop!"

I slid my gaze slowly in Imogene's direction. "*The* cookie shop?"

"The same one," Imogene said. "Veda's getting older, and she needs someone to take over so she can enjoy her golden years."

I wasn't sure, but it seemed to me that at over one hundred, Veda had passed her golden years and moved into daily miracle status long ago.

Willow beamed. She lifted a small container of macarons from the counter. "I made these this morning to celebrate."

I took in the pretty little cookies, recalling the way my troubles had seemed to fade while eating her fruit dip. "Did you make these at your new cookie shop?"

"Yes, and it was amazing. The place is absolutely magical," Willow gushed.

"That's what I keep hearing," I muttered. "Try one," I told Imogene.

Imogene hesitated. "I'm still full from lunch. I'll try one in a little while."

"What's wrong?" I asked, scrunching my nose. "You love macarons, and Willow made them to celebrate. You have to try one."

Imogene wavered. Concern puckered her brow.

Willow pulled the container back. "It's okay," she said. "You don't have to."

"She does," I said. I plucked a cookie from the tray and pushed it in Imogene's direction with a smile. I was usually the last person to believe Imogene's goofy stories about things that couldn't be explained, but I was almost positive the fruit dip Willow had made at my place had done something to me, and I had a perfectly cranky test subject to try my theory on.

Imogene took the cookie with a gracious smile and bit the tiniest crumb from the edge. "Delicious."

"You're so silly." I laughed. "You can't taste anything like that. Go on. Take a big bite."

Imogene slid her gaze from me to Willow, then sunk her teeth into the cookie at its center.

Willow and I stared. Willow was probably hoping Imogene would like the cookie, not realizing the opposite was impossible, and I was wondering if I was right and Willow was a real-life magic baker. The other thing that came to mind was how the magic worked. Did it have limits? Parameters? If Willow could bake her happiness into food, then what happened if she baked under duress or grief or after a bad breakup? Would all her customers take a bite and burst into tears? Leave their spouses? March themselves off a bridge or into the Mississippi?

I grimaced. Hopefully it only worked with happiness.

"Mmm," Imogene said, a smile blooming on her posy-pink lips. She took another bite, made the same noise, then shoved the rest into her mouth. "These are delicious."

"Imogene?" I asked as she reached for a second macaron. "How was business while I was away?"

"Not bad. You know how I like to meet new people."

"Uh-huh," I said, "and what did you think of the bull outfit I had on earlier?"

She tipped her head briefly over each shoulder. "I liked the way you added pants to make it more modest, and I bet you had a lot of fun down there being young and carefree, until those bulls tried to kill you."

I made a sour face. "Yeah. That put a damper on things. But you liked my outfit?"

She nodded, looking a bit mystified herself. "I didn't hate it."

I gave the macarons a long look and wondered briefly what would happen if Jack ate one.

Penelope meowed. "Oops!" I ran to free her. "Sorry, darling." The black cat that had been stalking Willow was seated outside the zippered door on Penelope's soft-sided carrier. When I opened the tiny drawbridge, Penelope slunk out stiff-legged and tail high. The cats circled each other while I tucked the carrier behind my counter.

"Would you like to come and see the cookie shop?" Willow asked. "I'm dying to show you. I'll bet we could bake a ton of pupcakes in there if you ever need to make a bunch in a hurry."

Baking in bulk was my life, and I had to admit I was curious about the magical cookie shop I'd heard so much about. I turned a bright smile on Imogene. "Mind covering for me again?" I asked.

"Not at all." She smiled. "I'll keep Penny too. Just leave these delicious cookies here with me."

"Will do," I said.

What I needed was two lifetime supplies of those. One for Imogene, and one for my mother.

The black cat leapt into Willow's arms and she snuggled it,

no longer the least bit put off by his clinginess. "Turns out this is Rune, my great-grandma's cat," she said. "Can you believe it? It's like he knew me the moment he saw me, and he's been keeping track of me since the minute I got into the city."

At the risk of sounding like Chase, I *could* believe it.

* * *

Thirty minutes later, we approached a storefront with a teal door and giant window I couldn't recall having ever seen before, on the corner of two crossroads whose names I immediately forgot. Willow stooped to set Rune on the sidewalk.

I tried the knob, but it didn't budge. "Are you sure this is the place?" I asked.

Willow set a palm on the door and it practically fell open. "Yep. This is it."

I followed her over the threshold into a shop pulled straight from the early twentieth century. Black-and-white-checked flooring. Teal walls and trim on the curved glass display case. White beadboard wrapped the counters, and the bay windows were lined in walls of exposed bricks and beams. A small black mat with white food and water bowls marked RUNE sat beneath a display table of pizzelles.

Scents of warm vanilla, caramel, and brown sugar hung in the air, punctuated with the mouth-watering zip of almonds and pound cake. I ran my fingertips over the twisted wrought-iron backs of chairs with little pink seat cushions and coordinating white round tables.

I drifted deeper into the room, admiring the rows of brightly colored cookies lining parchment paper–covered trays inside the case near a register that could have been a historic landmark on its own.

"This is marvelous," I whispered, turning in a small circle to take it all in.

I stopped as Rune slunk through the slowly opening door. Behind him, Henry LaSalle poked his head inside, a deep frown on his forehead. "Lacy?" he said, one hand on the doorknob and the other on the butt of his gun.

I did a little hip-high wave. "Hey."

Henri's gaze rose to meet Willow's, and his jaw dropped.

"This is Veda's great-granddaughter, Willow," I said. "Willow, this is Jack's former partner, Detective Henri LaSalle."

Willow smiled. "We've met. Unofficially."

"Veda gave this shop to Willow," I told Henri, unsure how long he planned to keep one hand on his gun.

Willow came to stand with me. "It's nice to meet you *officially*, Detective LaSalle," she said, a bit breathlessly. "I have the deed to the shop, if you'd like to take a look." She offered him the document, and he took it slowly, attention glued to her smiling face.

I got a little uncomfortable with all the googly eyes going on. "What brings you to the cookie shop, Henri?" I asked, scrambling to recall the shop's name or if it had one. Why couldn't I keep the details of this place in my head? I'd already forgotten exactly how we'd gotten there.

Henri relaxed his stance, finally dropping his hand away from his sidearm and apparently deciding there wasn't a need to shoot us after all. "I was making my rounds and saw the door was ajar, but Veda never opens until dusk. I assumed there was an intruder."

"Nope. Just us," I said, wondering how a woman over one hundred didn't open her shop until dusk, but my grandparents had eaten dinner at four and been in their pajamas by seven for most of my life.

"Can I get you a cookie, Detective LaSalle?" Willow asked. Her cheeks pinked and rounded with another big smile. She tugged the ends of her wild wavy locks.

"Please, call me Henri," he said, standing infinitely straighter, showing off his broad chest and shoulders and emphasizing his height.

Preening, I realized.

Willow hurried to her display counter and arranged a brightly colored cookie assortment on a small tray, then ferried it back to him.

I felt my mouth forming a little O as I waited for his cookie selection. The chemistry zigzagging through the room was already a little intoxicating. I wasn't convinced Henri could survive one of Willow's special cookies without going partially insane.

He shook his head. "No, thank you. I'm a vegan," he said, "but they sure do look delicious."

"Vegan?" Willow said the word with quiet reverence. "I'll have to think on that, but I'm sure I can make a cookie you'll love."

"No doubt," he said smoothly.

I stifled an eye roll. Good for them. They'd met five seconds ago, and they were completely into each other. That was wonderful. Lovely.

"You know what?" I said. "I'm going to go. You should get to know each other. You're new to our city," I told Willow. "Henri's an expert on it."

"I'd love to show you around," he said.

I lifted a palm. "There you go. Congratulations on your new shop." I gave Willow a hug and headed for the door. "Stop by and see me soon."

"Lacy," Henri said. His slow, thick accent stopped me in my tracks.

"Yeah?" I turned with a bright smile, hoping he wouldn't ask me about the bulls. I wasn't ready to talk about that again yet.

"You and Chase," he said, abandoning the sentence without finishing it.

I waited, and so did he.

I knew what Chase and I looked like together. Knew what Henri had seen when Chase had come to my rescue in Jackson Square. We were comfortable together, physically. Chase was doting and protective. He was a profoundly perfect and wonderful friend.

"No," I said finally. Even without knowing Henri's exact question, I was sure this was the answer.

Henri gave me a stiff dip of his chin. "Tell him," he said.

My stomach flipped as I contemplated what exactly he'd meant by the simple command, but I was too cowardly to ask.

Chapter Seventeen

Furry Godmother's advice for the bold: When things get fishy, go fishing.

I walked several blocks before digging my phone from my pocket and dialing Jack.

He answered on the first ring. "Oliver."

"Hey. It's me," I stalled, not quite sure why I'd called or what to say.

"Kristen?"

"Kristen!" I barked.

"Are you still up for that drink," he asked. The uncharacteristic pep in his voice balled my fingers into fists at my side. "I can meet you somewhere, or you can swing by here."

I shut my mouth before it completely unhinged. *Swing by his place?* Was he serious? Jack never invited anyone to his massive estate. His significant inherited wealth wasn't something he liked to talk about, and he never invited people over. The home was his oasis. His sanctuary. His Bat Cave. "It's two o'clock in the afternoon," I snapped, no longer able to hold my tongue. "Who is Kristen?"

Jack coughed. "Sorry. My mistake. Is this Jenny?"

I looked at the sky. "Never mind," I said. "This was stupid. I have to go."

"Hey." Jack's voice was suddenly low and confident, the steady, almost dangerous sound I'd come to know and love. "Lacy. I was just kidding. Your mom said you do that to her sometimes, and I thought it was funny. I guess I did it wrong. What can I do for you?"

I stopped walking and gave my heart a minute to settle, then cleared my throat. Twice. "How's the investigation going?"

He made an ugly throaty sound. "This pageant is one frustration after another," he said. "How are things going in the Quarter?"

I started moving again. "How do you know I'm in the Quarter?"

"Henri just called."

"Of course he did." I refused to ask what Henri had had to say. "Did he tell you he took one look at Veda's great-granddaughter, Willow, and fell in love?"

Jack released a long breath into the receiver. "It happens sometimes."

I hailed a cab and climbed inside. "Furry Godmother, Magazine Street," I told the driver. "I'm headed back to work,"

I told Jack, "but we should talk later. Will I see you tonight at the Tea Room?"

"Nah," he said. "Bomb threat. The Tea Room is shut down while the bomb squad goes through it."

"A bomb threat?" I yipped. Good grief! I tried to wrap my head around the words. "Is everything okay? Was there a bomb?"

"Not as far as we can tell," he said.

"That's why you thought I'd said *bomb* earlier, not *bulls*," I guessed.

"No. I guessed *bomb* because no one since the invention of the cell phone has called and caught someone in the middle of Jackson Square running from actual bulls."

I laughed. "You don't know that."

"I do," he said quickly. "I absolutely do. Your life is bananas."

I smiled at the passing scenery, enjoying the casual chat with the most intense man I knew. "You didn't mention the bomb when you stopped by Furry Godmother this morning," I said. "Why not? It's kind of a big deal, don't you think?"

"I figured you'd had a bad enough day, and you'd hear about it soon. The squad was running a sweep while I came to check in with you. Local cops were holding down the fort."

My other line rang, and I pulled the phone away from my cheek to see who was calling. "It's my mom," I said.

"Tell her I said hello, and I'll see you when I wrap things up for the day."

"You will?"

"If I'm lucky," he said. "Later, Crocker." Jack disconnected, and I smiled against the phone, drinking in the endorphins.

The phone rang in my palm, and I groaned. "Hey, Mom."

"Lacy?" she asked.

"Yes."

"This is your mother."

I rolled my eyes. "I know, Mom. Your name and face come up every time you dial me from your cell phone, plus I recognize your voice."

"There was a bomb threat at the Tea Room this morning, and they've decided to postpone the pageant until tomorrow," she said, ignoring me like she always did during that portion of our how-cell-phones-work conversation.

"I know."

"You know? How is that possible?"

I smiled.

"Jack," she said. "What else did he say?"

I rested my head against the sun-warmed vinyl upholstery of the cab as it crawled up to a red light. "That he will see me tonight."

Mom was silent for a long beat. "I was going to invite you for dinner. I have news."

"How about breakfast?" I countered.

"You said no to breakfast the last time I invited you to meet me."

I rubbed my forehead. "That was only because I'd already promised to meet Scarlet somewhere else. I'm free tomorrow. I'd love to meet you then."

"Fine, but I'm not cooking." She hung up before I could say goodbye.

I dropped my head forward. Somehow I'd managed to irk

my mother in less time than it had taken the light to change. That had to be a Crocker record.

* * *

I changed into cut-off shorts and a tank top the minute I walked through the door that night. Despite the million things I could have been stressed about, my mind had drifted back to Grandpa Smacker on repeat after seeing Willow's new cookie shop. I'd helped Imogene at Furry Godmother until closing time, but the entire bakery display case had already been empty when I got there at three. I wasn't a magical baker like Willow, but the things I made were special in their own ways. They were delicious and nutritious, for starters, plus they'd come to symbolize my successful reentry into the Garden District world. My pet-friendly recipes had gotten me the job at Grandpa Smacker, which had helped Jack with his investigation into his grandpa's death, and that investigation had brought me closer to Jack.

I tied an apron around my waist and got to work organizing the ingredients that were safe for pets on my countertop. I skipped the yogurt and peanut butter this time. I made enough sweet things already. It was time I made something savory. Something an owner could buy for lunch and share safely with their pet as they walked through the streets during the Fall Food Festival together.

I flipped the television on for background noise as I worked and waited to see the news coverage of the morning's bull fiasco. I found a rhythm in the kitchen that carried me through multiple recipes and most of the evening news.

When the doorbell rang, it took a minute for me to orient myself. I wiped my hands in the material of my apron and struggled to pull my mind back to the moment. It felt a lot like coming up from under water.

Scarlet dropped her keys on the coffee table before I could make it to the door. "I'm here to help," she said. "What can I do?" Scarlet stopped to look at the island full of still steaming products. Her faded NOLA Saints T-shirt and worn-out jeans made her look impossibly younger. The low-riding pigtails probably helped. "I thought you'd be upset," she said. "Chase told me you were almost killed today. Then my mother said your mother told her there was a bomb scare at the pet pageant. Are you okay?"

"I'm fine," I said for the millionth time. "I was trying to come up with a recipe for the Fall Food Festival. Taste this." I offered her a meatball on a toothpick.

Scarlet popped it in her mouth and chewed slowly. "I'm not going to lie," she said, "It's not great."

"Okay." I grabbed a pen and paper. "What's it missing?"

"Salt? Pepper? A little punch of something."

"Great." I set the notebook aside. "Now this." I passed her a napkin with a bacon-and-rice patty.

"What is it?" she asked, sniffing it first this time.

"Bacon, rice, chicken broth, bread crumbs, and an egg."

Scarlet's ruby-red lips pulled down on the sides. "Are you feeding me dog food again?"

"It's not dog food," I said. "I told you. I have to make a recipe people will enjoy, and their pets can safely share."

She imitated a crossing guard, raising a palm in my

direction. "No thank you. Find another guinea pig. It's bad enough Carter makes me try all the little jars of baby food, and that's actual people food, just pureed.

"One bite," I begged. "And this is all people food. I'm just trying to get the right combination, and none of it has been pureed. Here. I'll pour the wine while you think it over." I slid a glass of cabernet in her direction.

"One bite."

I waited while she chewed the bacon-and-rice patty. "This isn't bad. For dog food," she added, swigging the wine.

"I think you're too in your head about it being dog food," I said. "It's a combination of ingredients you eat all the time. I've just put them together, without any other ingredients that aren't safe for canines."

Scarlet finished the little patty, then pulled a laptop from her satchel and powered it up. "I didn't hate it," she said. "Now it's your turn. You have to watch some of these nanny applications with me. I've narrowed it down to the handful of applicants that didn't make my skin crawl."

"Interesting." I moved to her side of the counter and took a seat on the stool beside hers. "What kind of people sent nanny application videos that made your skin crawl?"

"You don't want to know."

The doorbell rang.

"Be right back." I went to answer the door and found Jack on the porch in dark-washed jeans and a fitted black button-down. The shirt was unbuttoned at the neck, revealing the curved collar of a black T-shirt beneath. His sleeves were rolled to the elbows, and his hair was still damp from a recent shower.

"I didn't realize Scarlet would be here," he said softly.

"Neither did I," I answered. "Come in." I took his hand and led him to the kitchen. "Scarlet came to check on me after the bull thing and to ask me to help her screen video applications from potential nannies."

Scarlet whistled as we walked into the kitchen. "Nice," she said, giving Jack an appreciative nod.

Jack gave her a crooked smile and shook his head. "Thanks."

"You going on a date?" she asked.

He flipped his gaze to me, then quickly back. "Just checking in on Lacy too."

"Good." Scarlet patted the stool beside her. "I'm glad you're here. I can't think of a better vetter than a cop."

Jack took a seat. He swiped half a chicken BLT off the counter and took a bite.

Scarlet and I watched as he chewed. "Now this," she said, handing him a meatball on a toothpick before he could take a second bite of the sandwich.

He took it, but he gave the array of food on the counter another look. "This is dog food, isn't it?"

Scarlet barked a loud laugh and clapped her hands. "She got me, too."

"It's not dog food," I argued.

Jack tried the meatball. "No," he said, spitting it into a paper towel. "Bad."

"What about the sandwich?" I asked.

He took another bite. "I like the sandwich, but it could use some mustard."

I raised my arms overhead in a V for victory. "Then it's decided. That's what we're serving to people at the Fall Food Festival," I said. "Every single ingredient is safe for pets, and it tastes good enough for people. I can blend up some special dips for the humans to use with their portions."

He ripped his half-a-sandwich down the middle and handed me one side.

I accepted, and he tapped his half to mine. "Good work, Crocker."

"Get a room," Scarlet said with a grin, "and pass me one of those sandwiches."

I obeyed, and Scarlet pushed play on the first video nanny application. "Pay close attention. This is my children's lives we're talking about."

"So, no pressure," I said.

The three of us sat silently through seven one-minute applications before Scarlet shut her laptop. "That's all," she said. "The rest were immediate nos. What did you guys think?"

"I liked the one who had a puppet," I said. "That was cute."

She wrinkled her nose. "It was a grown man with a sock and a magic marker," she said. "Jack?"

He tapped the screen of his phone for several seconds before turning it to face us. "The sock guy is a registered pedophile. I notified his parole officer."

Scarlet went sheet-white. "Oh my word. What am I doing?" She shoved her laptop back into its bag in a rush. "I can't leave my children with a stranger. What's wrong with me?"

"You're an exhausted mother of four who wants to get a little more sleep this decade?" Jack guessed.

"You'd like to leave the house without a pint-sized entourage at least once a week?" I asked.

She rolled her eyes. "At this point, I'd like to use the bathroom without a pint-sized entourage."

I made a puke face.

Jack laughed. "Wow."

Scarlet snapped her bag shut and did a whole-body shiver. "Never mind. I'm not getting a nanny. Everyone's crazy."

"Why not ask your old nanny?" I suggested. "I'm sure Imogene will take over for me when I need a nanny someday."

Jack turned on his stool to face me. "When are you going to need a nanny?"

"I don't know," I said, swiveling to face him. "I'm thirty. That puts kids on the five-year plan, I guess." I stopped to consider that a minute, then filled my glass with wine and took a long sip.

"What about you?" Scarlet asked Jack. "Is there a crew of Jack Juniors in your future?"

He looked from Scarlet to me. "I hope so." He stood and stretched. "I think I'll leave you to it," he said. "Let me know if you need anything."

I stood too. "Everything okay?"

"Yep." He nodded. "If you find a nanny you like, Scarlet, let me know. I'm happy to run a full background check."

She smiled. "Thanks, Jack. Sorry if I freaked you out by asking about kids."

"Wasn't that," he said. "I want kids." He headed for the door, and I followed.

"You don't have to go," I said. "You just got here."

"It's fine. It's not easy for Scarlet to get out and be alone with friends," he said. "Hang out. Have fun. Then give me a call. I think you and I should make that date soon."

"Okay," I said, unsure what was happening.

"What's wrong?" he asked, angling toward me, grouchy, thinking face in place.

I shook my head, unsure. "You said date, but it feels like you're breaking up with me."

His brows rose. "What? No." Jack took a tiny step in my direction and set a hand on the curve of my waist. "No," he repeated.

"Are you sure?"

"Absolutely. I'll see you soon, okay?" he whispered.

I nodded, then stood immobilized as he drove away.

Scarlet shut the door for me and steered me to the couch. "Sit down. I found news coverage of the bomb." She handed me a glass of wine and took the seat by my side. The BREAK-ING NEWS logo flashed over the screen, with prerecorded footage of the bomb squad, K-9 dogs, and a robot gathered outside the Audubon Tea Room. Jack was in the frame speaking with a uniformed officer. "You're going to explain what I just walked in on during the next commercial break," she said.

If only I could.

Scarlet and I watched silently as a local news crew covered the bomb threat at the National Pet Pageant, then recapped Viktor's death. The reporter caught Mrs. Smart and my mother heading into the building and stopped them.

"Oh no," Scarlet said. "Did you know your mom was interviewed?"

"No." I squinted, hoping Mom didn't do or say anything that would horrify her, or me, later. "She told me she had news when I spoke to her earlier. This must be it."

First, Mrs. Smart graciously answered a thousand questions about the pageant's history and her husband's involvement in making it a national event. Then she spoke confidently about the New Orleans Police Department and their ability to sort things out. When the reporter followed up with allegations about corruption within the event that might have led to the recent "bad luck streak," Mrs. Smart blanched, and my mother intervened.

"Hello," she said, stepping into the camera's view. "I'm Violet Conti-Crocker, president of the National Pet Pageant Welcoming Committee. I believe you're asking Mrs. Smart to speculate on the reason for a bomb threat and a murder." She made a gravely serious face and shook her head slowly in a perfect show of superiority and disdain.

The reporter shot the camera a worried look.

"Do you truly believe that this woman has some inside knowledge of these crimes?" she continued.

"Well, n-no," he stammered.

"Then you know she can't possibly speak to a criminal's motives with any degree of accuracy, but you still ask. Why is that? Are you colossally daft, or are you being intentionally ridiculous to stimulate ratings by acting a fool?" She lifted a perfectly sculpted brow, and the reporter went red.

The news cut to a commercial.

"Gotta love your mother," Scarlet said. "She set that man straight with a couple questions and an eyebrow."

"Did she look okay to you?" I asked. Mom had turned the unsuspecting reporter around and made it look effortless, but I knew her, and I thought I'd seen something unusual in her eyes. Worry? Maybe a hint of fear? "I'd better give her a call."

Scarlet sipped her wine. "Go for it." She scanned her phone while I dialed. "But when you hang up, you're going to tell me what Jack Oliver was up to."

"He invited me on a date," I said, mystified.

"A date-date?"

I nodded. "Yeah, I think so."

Scarlet kicked her feet onto my coffee table and smiled. "About damn time."

Chapter Eighteen

Furry Godmother's point to ponder: You might get more flies with honey, but honestly, who wants flies?

After a rousing breakfast performance of *has-everyone-lost-their-damn-minds* by my mother and multiple detailed recaps of all the ways she'd worked to troubleshoot any possible situation before the National Pet Pageant arrived, followed by a grand finale of *how-could-I-possibly-have-prepared-for-this*, I was on my way to work with a doggie bag of crepes and a budding headache.

Penelope was curled in her soft carrier beside me, strapped in safely by the seat belt and sunning her face in the lovely morning light.

I couldn't blame my mother for her foul disposition. She'd worked for months to make the National Pet Pageant's stint in New Orleans shine. She'd performed every manner of troubleshooting before the show arrived. She'd planned for scenarios no one had thought were remotely possible except her, and still this week had been a total nightmare. She hadn't planned for a murder or the complicated and terrifying aftermath.

If there was a silver lining for Mom, it was that there were only a few days left until she could put it all behind her and pretend it had never happened. Dogs performed tonight, assuming there wasn't another bomb threat, and tomorrow was a smaller, hodgepodge of performances, mostly of birds. Three nights from now, the winners would be crowned, and we'd have a legendary reception. Then the National Pet Pageant would move on.

I stopped at the next intersection and admired an expanse of plumeria pushing its beautiful white flowers through a nearby fence. I needed to recenter myself before I made it to work, but Mom's sheer exasperation was on a loop in my head. Dramatic as she could be, she was right about this week, and the awfulness seemed to be escalating. Viktor's death. My threats. Wild bulls. A bomb scare. Her lament about the fact that I hadn't called to tell her about the bulls had lasted through two cups of coffee.

I needed to get in front of this mess before someone else got hurt. Or worse.

I hit my blinker and checked the time on my dashboard. It was early, and I had only twenty minutes to spare, but I needed answers. Real ones. I motored across Mom's neighborhood to Coliseum Street and slid my Volkswagen against the curb outside an adorable Italianate cottage with a pristine lawn lined in stately iron fencing. A familiar white truck was parked across the street, and it took me a minute to remember where else I'd seen it. It looked like the construction company truck I'd seen outside the Saenger Theatre when Big Splash ran off. The rusty eyesore was out of place on a street where even the smallest home sold for two million dollars and laborers were kept painstakingly out of sight. I couldn't help thinking it wasn't a coincidence to find the truck here as well.

I grabbed Penny's carrier and hustled up the walkway to Eva's magnificent column-lined porch. The doorbell made an enchanting sound under pressure of my finger, and I smiled at all the hanging flower baskets and planters around me. With any luck, I'd catch Eva before she ran off to meet with Mom and the committee ladies. With even more luck, she wouldn't tell my mother that I'd shown up unannounced, first thing in the morning, without a gift or food of some sort. Mom had enough things to be upset about already. She didn't need another reason to question her parenting.

A scuffle on the other side of the closed door set me back a step. "Eva?" I called, loud enough to be heard through the door, I hoped, without irritating a neighbor. I leaned closer and closed my eyes to listen. The rasp of heavy whispering alternated with batches of silence.

I pressed the doorbell again. "Eva? It's Lacy Crocker."

"Coming," Eva called.

The door opened, and a man better suited for fitness modeling than home maintenance stepped out. A tool belt rode low on his hips and his shirt had a company logo to match the truck I'd seen parked across the street. He tugged on the brim of his ball cap and nodded in greeting before jogging down the steps and climbing behind the wheel of the white pickup.

I turned back to the open door.

Eva forced a tight smile. "Hi, Lacy." She tightened the ties of a short satin robe around her waist, then pushed a hand through the long brown waves tumbling over her shoulders. The nightgown beneath her little robe was black, silk, and not much longer than the short robe. She offered a small smile. "What are you doing here?"

I looked over my shoulder as the truck pulled away, then turned back to Eva, certain I had just put a couple of new puzzle pieces together without ever stepping inside. "I wanted to talk with you again about Viktor Petrov," I said. "I have a feeling Jack's getting close to arresting you, and I think you can stop it from happening if you'd just tell me what I'm missing."

Eva motioned me inside and pressed the door closed behind us. "Would you like some coffee?"

"Sure." I'd taken in enough coffee at my parents' place to launch a rocket into orbit, but seeing as how I'd failed to bring Eva a gift or warn her I was coming, the least I could do was be agreeable.

I followed her across high-polished heart-of-pine flooring to an airy room with large symmetrical windows and fresh flowers at every turn. The parlor's high ceilings were a delight to the eyes, lined in elaborately detailed moldings, pinched together at the corners by cherub cornices. The windows were crystal clear with fantastic views of an immaculately kept garden and flanked with white built-in bookcases. Her walls were a warm, buttery yellow and the furniture a crisp white with brightly colored throw pillows. A braided rug played anchor to an ornate coffee table where a carafe and service for two awaited.

Eva filled a delicate teacup to the brim with shaky hands. "I've told you everything I know," she said. "I'm not sure what else I can do besides trust that Detective Oliver will find the true killer."

I took a seat and rested Penelope's carrier at my ankles. "I'm sure Jack would love to know you have so much faith in him," I said, "but the thing about being framed is that all the available evidence will be pointed directly at you unless you can turn it around. Jack's good, and he's trying to get to the bottom of this, but there's only so much he can do if you're intentionally withholding information, which, by the way, is also known as obstruction."

Her cheeks flamed red, and she touched the tips of her fingers to her lips.

Her little nightie and mussy hair itched in my head. "Did that workman I saw leaving here sleep over last night?" I asked, hating to be rude, but needing the information more than I could afford to care about manners.

Eva folded her hands in her lap and made a strange sound.

"I don't care either way," I assured her, "but it seems to me that someone expecting a worker would have at least put on pants or found a hairbrush, and I know how things work in this district. Everyone you know would die of sudden collective heart failure if they knew you were dating a random laborer."

"Marcellus isn't random," she said, "and he's more than a laborer."

I sipped the coffee and smiled sweetly. "Oh?"

Eva puffed air through her little nose. "Marcellus is a second-generation Cuban American who started a handyman business in Holy Cross and plans to grow it into something big," she said. "He's a good guy. So much more fun than anyone in our snooty circle and more respectful than the bozos my parents fix me up with. Marcellus is brave and determined, kind and protective." She wet her lips and straightened her spine. "I think I'm falling in love with him."

My chest warmed at the unexpected confession. "He's very handsome, too."

She smiled. "Yes."

"Is he part of the reason you aren't telling anyone the real story about what happened in the balcony before Viktor fell?" I asked. She'd said Marcellus was protective. Was it possible that he'd caught Viktor pawing at her and had come to her defense, maybe even giving Viktor a shove that sent him stumbling for balance and toppling right over the rail? "Did something happen between Marcellus and Viktor?" I asked.

"No," she said, a look of confusion on her brow. "Of course not. They never met." A heartbeat later, her eyes stretched wide. She slid to the edge of her seat and leaned her elbows on her knees. "Marcellus wouldn't hurt anyone, and he wasn't in the balcony when Viktor fell."

"But he was at the theater?" So it had been his truck. I'd seen it when Big Splash ran off. "Did he know how Viktor treated you?"

"Yes, and he hated it. That was why Marcellus snuck into the theater to see me. He wanted to be sure I was okay. I slipped away to be with him," she said. "I told the committee I had a headache so they'd let me out of sight for a few minutes to go take an aspirin. I met Marcellus in the back hallway and took him to the upstairs office outside the soundboard and shut the door. We were . . ." She turned her eyes away from me. ". . . visiting . . . when we heard a commotion."

I slid forward too, unwilling to miss a single syllable of what she'd been hiding. "What did you hear while you were visiting?"

"Viktor's rumbling voice, mostly. There were a few muted sounds of movement, but nothing significant or out of the ordinary. I swear to you. If I thought I knew something that would help find his killer, I would've already told you or the detective, but I don't know anything."

"What did you do when you heard him outside the room where you were hiding?"

"I panicked," she said. "I knew if Viktor caught us, he'd make a huge scene over it and use his big mouth to be sure everyone in the theater knew what he'd seen. I assumed he'd be extra rude because I'd rejected his advances so adamantly. He refused to take no for an answer, which was why I'd eventually hit him. Then, to find me in the arms of someone like Marcellus"—she sighed—"it would have been a major blow to his fat-headed ego. There was also the possibility that Viktor would lash out, say something hurtful or cruel to me in Marcellus's presence that would make him fight back, and that was sure to end poorly, so I sent Marcellus out of the room first. I couldn't afford to be seen walking out with him. So he left, and I stayed to straighten myself up." Color crept over her freckled baby face as the implication of what she'd just confessed to settled in.

"That's why you didn't speak up," I said. "You were embarrassed."

"I had no reason to be in that office or upstairs at all," she said.

"Did Marcellus see anyone with Viktor when he left?" I asked.

"He said he didn't look. When he got downstairs, he heard Jack call a lockdown, so he angled his face away from everyone and kept moving until he was outside the building. All that he had on his mind was getting back to his truck without being noticed. He left before he could get caught inside the building and cause any trouble."

I tried to imagine the moving parts in her story.

Marcellus could easily have confronted and tossed Viktor over the balcony without a problem. He was strong enough, and no one had even known he was at the theater. It would be the perfect crime as long as his girlfriend didn't suspect him or tell anyone he'd been there. "Why didn't you tell Jack any of this?" I asked. "He doesn't care about district drama or politics. He doesn't care who you love or where you love him. He just wants to clear your name."

Eva kneaded her thin hands on her lap. "Marcellus asked me not to tell, and I agreed. I'd already lied about the headache, and I'm hiding a boyfriend no one will approve of." Her voice dripped with despair. "Everyone knows there's someone in my life right now. They just don't know who he is, and I'm not ready to tell them. There's speculation that I'm involved with a wealthy older man or some prince from another country. My parents will be horrified when they learn the truth. My friends will make fun of me."

I tried not to look as sick as I felt. "You said you love him."

"I do," she pleaded, lacing her fingers together and extending the knot in my direction. "I do, but it's not that easy and you know it."

"Important things rarely come easily," I said. I tried not to be angry on behalf of all the other women like Eva who felt they could love only someone preapproved by their parents. "What did you see when you left the room?"

She pressed her lips together and raised her shoulders. "Nothing. There was no one in the balcony, but I could hear Detective Oliver downstairs yelling and a few people were crying. I looked over the edge to see what was going on, thinking something had happened to one of the pets. I never expected to see Viktor." Her eyes glossed with tears.

"Eva," I said carefully, "I believe you, but I have to tell Jack what you just told me."

She slumped. "I know."

"I'll wait until I see him tonight, so you have time to do the right thing and make the call yourself."

She dragged her gaze up to meet mine, a mix of guilt and remorse in her eyes.

"And you should probably tell your family and friends about Marcellus or cut him loose," I said. "I'm no expert in love, but I can say as a fellow human being that I'd rather be dumped over someone else's issues and family drama than crushed because the person I care about thinks I'm something to be ashamed of. If you love him, do what's right by him." I stood and lifted Penelope's carrier into my arms. "Jack will be discreet with your personal information, but he'll want to talk to you again once I tell him all this."

Eva wiped the tears from her eyes and nodded but made no move to stand.

"I'll see you tonight," I said. "I can find my way out."

*　　*　　*

I arrived on Magazine Street in time to park two blocks away from Furry Godmother and run to the shop through scorching heat and humidity. I flipped the CLOSED sign to OPEN at precisely ten AM and thanked my lucky stars I had central air-conditioning.

I set Penelope free and loaded baked goods into the display case at warp speed, hoping to get ahead of the crowd.

Shoppers began to trickle in almost immediately.

I texted Scarlet to remind her she'd promised to find me a part-time shop keep before Imogene got completely fed up and quit.

Scarlet replied with a smile-face emoticon and a tiny thumbs-up. HAVE THE PERFECT GIRL. IRONING OUT DETAILS.

I breathed a little easier. Hopefully whoever she had in mind was less uptight and bizarre than the weird mix of nanny applicants she'd received. Then again, beggars couldn't be choosers, and right now, I was a full-fledged beggar. I could deal with bizarre as long as it showed up on time and helped customers.

By noon, I was spinning in circles from the bakery to the register to the telephone and all through the store, answering questions and taking orders on my own. I'd given Imogene the day off for a much-needed break, and I was partially regretting it already. I considered putting Scarlet's skates on for added speed, but I'd probably never wear those again without seeing that lead bull's flaring nostrils bearing down on me.

A group of ladies with humidity-resistant hair and high-end pastel ensembles moved toward the counter with practiced steps. Their small, steady smiles were Stepford quality, the definitive result of too many etiquette and cotillion classes.

I fixed a matching look in place to greet them.

"Hey, y'all," I said. "Out for lunch?"

The NPP Welcoming Committee ladies let their smiles drop. "We came to check on you," Elysia Mae Stevens said. "We heard about what happened with the bulls yesterday, and we thought we should drop in and see how you're holding up."

"I'm great," I lied. "Ready to get back to work tonight and see this pageant through."

A few of the ladies noticed the angry cuts and bruises on my hands and arms and stared. I forced myself not to hide them behind my back. "Where's Eva?" I asked, surprised to see she hadn't joined them yet and hoping it was because she'd decided to do the right thing.

"Home," Elysia said. "She told Reece Ann that Detective

Oliver was coming for a visit. Apparently, Eva had something else she wanted to tell him."

I didn't like the way Elysia shifted her lips into a tiny cat-that-ate-the-canary smile as she delivered the news, but I was proud of Eva for making the tough decision.

Reece Ann looked as if she'd been slapped. "She swore me to secrecy, Elysia. Why on earth would you go and announce it like that?"

Elysia slid her eyes in Reece Ann's direction. "You weren't so worried about keeping Eva's secrets when you were telling them to me."

I clapped my hands together. "Well, I'm glad Eva thought of something else," I said. "Maybe this will change things for her and be exactly what Detective Oliver needs to find out what really happened to Viktor." And hopefully Eva would put some clothes on before Jack got there.

"Rumor has it Eva is hiding a secret boyfriend," Elysia said. "You seem to know Detective Oliver better than anyone else. Any chance it's him?"

I clamped my jaw shut before it could swing open, then reapplied my practiced smile. "Hard to say," I told her, "but I'm sure if the rumors are true about Eva and a secret boy-friend, she's probably just trying to enjoy their time together before everyone starts sticking their noses in it."

The committee ladies broke formation at that, and most went to peruse my shop.

Reece Ann and Elysia stayed behind.

"I don't think the detective is seeing Eva," Reece Ann said softly. "She's only been hiding her guy for a month or two, but my brother saw Detective Oliver at a benefit auction in March, and he said women were coming on to the detective left and right, but he told every single one of them that he already had someone in his life and he wasn't looking to botch things up."

I fought the frown tugging on my features. Had Jack been blowing those ladies off politely, or was he hiding a girlfriend from me?

Why did everyone in this district have to keep so many secrets?

Reece Ann gave a beleaguered sigh. "I can't wait for this week to end."

"Amen," Elysia echoed. "The next time this district hosts a national event, I'm planning a month in France to avoid it."

"If it wasn't for your mother's fortitude," Reece Ann said, "this year's pageant would have been over before it started. First we were short an MC because the original one died. Then his replacement was disqualified for taking bribes. Now we're on our third MC, which means another judge will move up, and we'll need another judge."

"And they can't keep appointing judges from our commit-tee," Elysia said. "Lacy's already judging, and Eva's missing so much time over this nonsense murder allegation that we're working our tails off to keep up as it is. Then there are the venue issues. The Tea Room is pretty, but it's not a theater, and since we were forced to change locations on a moment's notice, the logistics are awful."

"Agreed," Reece Ann said. "Yet again, Mrs. Conti-Crocker saved the day. I bet no other city has a planning committee with a head like hers. The pageant is lucky it's having all this trouble in New Orleans, where we don't let things stop us."

Elysia nodded. "True. We've dealt with and overcome a bunch of unpleasant challenges so far, but I'm starting to worry about what might be coming next."

"So true," Reece Ann said.

They weren't alone in that concern, and I didn't want to venture a guess on what was waiting around the next corner. Whatever it was, experience promised it wouldn't be good.

Chapter Nineteen

Furry Godmother's advice for housekeeping: Pick up the pieces of your life before you trip on them.

I swung my car into the designated judges' parking outside the Audubon Tea Room, then hurried up the walkway toward the foyer doors. According to a text I'd received from Eva, she was glad I'd dropped in on her this morning. She'd had a long talk with Jack, and she planned to tell everyone about her relationship with Marcellus, maybe even tonight. I couldn't wait to congratulate her on her bravery in doing the right thing.

Mrs. Hams and the Llama Mamas waved as I approached. They'd set up a tiki hut outside the main doors to the Tea Room and dressed the llamas in grass skirts and leis. Anyone donating to their charity received a plastic coconut filled with shave ice and a "signed" photo of the llamas in hula attire. The signature was just a hoof stamp, but people were loving it.

Families crowded around the hut for a chance to donate, pet the animals, and spoon up the fruity dessert. I didn't blame them. It was ninety with a real feel of one-oh-two, and I could use some pineapple-coconut shave ice in my life. I stroked a llama's head, dropped some cash in the jar to support a local literacy program, then accepted a lei and mini cup of heaven. The whole scenario was beyond adorable and wildly effective. In other words, it was just the kind of thing to make my mother crazy.

I gave myself a brain freeze finishing the ice before reaching the Tea Room doors. I passed my lei to an exited child and puffed air against one palm, hoping Mom wouldn't smell the tasty sweets on my breath.

The foyer was crowded, but significantly cooler than outside. Members of the FFA lined one side of the space, holding fluffy yellow chicks and speaking to a handful of moms with kids in strollers about the adorable little peeps. On the other side of the room, the Jazzy Chicks were collecting donations for our local children's hospital, and the display table had a crowd three people deep in every direction, all angling for a chance to drop their money into the extraordinary machine Mom had gotten from her artist friend. The globe was nearly full of cash already, and I couldn't say for sure, but it seemed as if the Chicks might beat the Llamas this time around.

I slid a few folded bills from my wallet into the FFA's burlap sack before hurrying into the Tea Room. It didn't seem fair that Mom had nicked their donations with her fancy display, but the children's hospital was a wonderful cause. Still, even Mom would admit the poor yodeling farm children should get a little something for their efforts.

Mom shot me a proud grin as I passed. She was schmoozing with donators and clearly pleased as punch with her success.

I wound my way behind the judges' table and tucked my purse beneath the white linen skirt. Chase was holding court in the seat beside mine. A line of people and their pets were throwing rapid-fire legal questions his way.

I took my seat and watched as he unleashed his megawatt smile and sweet southern charm on the unsuspecting masses. Chase Hawthorne was one hundred percent as smart as he was pretty, and he never missed a beat. The line before him didn't stop until he was out of business cards and the lights were getting dim.

"Nice work; now skedaddle," I said. "The show's about to start, and I don't need a lawyer."

"You need something in that dress," he said, eyeballing me like a sailor on leave. "Protection, I think. Someone to stick close and guard your body."

"Oh my goodness," I chided, sucking in my stomach and squaring my shoulders. "Knock it off. The judge who sits there is going to be mad when he finds you in his seat."

Chase leaned on one hip and dug something from the pocket of his gray slim-fit dress pants. He slicked the name tag on the breast of his suit jacket. CHASE HAWTHORNE. JUDGE.

"Shut. Up." I laughed at the delightful surprise. "They made you a judge? Why?"

"I saw a need and offered my services," he said with a grin. "The fact that there are a limited number of impartial folks hanging around here who are both willing and available on a moment's notice probably helped my chances. Mrs. Smart and the other judges agreed and voted me in unanimously."

"Imagine that," I said with a smile. "You charmed an old lady and a bunch of women who are already in love with you to get what you wanted. Shocking."

He kicked back in his seat and stretched long legs beneath the table. "You think I'm charming."

Mom took the mic, and a spotlight splashed over her.

Chase leaned in my direction. "Cheer up. Your work here just got a lot more fun."

I swiveled forward before Mom caught me talking, then bumped Chase's shoe with mine. "I'm glad you're here," I said.

"Back at ya."

We watched dogs do things I didn't know dogs could do. Feats of speed and agility. Finding hidden toys. A conga line of poodles in every size. The tricks were hilarious and amazing. I clapped like a lunatic every time.

When Tippy, the shopping terrier, appeared, I had no idea what was in store. She pranced onto an adorable set painted to look like a miniature shopping center and went straight for a small silver cart. The pink apron at her waist was lined in white lace, and the matching bow on her head was perfection. Tippy's oversized shopping list hung from one side of her cart, easily visible to the crowd. EGGS, MILK, FLOUR, ICING. Tippy pushed the cart on two legs along the little aisle to a typical Muzak tune. She collected one of each item from the list, placed the selections into her cart, and pushed the cart to the checkout. Her trainer mimed ringing up the sale, bagged the items, then placed them in the back seat of a remote-control car. Tippy hopped into the front seat, and the music changed to Aretha Franklin's "Freeway of Love." The crowd cheered as Tippy took a couple of spins around her trainer while he traded the store set for a small kitchen, complete with pink appliances and bowls marked with Ts. The trainer moved Tippy's groceries to the counter, and then Tippy took a seat in front of the little stove until a small *ding!* interrupted the music. Tippy grabbed a towel that was tied to the handle of her little oven and tugged the door down. Then she did the same with a second bit of fabric tied to an interior shelf. The shelf slid out to reveal a small cake, and Tippy dug in.

I was on my feet with cheers and laughter. How could I not appreciate a tiny baking terrier?

When the night finally ended, I was completely exhausted from the thrill and still had hours of baking to do.

Chase walked me to my car at a leisurely stroll, tossing peanuts from the green room into the air and catching them in his mouth. "I'm still laughing at the wiener dog dressed as a wiener," he said. "I haven't laughed that hard since the last time we were judges together. We should do this again tomorrow."

"Deal," I said, "but I don't think those dogs like to be called wiener dogs. It's actually pronounced *ween-ie* dogs."

Chase laughed. "My bad. I'll try to keep it straight next time."

A black town car stopped beside us, and the back door popped open. Mom leaned her head out. The back seat was packed with NPP Welcoming Committee ladies. "Lacy?" Mom called. "We're going out for drinks. Why don't you join us?"

"Sorry," I said. "I'm beat, and I have a ton of baking to do before I can sleep. I've got to go home and get to it. If I have a drink first, I'll be asleep before the first round of kitty kisses come out of the oven."

"Don't worry about the drinks," Mom said. "You ride with us, and Chase can take your car to your house for you."

I looked at Chase. "Is she drunk now?" I asked. "I didn't say anything about not wanting to leave my car. I said I have work to do. I swear she only hears what she wants."

"If that was true," Mom interrupted, "I'd hear you agreeing right now."

Chase smiled. "It could be fun. I think you should go."

I gave Chase a crazy face, then turned to Mom and waved. "No thank you," I said. "Another night."

Mom scoffed. "Fine. Then will you at least run by your shop on the way home? Imogene left her silk scarf, and she's headed there now to meet you. She wants it for tomorrow morning. She's spending the day with her granddaughter, and it was a gift from her."

"She's going there now?" I asked. Had I missed something? Why hadn't she led with that information? "Why doesn't Imogene just use her key?"

"What do I look like," Mom asked, "a mind reader? It's bad enough she called me to ask you to do something. That woman, of all people, should know she'd have a better chance of getting that scarf if she asked anyone else to pass the request along, like maybe a vagrant or park squirrel." Mom shut the door. The car drove away.

I rocked back on my heels. "Wow. She really needs that drink."

"You probably should have gone," Chase said. "It's not too late. You can always call her. I'm sure she'd turn around."

"No. I just want to get the scarf for Imogene and go home," I said. "This week is catching up with me."

"Wait." Chase patted his pockets. "I think I dropped my keys."

I scanned the dark ground at our feet. "When? Outside or in?"

"I'm not sure." He made a lost-puppy face. "Will you stay and help me until I find them?"

I hung my head. "Okay, but we have to hustle, because apparently Imogene is going to be standing outside my shop in a few minutes."

Chase smiled. "Perfect."

We searched the walkway from the Tea Room to the parking lot, the mulch along each side of the walkway, the entire parking lot, and the ground around a dozen trees and shrubs near my car. When I finally insisted on taking Chase with me to meet Imogene and dropping him at home afterward, he found the keys.

In his pocket.

Weirdo.

I shook my head and said goodbye with a laugh. Maybe I wasn't the only one who was heavily sleep-deprived and distracted these days.

The streets were dark as I motored along Magazine toward Furry Godmother. Pedestrian traffic had thinned to the occasional couple or jogger. The shops were all closed, and most people had gone in for the night or out to a pub or show. Either way, the world before me seemed desolate. A row of ON DUTY cabs lined the block near my shop, forcing me to park farther away than I would have liked.

I checked my surroundings before getting out of the car, then moved quickly toward my destination. The wide, empty sidewalks were eerily quiet, and the full moon overhead cast ominous shadows across my path. Muted sounds of jazz lifted from the courtyard of a nearby café, and my mind conjured unwanted images of the Axeman of New Orleans, an early-twentieth-century serial killer I didn't like to think about. The Axeman was said to have targeted homes where jazz music wasn't playing. He broke into homes and killed the residents, more often the women than the men, and he basically terrorized the city for a year from 1918 to 1919 before stopping as suddenly as he'd started. His identity had never been discovered, but he was the reason I'd earned first chair in my high school jazz ensemble.

I moved a little faster, imagining the soft pat of footfalls behind me despite the fact that I was grossly alone. I palmed my cell phone and considered putting Jack's number on the screen in case I needed to send a quick call for help.

I stopped outside my shop. The door was ajar, but the space inside was dark.

I dialed Jack's number and hovered my thumb over the green SEND button while I tried to think.

The glass wasn't broken, and I distinctly remembered locking up and double-checking the door when I left, so whoever was inside had a key. Imogene wasn't waiting as I'd expected. Maybe she'd used her key to get inside after all?

Or maybe whoever had stolen Imogene's key was in there now.

I shook away the idea. No one had said Imogene's key was stolen. That was in my imagination. Like the footfalls I thought I heard again nearby. And the hundred-year-old Axeman I sensed watching from the corner.

I planted my feet and leaned forward at the waist, cracking the door open. "Imogene?" I called into the void.

My muscles tensed. I strained to hear an answer that never came. "Imogene?" I tried again, moving my thumb across the phone screen to dial her cell phone instead of Jack's.

A soft shuffling sound reached my ears, and I inched the door wider. Maybe she was in the back looking for her scarf? Maybe she hadn't heard me calling her name.

Or maybe someone had seen her inside Furry Godmother after hours, mistaken her for me, and hurt her.

The call connected, and Imogene's phone rang in stereo, both in my ear and inside my shop.

I swallowed a lump in my throat and flashed my cell phone flashlight over the space. Empty. I shoved my arm inside and slapped the row of light switches on the wall beside the door.

The room blazed to life, and a blast of happy voices and party horns erupted.

A deafening screech burst from my lips.

"Surprise!" the chorus repeated.

I flattened a palm to my chest, hoping to stop my heart from breaking my sternum.

Scarlet wrapped me in a hug. "Happy one-year anniversary of being the most amazing shop owner in all the land."

She released me, and more arms opened. I was passed, hugger to hugger, until the shock had worn down to something manageable and I was certain I wouldn't need an ambulance.

Mom, Dad, Imogene, and a collection of committee ladies stood with Mrs. Smart and a few of the judges, including Chase, near a buffet of delightful-looking finger foods and a punch bowl of something I hoped was spiked.

Mom met me at the end of a lengthy receiving line and squeezed my hand, a proud smile on her lips. "Sorry I had to be so short with you earlier. None of us could think of a way to get you to come back here when you were adamant about going home. I had to get my bossy pants on."

I took my first intentional breath since getting the fright of my life, then threw my arms around her shoulders. Maybe I was proud to know she was proud of me or honored that she'd taken the time to throw me a party when I knew she was so busy, or maybe I was just thankful to be alive, but emotion stung my eyes. "Thank you," I said.

Mom stroked my hair, then pressed a kiss to my head. "Anything for you, Lacy Marie. I know I get on your last nerves sometimes, but there is absolutely nothing in the world that means more to me than having you home, and I'm so proud of what you've accomplished this year."

Dad put an arm around Mom's back. He handed her his handkerchief, and she pressed it to the corner of each eye with a smile.

"I'm sorry I missed the exact date of the anniversary," Mom said. "I let the pet pageant prep take over my life for a while when I should've kept family first."

I reached around my parents in a group hug. "I didn't need a party. I know you're busy." The lump was back in my throat as I choked out the rest of my little speech. "This is really amazing. I don't think I know all these people. Where did you find them?"

Mom laughed and passed me Dad's handkerchief. "Silly. Everyone knows you. These are your neighbors, friends, customers, pet pageant affiliates, and local shop owners. I think every invitation I sent came back with an enthusiastic acceptance."

I pulled myself together and stepped back to look over the crowd. The number of pet pageant affiliates astonished me. "How did you get the committee and judges here before me? How could you have possibly made time to set this all up?" I looked at Chase and laughed again. "You told Chase to keep me busy."

Mom smiled. "How'd he do? He was my last line of defense in case you still decided to go home after we drove away."

"He made me search the ground for his car keys," I complained.

"Imogene met the caterer and took care of things here while we finished at the Tea Room."

I smiled. "You two have always been one heck of a dynamic duo."

The door opened behind me, and I spun around on instinct, still antsy from the surprise-party scare and images of the Axeman swimming through the back of my mind.

Jack strode inside, eyes searching. When his gaze caught mine, he slowed and smiled.

I went to greet him, my enthusiasm growing when I realized he wasn't alone. Willow and Henri walked in behind him.

"Hey!" I greeted them with hugs and thanks. My parents followed.

Henri had a bottle of scotch, which my dad helped him unload quickly, and Willow brought cookies, which my mom took for the dessert display.

"Sorry we're late," Jack said when my parents had gone. "It's not easy to keep these two on task." He hooked a thumb in the direction of his former partner and Willow.

"They're cute," I said, admiring the way they stood toe to toe and smiled through a private conversation, oblivious to the world.

"They knew I wanted to be here before you got here," he said. "Instead, we ran late and tailed you up the sidewalk, trying to stay out of sight. I missed your entrance."

I smiled up at him. "I'm just happy you were able to come and that I wasn't completely imagining those footfalls. I thought I was losing my mind."

"You can thank Willow for the sandals." His mouth shifted into a lazy half smile.

I looked at Willow's shoes, then Henri's and Jack's. Basically, he was suggesting that I never would have heard either of them coming without her. I didn't want to imagine the scenario where a man Jack or Henri's size followed me for nefarious reasons unnoticed.

I brightened my smile, focusing on the moment before me. "I was glad to hear you spoke with Eva this morning."

He nodded. "Thanks to you."

"It was the least I could do," I said, "and I should've done it sooner. I let her push me away before when I knew she was hiding something. I should've kept trying. I figured that might've been why you stopped by my place last night, so I wanted to see her before I saw you again."

Jack's brows knitted together. "You think I came over last night to talk to you about my murder investigation?" He let out a breathy laugh and raked a hand through his dark hair. "You know I'm constantly hoping you'll stay out of these things, right?"

"Yeah, but it's too late now," I said. "I'm all in on this one, and you have no idea how thrilled I am that this was a party and not a break-in."

He grimaced. "You thought this was a break-in, and you still came inside?"

"I thought Imogene might be in trouble," I said, "and I didn't come inside blindly. I turned the lights on from the doorway, and I'd already checked for burglars with my phone light."

He flashed me a disbelieving look with his ghost-blue eyes. Jack's eyes were the first thing I'd really noticed about him. They were cool and clear like glass. The faint color of rain on a windowpane. I'd known back then I could get lost in them, but he was accusing me of murder at the time, and it put a damper on things.

A sharp whistle broke the drone of voices around us, and Mom thanked Chase for the assist as he lowered his fingers from his lips. "I just want to take a minute to thank you all for coming," she said. "I know you love Lacy as much as I do and are just as proud and thankful for the opportunity to share this milestone with her." Her sharp gaze landed on me, and she smiled. "Heaven knows I have my faults, and I certainly have my moments," she said.

The crowd chuckled.

"And I've been called many things in my day, but my favorite of them all is *mother*." She moved in my direction and took my hand, leading me away from Jack. "Lacy, you are an amazing woman, daughter, business owner, and friend. Congratulations on the one-year anniversary of Furry Godmother."

I hugged her, and everyone cheered.

Chase performed a drumroll on my counter. His brother Carter and Scarlet joined in.

Imogene appeared in the hallway, pushing a wheeled table from the stockroom with a fancy silver cake stand in the center. A soft pink cloth draped over the top. "Time to cut the cake!" she called. Imogene positioned the cake in the room's center and pinched the pink cloth between her fingertips. "Congratulations, Miss Lacy!" With the flick of her wrist, the pink cover was whipped away like a magician's cape.

My favorite two-tier chocolate torte from Presto's Bakery

stood beneath a clear glass dome. Mini white fondant paw prints tracked whimsically across the chocolate frosting. A large silver knife was stabbed through the center, and something red oozed down the sides. The glass dome was streaked in matching red goo.

FINAL WARNING.

Chapter Twenty

Furry Godmother's words of wisdom:
It's fine to make hay while the sun shines,
but don't forget to dance in the rain.

Jack and Henri split up to question my guests while Mom, Imogene, Scarlet, and I packed the fantastic buffet of finger foods and appetizers into carryout containers. Willow distributed them to our extremely confused friends as they were dismissed from my party by off-duty homicide detectives.

A set of crime scene men had come to collect my cake, the dome, pedestal, and cart. They'd promised to return the property after processing, but Mom had told them to keep them.

Mom waved cordially to another round of dismissed partygoers, then fixed her wild blue eyes on me. "Would you please tell me just what the hell is going on here?" she hissed.

Imogene hummed a disapproving note at Mom's mild

cuss. She snapped the lid on another plastic container and raised her eyebrows into her hairline. "There's a whole lot of unsavory things going on in here tonight."

Chase smiled from behind the broom he was pushing across my floor. "Those Crocker women look sweet, but they've got mouths like sailors."

Mom rolled her eyes long and slow. "You'd better stick around, Chase Hawthorne," she said. "I might need to get out of a child abuse charge if Lacy doesn't start explaining herself."

Chase abandoned his broom to slide an arm around my back. "I'm afraid I would be forced to defend the child in that scenario."

Mom smacked her lips. "Of course you would."

"I told you someone was threatening me after Viktor died," I whispered through a careful smile.

"I had no idea it was still happening." Mom looked from me to Chase, then widened her eyes. "Was that what happened with the bulls? Someone intentionally sent them after you?"

"Maybe," I said. "We can't be sure, and I don't think bulls work like that, but someone did tamper with the gate, and I was there."

Dad poured another finger of scotch. His third.

Mom cast her attention briefly to Mrs. Smart and the committee ladies across the room. "What else?" she asked me. "You usually tell me as little as possible. So I know you left something out. What is it?"

I shrugged. "You already know about the paper lady on my shop door. There was a bike messenger delivery and a note in my judges' packet. That's it. And for the record, the bulls might be a coincidence."

Mom handed the last of the to-go containers to Willow. "What can I do?"

"Nothing," I said honestly, knowing the word killed her. Mom was a doer.

"All right." She rubbed a towel over shaky hands, then straightened her dress. "I guess. I'll call the car to take the ladies home. Your father can drive me."

"You okay?" I asked her, leaning against Chase at my side.

"No," she said. "I was excited for the pageant to arrive, but now I just wish it would all be over, so you will be safe and Mrs. Smart can go home. I can't take another minute of listening to her complain about how her husband's animal-lover's paradise has become nothing more than an overpriced cockfight."

I forced myself not to ask what constituted a well-priced cockfight. "I thought you liked Mrs. Smart," I said.

Mom looked exhausted. "I do, but if I have to hear one more story about how things were done in her time, I'm going to lose my ever-loving mind. Do yourself a favor and don't even get her started on Viktor Petrov. That's one woman who doesn't mind speaking ill of the dead."

"It's easy to understand," I said. "With Viktor, there was plenty not to like."

Mom rolled her eyes. "She blames him for the condition the pageant is in today. She says people only tuned in to see Viktor, and they were the wrong kind of people. She's even speculated that a crazed fan might've slipped in for an auto-graph, been rebuffed by the king of sass, and tossed him off the balcony for it."

I grimaced. I hadn't even thought of anything like that. I gave Mrs. Smart another look. "Do you think she's heard something?" *Could Viktor have had a stalker?* I thought of the notes Jack had mentioned. Letters telling Viktor to resign.

Jack moved into the mix of committee ladies and spoke with them as a group.

"I don't know what she knows," Mom said, "but I'm exhausted. I'm going to call the car."

An hour later, the shop was clean, and everyone was gone except Jack, Henri, Willow, and me.

Henri set his phone on the counter and put some music on to lighten the mood. "I am so glad that's over," he said. "I'm starving."

I handed him one of the leftover buffet boxes, then helped myself to one of Willow's cookies.

Jack picked one up, too.

"Careful," I said. "I don't know what she puts in these, but they're potent. One bite and your cares will start to drift away."

Jack shoved an entire petit four into his mouth and chewed. "Maybe I'll have two," he said.

"You'd be smarter to finish the scotch," I warned. "She is Veda's granddaughter, after all."

"Right," Jack said, taking a second cookie. "The one with the magical cookie shop I don't believe in."

"Correct." I nibbled the icing around the sides of my cookie, and my lips turned up in a smile.

Willow floated through the room, long hair and skirt billowing at her sides. "I love this song," she said, humming along to the tune. Eventually she spun herself to a stop beside Jack and me. "It's a real bummer about your cake, Lacy," she said. "It was beautiful except for that knife."

"Details," I said.

Jack grinned. "What's in these cookies?" He sucked filling off his thumb and watched Willow. "They're amazing."

"Just lots of added love," she said. "I kept imagining Lacy's smile and all the things I knew about her big heart while I was baking. Her love for this city, the district, her friends and family, animals, strangers, and fashion. Everything."

"That's a lot of love," Jack said.

I couldn't tell if he was making fun of me or Willow.

"Lacy took me in and made me her friend for no reason at all," Willow said. "People just don't do that anymore. I wanted the cookies to be perfect for her."

"Well, I think you accomplished your goal," he said, choosing another from the box.

Willow snagged a chunk of roasted cauliflower from Henri's mini-buffet sampler box. "Do you have any ideas about who's threatening you?" she asked me.

"Not really," I said. "Someone related to the pageant who wants me to stop asking questions about Viktor's death. That's all we know, and there are about one hundred and fifty people associated with the event. They'll probably all be gone before we know for sure who's behind any of this."

"Why?" she asked, her nearly perpetual smile slipping.

Jack rubbed his eyes. "About ninety percent of them are from towns across the country."

"Which is good and bad, "I said. "On the one hand, the killer might get away. On the other hand, my threats should stop."

Willow tented her brows. "Yeah, but you have to stay safe until then. That has to get tricky when you're working with the killer every night, and it looks as if whoever it was came to your party. Stood right here with us, eating your hors d'oeuvres and mingling with your friends like a psychopath."

I shivered.

"How many of the guests were from the pageant?" Willow asked.

Jack dusted his palms. "Twenty."

"Great." Willow perked up. "You just narrowed your suspect pool by more than one hundred."

She was right. Imogene had confirmed that the cake was perfect when it was delivered while she was setting up for the party. She'd put it in the stockroom herself, but the stockroom was right beside the bathroom at the end of the little hallway, where anyone from the party could have slipped away without drawing attention.

"I was thinking," Willow said. "Of those twenty suspects, who has the most to lose?"

"What do you mean?" I said.

Jack shifted his weight and pressed his palms against his hips, apparently also waiting for the answer.

She cocked her lips to the side for a long beat. "It's been my experience that most people are selfish. They want things for themselves and don't care what happens to the people around them as long as they get what they want. The money, the glory, the girl. I suppose it comes down to pride," she said. "My mama always said pride was both powerful and delicate. Some folks will do anything to increase theirs; others will stop at nothing to protect theirs."

I considered her take. "She's not wrong," I told Jack. My pride was fragile, and I'd gone out of my way to protect it many times. Maybe there had been an issue of pride happening between a pet owner and Viktor, or maybe someone just needed a win for all they'd given up. "It could be one of the pet owners," I said. "Some of them have sacrificed everything to be here, and they'll lose even more if they're put in jail for murder."

Willow nodded along. "And you just keep coming for them, which gives them strong motive to dissuade you."

"It could also be a PA," I said. "Viktor belittled them regularly." A powerful hit to their pride. "Veronica." I touched Jack's arm. "Veronica sent compromising pictures of herself to Viktor, and he rejected her."

Jack nodded. "I've been looking into her."

"Did you find her emailed photos?" I asked.

He glanced at Henri, then back to me. "Yeah, along with some follow-up correspondence. Veronica didn't like being ignored."

I bit into another cookie and chewed. *Pride.* A motive for murder I'd never even considered.

Henri swirled scotch in a plastic cup and gave Jack a pointed look. "Tomorrow's my day off. Why don't I meet you

up here and help you review the notes on the original interviews and statements for the pet owners who were here tonight?
Maybe talk to the handful of PAs and crew on the guest list,"
he said. "I'll follow up with Veronica too. I saw her when we
got here, but I don't remember talking to her at the end. Which
means she left before the cake was uncovered."

Not good, I thought. Veronica had had access to the cake
when it was still in the stockroom, then vanished before the
big unveiling. She'd seen me outside Viktor's dressing room
immediately after his murder. She'd been questioned by Jack
and me. She knew I was hunting down leads. Maybe she
thought I was on to her.

Jack shook Henri's hand. "Thanks, man."

"You know I love to get the bad guys," Henri said, "and
someone's got to protect your girl." He winked at me.

My cheeks heated. The first time I'd met Henri, he'd called
me Jack's girl. Jack hadn't argued then either.

"Do you want to get out of here?" Willow asked. "The party
was really something, but I'm ready for a walk under the stars."

I locked up as we moved onto the sidewalk. Rune was
seated on the bench outside Furry Godmother. He wound
immediately around Willow's feet.

Warm summer wind blew my hair out like a cape behind me.

My dress was a different story. The form-fitting material
clung to my skin from the strapless neckline to just above my
knee. I'd chosen it for the simple lines that emphasized everything I still liked about my figure and forgave the things I
didn't, but it also turned out to be perfect for walking in a
brewing storm.

Willow kissed Henri under a streetlight, and I headed in the other direction, enjoying the blustery night. Jack fell into step beside me.

"I love nights like these," I said, watching wispy gray clouds skate across an inky black sky, a million visible stars twinkling around a broad white moon. The next gust of wind sent a shiver down my spine.

Jack slid his black suit jacket from his shoulders and draped it over mine. "I think I felt a raindrop. We can head back."

"No." I turned my head to inhale the scent of him in the jacket fabric. "I like the rain."

"Me too," he said, "and I love walking these streets, but I don't spend enough time doing it. I'm always in a hurry somewhere."

"Yeah. Same," I said wistfully.

"When did we get so busy?" he asked.

I wasn't sure, but I was determined to make the most of the time I had before the rains came. Who knew when I'd take the time to walk Magazine Street at night again?

I admired the stately homes and ancient oaks, the historic storefronts and iconic horse-head hitching posts, lined up like soldiers along the curb, all remnants of another time. Thanks to New Orleans's continual efforts to preserve history and everything that made our town significant and beautiful, the scenery was slow to change. "I like to imagine some other couple walking this patch of sidewalk in a hundred years and having the same conversations we do, just like the couple that walked here one hundred years before us, and I especially love that the sights we all see will be largely the same."

The back of Jack's hand brushed against mine as we strode along. A moment later, his long fingers hooked on mine. I dared a look in his direction, and he held my stare as he turned his palm over to lace our fingers together. "Did I tell you how beautiful you look tonight?" he asked.

I shook my head, unable to find my tongue.

"I think that dress is one of my new favorites."

I wasn't sure what to die about first. The fact that Jack Oliver was holding my hand under a full moon on Magazine Street, that he thought I was beautiful, or that he knew my wardrobe and had favorites.

Jack slowed outside a bustling café that smelled like my best dreams and had a solo artist singing "Stand by Me." "In that story about the couples walking this street, you called us a couple," he said.

I stopped with him to enjoy the song and think about how to respond. *Busted* came to mind.

Jack turned me to face him and caught my other hand in his, raising it to his shoulder and bringing me closer with the effort. He lowered his hand to the small of my back and began to lead me in a slow dance. Café patrons turned to watch. The vocalist sang a little louder. Across the street, Henri and Willow hooted, then began to dance too.

Laughter bubbled up from my chest and I buried my face in the fabric of Jack's shirt for a long moment before pulling back to look at his deadly serious face. I didn't know what was happening to my previously ruined night, or if it was the work of Willow's cookies, but I didn't care. I'd never had a perfect moment before, one I'd want to bottle up and keep forever so

I could take it out to enjoy again and again, but this seemed like exactly that. My cheeks ached from the smile.

"So," Jack said, leaning forward, cocooning us in a private little world as we danced. "You called us a couple in your story."

"I did."

"Why?" he asked. "Was it just because it fit the point you were making, or is that how you think of us?"

"It's how I think of us," I admitted, then laughed at my sudden candor. "I know it's ridiculous, but in my glitter-and-sunshine-soaked mind, you're mine. I'm yours. We're a thing, and this is our endgame." I released his hand and stepped back, embarrassed to the core by my confession, timing, and word choice. My arms fell limply at my sides as I waited for him to let me down gently. Politely.

His brows furrowed deeper.

I pressed my lips shut before I said anything else I'd regret.

"When?" he asked. The low, gravelly quality of his voice sent another round of shivers down my spine.

"When what?"

"When did this start? How long have you thought of us as a couple?"

I glanced at the people sipping drinks a few feet away. At the man still crooning one of my favorites songs. I'd already put myself out there for Jack to crush, and I didn't want to say any more. I wet my lips, scrambling for a change of topic.

"Lacy," he prodded. "Please answer."

I chewed my bottom lip. "Do you remember when we met?" I asked. "You were always grumping around, telling me to stay out of your investigation."

"I still do that."

"Yeah, but do you remember the night you showed up undercover at a bar where I was trying to get information about a criminal I thought was a killer, and you got into a big bar fight?" Heaven help me, but I couldn't keep my mouth shut tonight. I was a fully-shaken Lacy soda and Jack had loosened the lid.

"Yeah." He crossed his arms and widened his stance.

"That was the night I stopped caring about your angry looks. That was the night I knew you cared about catching the killer as much as I did, even though I was the one whose business and reputation were on the line. That was the night I saw beyond the handsome face and shiny badge, and I saw you. Honest and steadfast. Trustworthy and brave. A protector. *My* protector," I said. "I wanted you in my life because I realized you'd already found a way into my heart."

The song ended, and everyone clapped.

I looked away, fighting a heavy blush and potentially renegade tears. I begged my mouth to never open again.

Jack reached for me. His furrowed brow had vanished, replaced by a brilliant smile that lit his enchanting blue eyes. "That's the same night for me, too," he said. "I hadn't had a connection like that with someone in a very long time, but all at once, with you, I wanted to."

He took my hand and we moved on through the windy night. "Can I tell you something else?" he asked. "While I'm making confessions?"

My heart leapt. "Please."

CAT GOT YOUR CROWN

"I like Chase Hawthorne," he said with a sudden bark of laughter.

I laughed too. "What?"

Jack shook his head in awe. "That guy should be on my hit list, but I really like him. He makes it impossible not to, and he makes you smile, so I've got to give him credit."

Jack stopped on the corner to push windblown locks off my face and frown. "I don't like how right he is for you. Your families are close. Your history is shared. Your best friend is married to his brother, for crying out loud, and I've seen you and Chase together. I've even had the significant displeasure of seeing you almost kiss him outside your shop. I think that was the closest I've ever come to coldcocking him."

Thunder rolled across the sky and a flash of lightning lit our world. I smiled as a pattering of fat drops of rain fell over us. Jack would never have hit Chase, but I liked that it had crossed his mind. I'd had the same irrational pinch of anger when Jack had teased me on the phone, pretending to think I was someone else.

"I don't want to be selfish with you," he said. "I want what's best for you, and Chase checks all the boxes. The two of you have something good and real."

I reached for his hands and lifted them between us, lacing our fingers the way he had earlier, enjoying the ease of his acceptance of my touch. "We have something good and real," I said.

The skies opened, and the few fat drops became a downpour. Thunder roared, and the wind whipped into action, threatening to tip me over where I stood. Sheets of rain slapped my skin and poured over my face as I rose onto my toes and repeated my statement, louder, determined to make him hear me. "*We* do, Jack. *Us.*"

Around us, people squealed and laughed and ran for cover, but he stared down at me, his sopping dress shirt clinging to his skin. The furrowed brows were back as he batted rain from his eyes. Then, slowly, he nodded. "We do."

"We do," I echoed. "So, what are you going to do about it?"

Chapter
Twenty-One

*Furry Godmother's advice for life: If there's a bee in
your bonnet, get a swatter.*

Jack freed his hands from mine and pulled me against him in
a move so confident and tender that my already racing heart
hit overdrive. Our lips met. Tentatively at first, then with added
purpose, and my bones went soft. When he pulled back, there
was awe and question in his eyes, so I kissed him again. Several mind-numbing moments later, I was fairly certain the
strong arms he'd hooked around my back were the only things
keeping me upright.

"You want to get out of here?" he asked.

"Yeah."

Jack called Henri on our way back to his truck, splashing
through puddles at intersections in the driving rain. Henri and
Willow had already gotten comfortable inside a restaurant

and ordered drinks. They thought we should join them. I thought they were nuts.

Jack set the heaters inside his truck on low and pointed the vents my way, presumably to counter the rain's deep chill, but that wasn't what had my limbs shaking.

He held my hand on the seat between us while I began to overthink everything.

"What's wrong?" he asked at the next red light, the pad of his thumb running across the back of mine in gentle sweeps.

"Nothing," I said on instinct, still putting words to the issue internally.

His smile reshaped into the more typical look of concern. "I can take you home, if you'd rather."

"No." I shook my head. "It's not that."

"What then?" he asked, pulling forward as the light turned green.

I still wasn't sure. It was a lot of things. Lately, my thoughts had been trapped in a perpetual state of panic and fear, but suddenly I was kissing handsome detectives on street corners in the rain? On the same night I'd had my party crashed with another bloody threat? There was too much happening this week. The good and bad had all mashed into a ball of complexity that I wasn't sure I could sort when it ended.

"Was it the cake?" he asked. "The kiss? Timing?"

"No." I turned worried eyes on Jack as a new concern presented itself. What if I was right about Willow's cookies? What would happen when the effects wore off? Was I completely losing my mind, or was that a real possibility?

I rubbed my temples. The week's stress had come to a head, and I was going round the bend.

We rode in silence the rest of the way to Jack's place. He parked in the garage, then settled the engine and turned to me. "Is it something I said? Something I did?"

"No." I forced a smile. "It's nothing." Clearly, magic wasn't real, and I was absolutely calling my therapist in Tahiti tomorrow. "I'm over it."

"Is it Chase?" he guessed.

I bristled. We'd talked about that already, hadn't we? "Of course not."

Jack raised his brows in challenge. "You sure about that?"

Jack got out. He rounded the hood and opened my door to help me down from his giant pickup. "Talk to me, Lacy. You're not the only one feeling exposed right now." He looked almost vulnerable, for a six-foot former solider and current lawman with a gun on his belt.

"Fine." I screwed my face up, then let him have it. "I was just wondering if you really wanted to kiss me, or if you were just feeling the effects of Willow's cookies."

Jack stepped back and scrutinized my fast-flushing face. His eyes narrowed. "The magic cookies?"

I nodded. "What if you're doped up on magic, and I took advantage of you? Does that make me a sex criminal?"

His lips twisted in an attempt not to smile. He rubbed them with a heavy palm when that failed. "You think you took advantage of me?"

I made another face.

"And you were quiet all the way here, not because you regret anything, but because you're worried you might be a sex criminal?"

I lifted my brows.

Jack rolled his eyes and caught my wrist in his hand. "Come on, Crocker." He towed me inside and dragged me down the hall to his master bedroom.

"What are you doing?" I gasped, as he pulled me over the threshold and released me.

He left me standing dumbfounded as he cut into the next room. Water sprayed on, from a shower, I realized. He returned with a stack of spa-quality towels and an outfit. One navy T-shirt, a pair of cut-off sweats with a police academy logo on the bottom corner of one leg, and a matching hoodie with OLIVER written across the back in white block letters. "Help yourself to the shower and dry clothes. We can toss your wet things into the dryer when you come out. I'm going to make some hot tea and a sandwich." There was fresh heat in his tone, and it wasn't the good kind.

I stared, dumbfounded. "Why are you mad? You told me to tell you what I was thinking, so I did. You're not allowed to be mad about it."

Water dripped from his sodden suit and hair into a puddle on the plush carpeting beneath his feet. He shifted his weight uneasily. "I've been trying to tell you how I feel for a year, but it was never the right time. Something always came up. Now, I finally say it, and you don't tell me to go away. You reciprocate." He stopped, eyes searching mine. "For one split second, everything was right in my world."

My heart softened. "Then I ruined it?"

Jack released a long sigh and let his head tip over his shoulder. "I don't need a damn magic cookie to know how I feel about you."

"Tell me how you feel again," I said, moving in close and angling my face up to his.

"You're killing me, Crocker."

* * *

Thirty minutes later, I was dry and snuggled into Jack's clothes. I'd rolled the waistband on his shorts until I was sure they wouldn't fall off, then done the same to the hoodie sleeves until my hands poked out. My skin was delightfully pink and warm from a nice long shower, and I smelled like Jack after using his shampoo and body wash.

I padded along high-polished wood floors to the tile mosaic in his blessed temple of a kitchen. The space was something out of my dreams, only better, and complete with a scrolling S embossed in the endless copper backsplash. *S for Smacker.*

Jack was busy in the kitchen when I got there. He'd stacked the halves of toasted cheese sandwiches on a platter and put a kettle on as promised. I admired how comfortable Jack was in the kitchen, a side effect, no doubt, of being raised by Grandpa Smacker.

"Smells good," I said, announcing my entrance, as if he hadn't probably tracked my approach from the moment I turned the bedroom doorknob and emerged.

"I hope you're hungry," he said.

"Always."

His cat, Jezebel, loped in my direction and collapsed at my feet. Her flat face and dark muzzle made her a dead ringer for the grouchy Internet cat everyone loved. I scooped her into my arms and cuddled her before putting her back where she came from.

Jack held my gaze as I climbed onto a high-backed stool at the counter. "I shouldn't have snapped at you earlier."

"I shouldn't have taken advantage of you while you were under the influence of magic cookies."

Jack snorted, then came to stand before me. He lifted my chin with strong fingers and kissed me. "I'm not going to get used to the fact I can do that for a while, so bear with me."

I smiled.

He headed back to the stovetop and flipped another sandwich. He'd changed into an outfit nearly identical to my own. Sweat shorts and a T-shirt. He'd skipped the hoodie, but considering the fact that my delicates were drying in his bathroom, the hoodie was a good choice for me.

"Will you stay with me tonight?" he asked. "I don't like the idea of you being anywhere alone right now."

"Sure." I nodded, feeling the butterflies return. I set my phone on the counter and texted my mom. "I'd better tell my parents where I am so they don't worry." I gave Jack a careful look. "You're in charge of keeping me safe. What do you think Mom will say about me sleeping over?"

"I think she'll be glad you aren't alone tonight. That cake terrified her, and she's seen you in grave danger once already this year."

I blew out a puff of breath. "I meant about us. Do we tell her, or should we keep it quiet a while?"

"She knows," Jack said.

I nearly dropped the phone. "What? How? I just found out."

"She saw right through me the first time I spoke to her about keeping you safe. She reads people. It's what makes her such a good leader, and it's the reason people choose to follow her. She would've made an excellent detective if the position of all-powerful socialite had already been taken."

I thought of the way she'd warned me about falling in love with a cop. She'd known exactly how Jack felt when she'd cautioned me against the potential heartache. "She knows how I feel, too."

"Probably," he said with a wicked grin.

I snagged a slice of apple off a plate on the island and smiled as I dragged it through a peanut butter mix he'd set out. I thought about how much fun Chase, Willow, and I had had eating her fruit dip and dancing. I'd had a horrible day before picking her up on my way home. If the dip wasn't magical, then what? *Maybe I was just really relaxed and happy with the company that night.* And Jack was feeling the same way tonight.

Willow's cookies had put Imogene in a good mood, too, but maybe they were just delicious cookies, and Imogene was thrilled to know her best friend had finally found her great-granddaughter.

Jack flipped the burner off on the stove and grabbed the kettle. "New Orleans's magic is in our history, music, food, and people, not some hippie's mystical powers."

I laughed. "Willow is a total hippie. I really like her."

"Me too," he said. "She'll be good for Henri. He can be uptight."

I laughed again, then helped myself to half a grilled cheese. The bread was golden brown, and the cheese was stringy. There were thin slices of ham and pickle inside. "I think Willow was right about figuring out who had the most to lose," I said. "Veronica's burnt pride aside, do you know how many people were paying off the MC and judges? Do we have names? Were any of them at my party tonight?"

"We're looking at Viktor's financial records, but it's a slow process," he said. "We're hoping we can trace something back to someone in New Orleans this week, but we know Viktor accepted cash. There's a good chance there won't be any records to find."

"What about relationships?" I asked as Jack set two cups of tea on the island, then climbed onto the seat beside mine. "If it wasn't about the money, it could have been about love or jealousy. Do we know if Viktor was involved romantically with anyone? Maybe that person had another lover or spouse that found out about the cheating?"

Jack swigged his tea. "I'm on that now. I've been digging through everything in Viktor's computer and phone records, trying to link him on a personal level to one of the pet owners, PAs, or crew. I'm also looking at peripheral players, like his agent or an ex-wife, things like that. Anyone who might've reasonably come to visit him, then killed him and left unnoticed."

I chewed a bit of sandwich thoughtfully. "You said Viktor

came to you to ask about safe neighborhoods. He was planning to stay here."

Jack nodded. "He got some vague threats demanding that he resign, so he planned to step down after this show and start something new."

"Did he have any idea who was threatening him?"

"Not really," Jack said. "He thought it might've been an obsessed fan of the show."

"That's Mrs. Smart's theory too," I said. "Mom mentioned it tonight."

"It's not a bad one. Could be someone obsessed with him or someone who didn't like his outlandish behavior onscreen." Jack shook his head. "The same over-the-top antics that ticked some people off also got the show's ratings up and earned Viktor all those spin-off deals and media attention."

I set my sandwich aside and reached for my tea. "Whoever killed him might've been the same person demanding he resign."

Compassion pooled in Jack's eyes. "Yeah, and he was going to do what they wanted in less than a week, but he never got a chance to make the announcement."

I cradled the mug between my palms and inhaled the sweet scent of chamomile. "That's tragic. He didn't have to die and the other person didn't have to become a killer. Everything would have worked out if the angry party could have held his or her temper a few more days."

"That would be true," Jack said, "*if* that theory is correct."

"You don't think it is?"

He tipped his head. "I don't know. I'm still looking at some other leads."

I sipped my tea and tried to look less eager. "Like?"

"Eva Little's boyfriend, for starters."

I'd completely forgotten about him.

Jack stretched back in his seat. "I'm going to double down tomorrow, hopefully find a link between Viktor and someone who was bribing, blackmailing, or threatening him, maybe even someone he was bribing, blackmailing, or threatening. I haven't ruled out any possibilities. Henri will be the footman, reviewing interview notes with fresh eyes and visiting anyone we need more information from, including Eva's boyfriend." He set his palm on my knee and gave it a gentle squeeze. "I think you should stay with me until it's time for the pageant tomorrow night. Don't go to work. Don't go anywhere alone. I can work from my office here, and you can relax. Swim in the pool. Sleep. Whatever you need. Then I'll drive you to the Tea Room tomorrow night and stick close during the event. We can swing by your place after breakfast to collect Penny and Buttercup."

I set my hand on his, immensely thankful Willow's cookies weren't magical.

Chapter Twenty-Two

Furry Godmother's advice on breaking news to your mother: Bring a flask.

Imogene opened Furry Godmother on her own and stayed until lunch. She promised to put a sign in the window on her way out announcing we were closed for the afternoon. It was the first time I'd slept past eight in over a year, and it was glorious. I made a mental note not to wait until someone else threatened to kill me before taking another morning off to rest and pamper myself. On my third lap through the warm saltwater of Jack's pool, I had an epiphany. What if I spent half as much time giving myself the things I needed as I did on fulfilling the needs of my store? I'd never had balance before. I'd juggled too many things all my life, letting the chores and responsibilities consume me. But what if I didn't?

I made lunch for Jack and took it to him in the living

room, where he sat surrounded by printed reports and files, his laptop balanced precariously on the arm of the couch. "Hungry?"

He seemed startled at first, as if he might have forgotten I was there, or where he was. *Consumed*, I thought. Another thing Jack and I had in common. A slow smile spread over his face, and he patted the cushion beside him. "Absolutely."

I cleared a couple of feet of space on the coffee table to set the lunch tray down, then took a seat and pulled my feet up beside me. "What are you working on?"

"I'm reviewing the details Eva gave me about her and her boyfriend. He's got a bit of a record, but I spoke with him after I spoke with her, and he corroborated her statement. So, they either got their stories straight before that, or they're both telling the truth."

"But you believe Eva," I said.

"Yeah. My gut says she's as clueless about Viktor's death as she says, but I'm torn because the new love of her life isn't someone I thought she'd share the same sidewalk with, let alone a bed."

I blushed on Eva's behalf. "Maybe he tricked her, and she doesn't realize he's not who he says he is."

Jack helped himself to an apple. "I just want to be sure he didn't trick me."

* * *

I baked all afternoon in the most glorious kitchen on earth, stocking up on treats for Furry Godmother and tweaking the sandwich recipe I would present to Grandpa Smacker for the

Fall Food Festival. It was a much-needed vacation and personal respite just ten minutes from home.

Jack spent the bulk of his day on the couch, accompanied by stacks of files and a laptop, but at five o'clock sharp, we were dressed and ready for whatever the night would bring. Fifteen minutes later, we parked outside the Audubon Tea Room, facing the final night of the National Pet Pageant. Tomorrow's crowning ceremony would be short, sweet, and thankfully without need of judges.

"You ready for this?" he asked, pressing his shifter into park.

I checked my hair and makeup in the visor mirror, then adjusted the deep V of my vintage pinup-style gown. "I think so. How do I look?"

To his credit, Jack's eyes never dropped lower than my lips. He shook his head and laughed quietly. "Like I must be dreaming."

I kissed him for that one, then reapplied my lipstick before climbing out of his truck in my new favorite gown. The dramatic red soft chiffon was fitted at my torso and covered in a layer of silver sparkles that twinkled with my every move. The skirt was a thousand layers of the same, draping all the way to the ground, where it met a matching pair of red stilettos. The gown was nowhere near pastel, but it did match my lips, nails, and clutch, so I called that a win.

I hooked my hand in the crook of Jack's arm as we moved toward the Tea Room doors. He was stunning in black Armani. His coordinating red pocket square was a quick addition made after he'd taken one look at me in my new dress.

We cut through the foyer and headed to the green room in search of my mother. Eva was with the committee ladies in the green room and beamed when she saw us.

"Lacy!" She wrapped me in a hug, then shook Jack's hand. "Thank you both so much for speaking with me. It feels great to breathe again. To know the truth is out to the people who matter most and will be out to everyone else very soon. It's really freeing, you know?"

Jack squeezed my fingers, and I smiled.

"I know," I said.

"Lacy?" Mom's voice cut through the white noise of the room as she headed our way.

Eva glanced at my hand in Jack's and made a worried face before kissing my cheek and getting out of there.

"What's this?" Mom asked.

"I know it's not pastel," I said, releasing Jack's hand to lift the layers of my amazing skirt, "but I love it." I curled an arm protectively around my middle.

Her gaze swept appreciatively over the dress. "The gown is spectacular, but that's not what I meant." She turned her stare from my eyes to Jack's. Her hands dropped to her sides. "You told her," she said.

"Ma'am?" he asked, stiffening slightly at my side.

"You told her how you feel, and now you're a couple." She clucked her tongue.

Mrs. Smart and the committee ladies moved in our direction, curious eyes sweeping over us.

Jack bowed his head to my ear. "Told you."

I smiled sweetly, wishing we didn't have a little audience

but recalling that this was Mom's kingdom. Her Garden District socialite life was also mine, and it wasn't so bad when the spotlight was off. "What are you and Dad doing after the pageant tonight?" I asked Mom, hoping to reschedule the current conversation to a place more private in case she killed me. "Maybe Jack and I can swing by for coffee." *Or a stiff drink.* At least Jack carried handcuffs in case Mom went completely bonkers.

She scrutinized us. "You're both coming?"

I nodded.

"And we'll talk about this?" she asked, turning her eyes back to Jack.

"Yes, ma'am," Jack answered.

I shook my head at him. "You're going to have to be less agreeable to her now."

Mom's lips twitched before curling into a small, mischievous smile. "Fine. I'll let your father know, and we'll be waiting. Don't dally."

"No, ma'am," Jack said.

I elbowed his ribs. "Knock it off."

Mom heaved a sigh. I couldn't tell what it meant, but I was sure I'd get plenty of details at her place later, so I let it go. "Well, Jack," she said, "I guess you're keeping her close, which means she's safe, but where are you on finding the person who's threatening my daughter?"

"Working on it," I interjected, "and getting close, so I don't want you to worry." I swung my gaze pointedly at Mrs. Smart. There was no reason for her to continue to worry about the state of the pageant. Jack was cleaning up any remaining

bribers and extortionists. Henri was reviewing every interview and revisiting every witness or suspect. And I had complete faith in the both of them.

"How close?" Mom asked.

"Very," I vowed. "It won't be long now."

I grabbed a bottle of water and some snacks for the judges'
table while Mom and Jack had a little conversation I wasn't
sure I wanted to hear. He kept a close eye on me as I moved
through the room, and Mom broke away before I returned.

She met me near the nuts and mints and caught my arm
as I passed. "Are you sure about this?" she asked in a voice I
could barely hear. I followed her gaze to Jack.

"Yes, ma'am," I mocked, a broad smile on my lips.

She smiled back. "Good, because I might've been wrong
before."

I kissed her cheek. "I'll see you tonight. Don't embarrass me."

I headed back toward Jack, ready to take my place with
the judges before the lights dimmed.

"There you are," Chase said, smiling brightly as he strode
into the green room. His sandy hair was perfectly gelled. His
pale-gray suit was cut to fit and generously reflecting the bright
green of his eyes. "Whoa." He stopped to take in the dress,
then circled a finger, indicating I should spin.

I obeyed with a coy look over one shoulder as I turned. The
airy material of my dress lifted, floating around me as I spun.

"Oo la la," he said, catching me with one long arm as I
finished and pulling me against him in a strong rocking hug.
"Wait." He set me free. "What's wrong?"

My gaze flicked to Jack, who watched silently from a few feet away.

Chase's brow creased. "Oh." He dragged the word out for several syllables. "No, no no."

I moved back to Jack. "Guess what?" I said.

"Ugh." Chase dropped his head forward and mimed stabbing himself in the chest.

"I'll let you take care of that," Jack said, motioning to Chase, "and I'll meet you at the judges' table." He tucked his phone into his pocket, kissed my cheek, then extended a hand to Chase. "Sorry, man."

Chase groaned. "Liar."

Jack smiled, then walked away.

"He's not sorry," Chase said.

I laughed.

*   *   *

Chase continued to pepper me with questions about Jack for an hour after the show began. I did my best to answer the least obnoxious of his inquiries while scanning the crowd for someone who looked like they wanted to kill me.

No one fit the description.

"At least tell me the two of you are planning to take it slow," Chase said as Mom took the podium to announce intermission.

"What's that supposed to mean?" I asked. "Slow compared to what?"

Chase made a series of strange faces.

"Are you choking?" I asked.

He heaved a sigh. "You know exactly what I'm saying," he said as Jack approached behind him.

I wrinkled my nose. "I assure you I do not."

The room burst into motion, and I stood. Intermission had commenced, and I needed a break.

"I'm going to powder my nose," I told Jack, turning my eyes to the ladies' room directly across from us. I preferred the roomy, better-appointed private restrooms reserved for event staff, but those were down the hall past the green room, and I wanted to stay within Jack's line of sight. "Meanwhile, Chase has a lot of wonderful questions. I'm running short on patience, but maybe you can help him with some of the vaguer ones involving my virtue."

Jack kissed me chastely, and Chase dropped his head onto the table as I hurried away.

I beetled into the ladies' room to freshen up before the line got too long, and I tried not to think about how incredibly stupid it might have been to leave Chase and Jack alone. I checked my reflection in the mirror and fluffed my hair while I waited my turn at the front of a long line of stalls.

I dialed Scarlet while I waited. We hadn't spoken since my party last night, and there was plenty I needed to tell her. "Hey," I said when the call connected.

"Lacy?" she asked. "Everything okay? Aren't you supposed to be judging the pet pageant right now?"

"Intermission," I said.

"What's up?"

I wanted to tell her about Jack. After a public outing like

this one, news was sure to travel through the district grape-vine by morning, and Scarlet would probably hear sooner if Chase stopped by her place on his way home to tell his brother all about it. Jack was the reason I'd called her, but now that I had her ear, I couldn't get my mind off of how a killer was likely in the building with me, and maybe even in line for the bathroom or listening to Jack and Chase discuss my virtue.

My phone buzzed with a text message. Eva's number was on the screen. "Hold on," I told Scarlet. "Eva's texting me."

I checked the message.

CAN WE TALK?

I responded with a quick SURE. Then I promised to call Scarlet right back.

Eva's next text came immediately.

I LIED BEFORE. I SAW WHAT HAPPENED TO VIKTOR, BUT I WAS AFRAID TO TELL YOU, AND NOW I THINK I'M IN BIG TROUBLE.

A jolt of panic swept through me. Eva was in trouble. Was Jack right about Eva's ex not being who he said he was? Maybe that guy wasn't a bighearted underdog making a life for him-self. Maybe he was a killer using the most innocent and trust-ing person I knew to cover his crime. My blood began to boil. I responded before she changed her mind about talking.

YOU CAN TELL ME ANYTHING, AND JACK CAN PROTECT YOU. WHERE ARE YOU?

I stepped out of line to wait on her response and location. She couldn't be far. I'd seen her with the other committee ladies during the last act.

OUTSIDE. ON THE ZOO BRIDGE. PLEASE DON'T TELL JACK YET. HEAR ME OUT FIRST.

I couldn't make her any promises on the Jack request. He and I had crossed into new territory, and I wasn't going to mess it up by keeping a secret this big. Whatever she wanted to tell me, she really needed to tell him.

I slipped out of line and checked the time. She and I had spoken on the bridge before, and it wasn't far. If I hurried, I could get her and be back in my seat before intermission ended. I forwarded her texts to Jack, then asked him to come along. If Eva knew what had happened to Viktor, then we had to protect her. Someone had been threatening me all week, and I was only looking for answers. I couldn't imagine what would happen to Eva if the killer found out she'd seen everything and planned to tattle. Satisfied I'd covered my bases by alerting Jack, I sent one more text to Eva.

I'M COMING.

Chapter
Twenty-Three

Furry Godmother's proverbial advice: Beware of a fox in sheep's clothing. She'll pull the wool over your eyes.

I raced from the restroom and stopped at the sight of Chase sitting alone at the judges' table. I inched out of the way as folks streamed around me in every direction, hurrying to make the most of our short break. I considered rushing to him to ask what had happened to Jack, but the idea of threading my way through the giant congested room seemed like a waste of precious time. Eva was waiting, possibly changing her mind at any second or worse. What if she was in danger? What if the person she was so afraid of had found her?

I texted Chase as I scanned the sea of faces for the one I desperately needed. WHERE'S JACK?

Chase's response came back fast. JACK WENT TO FIND YOU AND TALK TO EVA. ARE YOU OKAY?

Yep.

I was perfect. Jack was already on his way to the bridge, which meant Eva would be okay too.

I worked my way through the crowd as fast as I could in stilettos and an amazing vintage gown, then ducked outside and broke into a jog on my tiptoes. I'd sent the texts to Jack only a few moments before, so I had a good chance of catching him if I hurried. He must've assumed I'd gone ahead without him, but I'd learned my lessons about rushing headlong into sketchy situations alone. This time, I'd arrive with Jack and use my friendship with Eva to set her mind at ease. Then we could bring her back with us and keep her safe until local authorities could make the arrest I'd been waiting for all week.

I darted through the night toward the arching cobble-stone bridge. "Eva?" I called, squinting into the darkness. The path was darker than I recalled and the bridge significantly steeper, though it was admittedly my first trip there after dark and in stilettos. "Jack?"

I slowed at the crown of the bridge, utterly alone. My skin crawled as I double-checked my phone screen to be certain I hadn't misunderstood Eva's texts, but something wasn't right. Where was Jack? Where was Eva? They couldn't have had time to meet up and leave already. Could they? And even if I'd missed their rendezvous, I should have passed them on their way back to the Tea Room. Where else could they have gone? The zoo?

I turned to study the massive wrought-iron gates. The zoo was closed. Jack and Eva had to be *here*. Right where I was standing.

But they weren't.

Behind me, muffled cries rose into the night. I spun to find the Tea Room completely dark, and the path before me significantly dimmed from the loss of the building's ambient light.

My muscles went rigid and my mind on alert as I teetered on the bridge. Go forward? Go back? Was the danger here or there? Were Jack and Eva caught in it somehow?

The Tea Room's emergency lights flickered on before I could decide what to do. The new lights cast an eerie glow over the building and its surroundings. A repetitive bleating groan echoed from the walls. A moment later, the doors flung open, and people poured out in a panic.

Another bomb threat? Something worse?

I dialed Jack's phone.

"Where are you?" he barked without saying hello.

"I'm on the bridge," I said, his tension adding to my own. "Why aren't you here? Where's Eva? What's happening at the Tea Room?" The questions poured out of me, and there were more mounting by the second.

Jack spoke again, but I couldn't understand him. The chaos on his end of the line mixed with the increasing drone of people spilling outside in a frenzy. The combination was near deafening. "What?" I asked, unsure if he'd answered me or someone else. I pressed a palm to my opposite ear and closed my eyes to concentrate.

He called out a series of instructions, and I realized he was directing people to the exits from inside the Tea Room. The edge in his voice tightened my stomach into knots.

I longed to run back toward the chaos and find Jack, but

my cowardly bones were frozen, unwilling to carry me through the short expanse of darkness cloaking the path. I jumped at the sound of cracking twigs, but there was no one there. Just my tension and nerves playing tricks on a rattled mind.

"Lacy," Jack snapped. "Get back here. Now!"

"What about Eva?" I asked, turning back to watch the distant crush of people outside the Tea Room. "What if she's hurt?" *Or worse?* "She said she'd be here." An awful thought wiggled into mind, and my heart jerked into a sprint. "What if whatever is going on at the Tea Room is the killer's way of flushing her out? Whoever did that might not know she's out here. We've got to find her!"

"Dammit, Lacy," Jack growled. "I'm with Eva!"

"What?" His words crashed and banged in my mind. I scanned the area around me again. How was that possible? Why would she ask me to meet her on the bridge, then go back inside? Had I misunderstood? Had she lied? Why? "I don't understand."

I stared back at the streams of people, baffled.

"I got your texts about the bridge," Jack said, sounding more frightened than angry.

The low cries of emergency vehicles had swollen in the distance, and I suspected he felt the relief of knowing help was on its way.

"I went to stop you from going out alone," he said. "I saw Eva in the crowd on my way and flagged her down."

"She never made it outside?" I asked.

A large splash turned me around on the bridge. My muscles ached with tension as I peered over the edge. Something large and dark floated in the water below. A man's jacket? *A man?* "Oh no!" I yelled into the receiver. "Someone's in the water!" I leaned forward for a better look, gripping the ledge at my middle and pinching the phone between my head and shoulder.

"Stay put," Jack snapped. "Do not engage! I'm coming!"

My stomach churned as I watched the silhouette's arms float to the water's surface. His features invisible in the night.

I forced myself not to wonder if he'd fallen in, of if he'd been thrown in by the same killer who was hunting me. My heart clenched as I stretched my right arm behind me, working the strap of my stiletto over my heel with shaking fingers. I had to try to save him. I said a silent prayer that we would both survive whatever was happening.

"Lacy!" Jack yelled. "Do not engage," he repeated. "Eva didn't send you those texts. Someone stole her phone. You were tricked, Lacy, and you're in trouble."

I froze, one foot up, fingers curled beneath an ankle strap. *Trouble.* The word sent ice splinters through my soul.

Before I could form another solid thought, my left foot was swept out from under me by the sharp crack of something hard and fast. Two angry hands shoved my bottom up and over the narrow cement ledge, and my cell phone plummeted in with a splash. My palms pivoted on the hard surface, and I scrambled for purchase to keep from going the way of my phone. The water was far too shallow and the rocks too thick for anyone to survive a fall from this height.

A string of emergency vehicles raged to a stop outside the Tea Room. Their sweeping carousels of lights washed over the darkened path, repeating and circling, not quite reaching the bridge. "Help!" I screamed.

Mrs. Smart's placid face came into view just opposite the ledge where I clung.

Ice formed on the back of my neck as I realized I'd overlooked the most obvious killer.

"You," I whispered.

"Me," she agreed, raising her duck-head cane overhead with a scowl.

"All to save your husband's precious pageant."

She frowned. "All to save his reputation and preserve his legacy." She brought the weapon down on my clutching fingers with a sharp crack.

I screamed until my throat was raw, and my nails ground into the cement, tightening their grip on the ledge when pain and instinct urged me to let go. "Stop!" I cried. "Please, don't!"

The cane bounced against the cement, having caught a few of my fingers and missed the rest. I realized it was probably the same object that had been used to whip me off my foot. Heat pooled beneath my sweaty palms, now doubly slick with blood where the soft skin had been torn as I'd struggled not to fall. I kicked my feet uselessly, wishing I could find something beneath the bridge to use for a foothold.

My unfastened stiletto jostled free and landed in the water with my phone and the man. I swallowed another cry for help, begging my heart to settle and my mind to think clearly. Who would hear me through the chaos outside the Tea Room? *Save your strength*, I thought. *Think.*

"Let go!" Mrs. Smart yelled. Her pale, wrinkled face was menacing in the moonlight.

"Why are you doing this?" I gasped.

"You know why," she said, frustration pooling in her angry blue eyes. "You looked right at me in the green room tonight, and you told me that you know what I did to Viktor."

"What?"

She nodded. "You said you're close to proving who did it. You said it won't be long now."

My mind reeled. I had said those things, but I hadn't meant it the way she thought. That had been her guilty conscience speaking.

"Well, I'm not giving you time to prove it," she continued. "I killed Viktor to protect my husband's good name. I can't very well go to prison, or the whole thing would have been for naught."

A dozen recent memories rose to the surface of my terror-filled mind. Mom had told me that Mrs. Smart blamed the pageant's demise on Viktor. She thought he brought the wrong kind of people and the wrong kind of attention to the event. She'd told me as much herself the day I met her. And I'd still been too blind to see it.

"What about the bomb threat?" I asked. "Was that you, too?"

"I hoped to get the whole show canceled before it went down in infamy," she said, pinching the cane against her side with one elbow, "but that didn't work, so I decided to keep it simple. Pretend I had no idea what happened to Viktor and be glad he'd finally be replaced." She pressed a soft palm to the back of my hand and began to pry my fingers off the cement, one by one. "Every time I saw your mother, she assured me that you'd know who killed Viktor soon, and I shouldn't worry because you'd find the culprit. You'd figure it all out."

"You don't have to do this," I said, curling my fingers over hers as she freed them. "I won't tell anyone. I swear. No one else has to die."

"You're wrong," she said, peeling another finger free.

I dared a look at the drop beneath me. "Who's in the water?" I asked.

Mrs. Smart pulled my right hand free and gave it a toss.

I screamed and threw my hand back against the ledge.

"That's just a jacket in the water," Mrs. Smart said, going to work on my other hand. "I took it from the back of someone's chair."

I gave the dark shape a closer look. It wasn't a body. Just a cast-off item of clothing. "The splash," I argued. "I heard him fall in."

"You heard a rock," she said, moving on to my third finger.

I jerked free and repositioned my hand on the ledge.

"Darn it!" Mrs. Smart freed her cane and smacked my hand again. "Stop that."

I ground my teeth and bit back a sob.

"You should run while you still can," I said. "Jack's on his way. He knows I'm here, and he's coming to help me. You'll be caught if you stay." I found a cleft in the stones beneath me and wedged the toes of my bare foot into it until I felt the sweet relief in my hands and shoulders.

She glanced in the direction of the Tea room, then doubled down on her efforts to pry my hands loose. "I can't leave a tattletale behind to tell on me."

Fatigue racked my aching muscles, weakening them by the second, and all I could think about was how stupid I'd been.

The real killer had been right in front of my face all along. I'd spoken with her minutes after she'd killed Viktor, and I'd had no clue. I'd shared coffee with her at my shop after she'd stabbed my cake and ruined my party, and I'd had no clue. She'd been right there at every turn, and I'd only seen what she'd wanted me to see. A cranky, clueless old lady.

She groaned. "Your hands are bleeding everywhere."

She took a break and stared at the ground, hopefully rethinking her plan.

My left shoulder shuddered from the strain, and my arms burned from their burden. I needed a better foothold. Needed relief for my hands. Needed ground beneath my feet.

"This is all your fault. The police would've cleared your friend eventually," Mrs. Smart said before ducking out of sight, "if you would have left things alone. All you had to do was wait." She stood again, popping back into view. This time there was a large chunk of broken concrete in her hands. She raised the mass high above her head and locked her gaze with mine. "Forgive me," she whispered.

"Freeze!" Jack's voice boomed through the night, sending waves of thanks, relief, and gratitude through my desperate, trembling frame.

A pair of big warm hands were suddenly on mine, curling their strong fingers around my burning wrists and lifting me to safety. I recognized Chase's touch before I saw him. When he heaved me over the ledge and into his arms, the look on his face was foreign, as if it belonged to someone else, someone years older, someone who'd nearly lost something irreplaceable. His usual jovial expression was eerily absent, replaced by sheer terror.

Mrs. Smart's face went bright with the beam of a spotlight as Chase whirled me away from the ledge and eased me back onto land. My knees buckled beneath my weight, and Chase whipped my legs up like a bride carried over the threshold, unwilling to let me fall.

I buried me face against his chest and sobbed as he lowered us to the ground. He pressed his back to the bridge and peeled my bloody hands from around his neck to examine them closely.

Jack's voice was cold as ice and sharp as a razor reading Mrs. Smart her rights.

I pressed my cheek to the curve of Chase's warm neck and tuned in to his pulse as it tapped too quickly against my skin.

Jack pushed the old woman into the grasp of a uniformed officer, then came to stand before us. He extended a fist to Chase, who bumped it gently with his. "May I?" He reached for me, and Chase helped me onto my feet and into Jack's arms.

I wobbled unsteadily, still weak from exertion, and tilted significantly between one bare foot and one stiletto. "I lost my shoe," I cried.

The hint of a smile twisted his troubled face as he scooped

me into his arms and headed down the darkened path toward the Tea Room. "You're a mess, Crocker."

"But we got the bad guy."

Jack slid emotion-filled eyes in my direction, his mouth still fighting the smile. "Yes, we did."

Chapter Twenty-Four

Furry Godmother's hard truth: Life is short.
Eat the cookies.

I handed my car keys to the valet outside my parents' home and jogged up the walk, running late as usual. Half the district seemed to be there, but experience said my estimate was low. White bistro lights hung in the reaching limbs of the ancient oaks along their property, dangling from beautiful overhead canopies and illuminating the beards and wisps of moss. A warm night breeze tousled my hair and scented the air with my mother's begonias, and I smiled at the nostalgia that came with it. There was nothing like a southern summer night.

When Mom had insisted I come for drinks at her place after closing Furry Godmother for the evening, and Imogene had abandoned her shift early for vague, personal reasons, I'd suspected they were in cahoots on something. The party was no surprise either. It was a day ending in Y, after all, and with the National Pet Pageant out of town, Mom had time on her hands again, at least for the moment. I'd stopped at home to trade my casual yellow sundress for a classic black slip dress that made me feel fabulous and headed right over.

In the weeks since the NPP had ended and Mom's NPP Welcoming Committee had disbanded, she'd fallen back into her routine of throwing elaborate dinner parties and meddling in my personal life. All in all, it was a welcomed return.

I slowed on the narrow walkway, long ago misshapen and upended by the tenacious roots of mammoth historic oaks. I took in the familiar sights and sounds I'd done everything in my power to dodge a year ago. These days, I didn't mind. I found instead that I liked seeing everyone, hearing what they were up to and feeling like a part of something bigger.

I caught sight of Dad on the porch and went to kiss his cheek. We hadn't spent enough time together lately, and I missed him. "Tell me the truth," I said. "How long have you been out here hiding?"

He checked his watch. "'Bout twenty minutes. When your mother asks, I tell her I'm keeping watch for you."

I laughed. "I love you. You know that?"

He lifted my still partially bandaged hands to his lips and kissed them. "How was physical therapy this morning?"

I exaggerated the genuine shudder to make it look contrived, then forced a big smile.

He smiled back, but I knew he saw right through me.

"Not bad," I said. "My hands will be good as new in time." That was true. My hands were healing nicely, despite some fairly extensive damage to my joints and ligaments, but the deeper problem wasn't with my hands. I'd set a standing appointment with my therapist the minute she returned from her trip, and I attended faithfully. Every week.

Dad hugged me. "I hate the things that have happened to you," he whispered, stroking my hair where it draped down my back. "I promised you the moment I met you in that delivery room that I would protect you from everything every day of my life, and some days I can't get over how miserably I've failed."

"Dad," I said, pulling back for a look in his glistening blue eyes. "You can't protect me from everything. I wouldn't want you to."

"You don't understand," he said. "If you choose to have children one day, you'll see." He laughed softly. "The joy comes with a whole lot of pain."

"I'm sorry I've scared you badly and so often," I said. And I meant it in my marrow.

He pressed my hands gently to his heart. "I'd do it over a thousand times for you."

I freed my hands from his so I could hug him tightly in my arms, careful to keep the pressure off my hands and fingers.

My small motor skills would take some time to perfect again, but therapy was helping, and I was a fighter. I would heal, and I was certain that, with time, my tight and professional hand-stitching would be nearly invisible once more.

Dad kissed my head. "All right. I'll let your mother know I saw you pull up. If you haven't guessed, this is your surprise party do-over. Act shocked when everyone yells."

I hadn't guessed, and I was a little excited at the prospect. I gave a weird salute, then counted slowly to twenty before following him inside.

"Surprise!" the crowd of family and friends yelled out.

I did a *what-is-all-this* face, then bowed and curtsied and acted a mess until I was sure everyone bought my terrible acting. When that was done, I nabbed a flute of champagne from a passing waiter and went to investigate the dessert situation.

Mom moseyed to my side, a faux but believable smile in place. "You knew," she said.

"Yeah." I popped a strawberry into my mouth. "Thank you for this. Everything looks so beautiful, and there's a ton more room here than there was at my store. It's perfect." Plus, I was still unbelievably glad to be alive to enjoy it.

"I had them move the furniture when they set up the tables," Mom said. "There was an overwhelming response to this invitation." A prideful smile bloomed on her lips. "You've done well for yourself, Lacy. Without a medical degree or a fancy title or rich husband. Without so much as a penny from your father and me. I don't know why you choose the hard way, but I marvel at your perseverance."

I smiled. It was quite possibly the highest praise my mother had ever given anyone in her life, and she'd given it freely, *to me*. "Thank you," I whispered, feeling the tug in my chest.

She nodded. "I guess I should have expected you'd figure out I was planning something. You've become quite the amateur sleuth, and you did inherit half my genes."

I rubbed the backs of my hands gently and gave the room a long look. Mom had spared no expense as usual, from the crisp black linens and high-top table rentals to the elaborate spread of food and drinks. She'd even hired a harpist and ordered my favorite cake from Presto's Bakery. Again. "I think you've outdone yourself."

"Not even close," she said. "Keep that in mind if you ever need to throw a really important party. I'll knock your socks off." She lifted her gaze to the sexy six-foot homicide detective approaching from across the room.

"Looks like you're warming up to him in my life romantically," I said. "I appreciate that."

She shrugged. "He'd take a bullet for you, and he's easy on the eyes. Who can be mad at that?"

I laughed.

"His chosen profession is awful, but net worth is admirable."

I rolled my eyes. *That's the Mom I know.*

She sighed. "And how could I fault anyone who looks at you like that?"

Jack pried his gaze off me and squeezed her hand. "Violet."

"Jack."

He was breathtaking in black dress pants and white dress shirt, sleeves rolled to the elbows, buttons undone at the neck. He fixed his attention on me, a wicked gleam in his clear blue eyes. "You look stunning."

I blushed the way I always did when he said that, like it was the first time I'd ever been told.

Jack selected a cookie from the dessert spread and grinned. "Willow's?" he asked.

Mom nodded. "Imogene thinks they're magical. They're

certainly delicious. If you have any important engagements in the future, I'll be sure to make them available."

I groaned at the way she emphasized the word *engagements*.

Jack bit into the cookie with devout seriousness. "I'm planning something pretty big, actually. I'll let you know."

"What?" I asked, curiosity piqued.

Mom clasped her hands in front of her. "Lovely."

"What?" I repeated.

Jack handed me a cookie and winked.

"I have no idea what that means," I said, as baffled by his pointed looks and intent expressions as ever.

Mom ducked away to chastise a server without a full tray, and I turned on Jack. "What are you up to, teasing my mother with the opportunity to throw a big party?"

"It makes her happy," he said, "and she's remarkably good at it, plus I wasn't teasing."

Willow's blonde hair caught my eye where she twirled on the veranda outside. She caught me looking and waved.

"Willow came," I said, feeling my smile widen.

"Henri too," Jack added. "Shall we?" He took my free hand gingerly and led me across the room toward the open patio doors.

Someone clanked a spoon against a glass as we neared the foyer, and the crowd quieted. "Hello, I'm Scarlet Hawthorne," Scarlet said, moving onto the steps, where she could be seen more easily.

Jack and I stopped to listen.

Henri, Willow, and Chase moved inside from the veranda and came to join us.

"As most of you know," Scarlet said, "I've been Lacy's best friend since diapers, and I love her like family because that's exactly what she is. Tonight, we're here to celebrate the one-year-*ish* anniversary of her return to our town, the opening of her shop, and her reintroduction into our lives. I don't know what I'd ever do without her, and I don't want to find out. So, Lacy, I want you to know I adore you. You are the sister I never had. Godmother to my children. Best friend of my brother-in-law."

Chase lifted a flute of champagne overhead and smiled.

"Also, I am proud to announce that I have found the perfect part-time shopkeeper to help you and Imogene at your store. A woman who will be worthy of your employment and make you smile every day that she works, but never before nine or after two because she has to drive carpool."

My jaw dropped. "You?" I looked from Scarlet to Carter. He smiled and nodded.

Scarlet pressed a hand to her chest. "Me!"

Imogene looked at the ceiling and signed the cross.

I ran to hug Scarlet, and the crowd clapped.

Chase hugged me next. "What she said." He grinned. "But not the part about working at your shop."

"Got it," I said.

"How's Jack treating you?" he asked, eyeballing the man at my side.

"Like a princess," I said. "A delightfully headstrong princess."

Jack nodded in slow, emphatic agreement while catching his own drink from a passing waiter.

Chase laughed. "It takes a special man."

I kissed his cheek. "You're a special man, and you really are my best friend, right after Scarlet, of course."

"Of course." Chase smiled back. "Well, you know where to find me when you come to your senses and realize my proposal still stands." He did a long stage wink.

"I do," I said.

"Excuse us," Scarlet butted in. She gave me another hug. Chase walked away.

"You really get to work with me?" I asked. "How is that possible? Did you find a nanny?"

She nodded. "I took your advice and called my old nanny. As it turned out, she was looking for a part-time job, so she'll watch the kids after school and on weekends for up to four hours a day, which means I can get away from the house and help you. Nanny will cook, clean, whatever needs done while I'm away, and when I come home all will be well."

"Love it." I smiled.

Scarlet leaned against her husband. It was hard to believe that high school sweethearts still made it into successful marriages, but they had, and I admired them for it.

Jack pulled me to his side and made a puzzled face. "Chase Hawthorne proposed to you?"

"Not officially," I said. "There was no ring. It was more of a standing offer," I said.

Jack made a crazy face, eyes on something in the distance, presumably Chase.

"So," Carter said, "how are you doing, Lacy?" His eyes slid to my bandaged hands.

I gave a nervous smile. "I'm doing okay."

"Good," he said, moving his attention to Jack. "Whatever happened to the old lady?"

I felt my insides twist painfully at the mention of her. The fine hairs along my arms stood at attention, and heat rushed through the back of my head in a blazing burst that spread across my cheeks and down my throat.

Jack held me a little tighter. It was a question I knew the answer to, and one I'd heard asked and answered a dozen times over the past month, but reliving those awful moments on the bridge never got any easier. "It's okay," I said, rubbing my injured hands carefully. "Go on."

"Mrs. Smart was charged with physical assault, stalking, and menacing," Jack began. "We were able to tie her to Lacy's threats, from the bike messenger delivery to the vandalism of her shop door to the destruction of her cake, and we got her on inducing panic for calling in the bomb threat and pulling the fire alarm. We were also able to connect her to a series of threatening letters demanding Viktor's resignation in the months before his death, and a tourist's home video from the French Quarter puts her outside St. Louis Cathedral near the time of the mini stampede." He inhaled deeply and squared his shoulders. "Plus she confessed to Viktor's murder and the attempted murder of Lacy."

I kept my chin up, but I wanted to run. Senselessly, of course, but the adrenaline was always there at the sound of her name, pooling just below the surface. I imagined it would be that way for a long time.

"Lacy?" Eva's smile was small and timid as she moved into our little circle. Tension rolled off her in silent waves. "Sorry I'm late."

"I think you're right on time," I said, wrapping her rigid body in a gentle hug. "Everything okay?"

She pursed her lips. "I broke up with my boyfriend."

Scarlet, Carter, and I did a soothing round of *aw* and *I'm so sorry*.

Jack said, "Good."

I whacked his arm.

He shrugged. "I ran a background check on him when I thought he might've had something to do with Viktor's death. That guy's arrest record is extensive and varied. As far as I could tell, he only drives that old construction truck so he can look like a productive member of society. He's really a professional criminal, and not a very good one. He's been charged with a little bit of everything, including multiple domestic violence charges."

My jaw swung open. "Oh my gosh! Eva. Are you okay?"

She bobbed her head. "I will be. I'm just glad I found out I was being lied to now rather than later."

Chase reappeared with two flutes of champagne and handed one to Eva. "I'm glad you decided to come."

She took the drink. "Thanks for encouraging me."

I raised my eyebrows at Chase.

"What?" he said. "You inspired me to set down roots and embrace this life. I'm glad I did, so I thought I should pay it forward. Maybe help a fellow straggler to find herself too."

Eva leaned against him. "Chase told me about his return to the district and a little about Lacy's readjustment. Then we talked about figuring out who I am, and who I want to be. I'm not exactly the outgoing socialite my family always wanted, but I'd love to open a bookshop and sell tea."

"Do it!" we responded in a group cheer.

She smiled. "Maybe I will."

Jack tipped his glass in her direction. "Cheers."

We all put our glasses together.

"To breaking molds," Scarlet said.

"And doing what we want," Chase added.

"To friends," I said.

* * *

I followed Jack to his place that night because he'd promised me a surprise.

He led me to his kitchen with an apprehensive smile. The massive marble island was covered in fresh produce and bags and boxes of every ingredient under the sun.

"You bought me groceries," I said with a laugh.

He lifted my hand in his. "I thought we could brainstorm ideas for new recipes. I'm off work tomorrow and Imogene is opening for you, so I bought everything I could think of, and we have all night to play around with your ideas."

I sagged against him in an easy hug. "Thank you. Is it super dorky to say this is my idea of a perfect night?"

He pulled back and looked at me with a warm, familiar smile. "I have something else too."

He selected a worn leather journal from the line of cook-books on his counter and presented it to me like a gift. "I want you to have this."

I reached for it greedily. "I love old cookbooks," I said, flipping the cover immediately.

"This one is very special to me."

The pages were handwritten like a journal and interspersed with recipes, some reworked a dozen times, others completely scratched out. I ran my fingers down the fading ink inside the cover.

Wins and losses in the kitchen, my quest for perfection.
by Jack M. Smacker. 1952.

I raised my startled gaze to his. "Your grandpa wrote this."

"You would've liked him," Jack said, a touch of grief in his beautiful eyes.

"I know."

Jack stepped closer, something still puckering his brow. "Grandpa journaled everything. Recipes as they originated, the results, the changes. New results. All of it. He's the only person I've ever known who loved the kitchen as much as you. I thought you'd find his trials and corrections comforting. A few of these recipes are really good, too. I hoped those would inspire you."

I hugged the journal to my chest. "You inspire me," I said.

The night buzzed by in a cloud of sifted flour and unfil-tered laughter. I sang, danced, and relaxed in ways I hadn't in months as Jack and I compiled and tested a half dozen recipes over a shared bottle of wine. It was my second favorite night so far. The pet pageant was over. My assailant was in jail. Scarlet was going to help me at my shop, and I was falling head over heels for the man at my side. It was an ending I never could have seen coming a year ago, but New Orleans was like that. In my city, in this life, anything was possible.

Acknowledgments

Thank you, dear readers, for picking up another one of Lacy's adventures. You make my dreams possible, and for that I am eternally grateful. Thank you, Crooked Lane Books. Jenny Chen and Sarah Poppe, I can't possibly tell you how important you are to me. You make my work better and this job so much more fun. Thank you, Jill Marsal, my blessed literary agent, for believing in me. Without you, I'm not sure what I'd be doing with my life, likely not this. To my critique girls, my family and my squad. You know what you do. There simply aren't words. But thank you. I love you.